JACK DANIELS

STORIES

by JA KONRATH

INTRODUCTION

There have been seven Jack Daniels novels so far (Whiskey Sour, Bloody Mary, Rusty Nail, Dirty Martini, Fuzzy Navel, Cherry Bomb, and Shaken—coming in 2010.)

The continuing cast of characters in the Jack Daniels books are one of the reasons I enjoy writing them so much. Having established early on that the series is a mixture of humor, scares, mystery, and thrills, I have complete freedom to write short stories in any and all of these sub-genres.

I use shorts to take my characters in places they wouldn't normally go in the novels. Jack can function as a traditional sleuth, solving crimes like Sherlock Holmes or Miss Marple. But she can also star in nail-biting thrillers without any element of mystery. She can even be delegated to sidekick role, letting someone else take center stage.

Harry McGlade can be even goofier in short stories than he is in the books. When I write a McGlade short, I play it for laughs and cross over into parody, which would never work in the novels.

Phineas Troutt is ideal for hardboiled tales. Because he's a criminal, I can walk on the dark side with him, and have him do things that Jack, with her moral compass, would never do.

Plus, I can get away with things in short stories that I can't in my books. I don't have to worry about having lines cut, or having my characters' motivations questioned. For a writer, it's the ultimate indulgence, and the ultimate freedom.

It also allows me to do some pretty fun shit.

And for the completists who want to make sure they have every story in the Jack Daniels universe, there are four novellas (Suckers, Truck Stop, Planter's Punch, Floaters) that aren't in this collection, but are available separately on Amazon Kindle and on my website, www.JAKonrath.com. I've included excerpts at the back of this ebook. Jack is also a supporting character in my thriller novel Shot of Tequila, which takes place in the 1990s when she's still a rookie detective, still married, and her partner Herb was thin. She also appears in a cameo in my upcoming sci-fi book Timecaster Super Symmetry under my pen name Joe Kimball. Jack's grandson, a 2054 Chicago cop named Talon Avalon, is the hero of that series. His best friend is Harry McGlade the Third.

I may very well write about these characters forever...

Joe Konrath, February 2010

CONTENTS

On The Rocks

After landing my first three-book deal, I started writing short stories like crazy, trying to get my name out there. I always liked locked-room mysteries, and decided to do one featuring my newly published detective, Lt. Jacqueline "Jack" Daniels of the Chicago Police Department. Here, Jack takes a break from serial killers to solve a classic whodunnit. This sold to Ellery Queen Mystery Magazine, and was placed in their Department of First Stories, which thrilled me because I've been a fan of EQMM since childhood.

"She sure bled a lot."

I ignored Officer Crouch, my attention focused on the dead woman's arm. The cut had almost severed her left wrist, a flash of pink bone peeking through. Her right hand was curled around the handle of a utility knife.

I'd been in Homicide for more than ten years, and still felt an emotional punch whenever I saw a body. The day I wasn't affected was the day I hung up my badge.

I wore disposable plastic booties over my flats because the shag carpet oozed blood like a sponge wherever I stepped. The apartment's air conditioning was set on freeze, so the decomposition wasn't as bad as it might have been after a week—but it was still pretty bad. I got down on my haunches and swatted away some blowflies.

On her upper arm, six inches above the wound, was a bruise.

"What's so interesting, Lieut? It's just a suicide."

In my blazer pocket I had some latex gloves. I snapped them on.

The victim's name was Janet Hellerman, a real estate lawyer with a private practice. She was brunette, mid thirties, Caucasian. Her satin slip was mottled with drying brown stains, and she wore nothing underneath. I put my hand on her chin, gently turned her head.

There was another bruise on her cheek.

"Johnson's getting a statement from the super."

I stood up, smoothed down my skirt, and nodded at Herb, who had just entered the room. Detective First Class Herb Benedict was my partner. He had a gray mustache, Basset hound jowls, and a Santa Claus belly. Herb kept on the perimeter of the blood puddle; those little plastic booties were too hard for him to get on.

"Johnson's story corroborates?"

Herb nodded. "Why? You see something?"

I did, but wasn't sure how it fit. Herb had questioned both Officer Crouch and Officer Johnson, and their stories were apparently identical.

Forty minutes ago they'd arrived at apartment 3008 at the request of the victim's mother, who lived out of state. She had been unable to get in touch with her daughter for more than a week. The building superintendent unlocked the door for them, but the safety chain was on, and a sofa had been pushed in front of the door to prevent anyone from getting inside. Crouch put his shoulder to it, broke in, and they discovered the body.

Herb squinted at the corpse. "How many marks on the wrist?"

"Just one cut, deep."

I took off the blood-soaked booties, put them in one of the many plastic baggies I keep in my pockets, and went over to the picture window, which covered most of the far wall. The view was expensive, overlooking Lake

Shore Drive from forty stories up. Boaters swarmed over the surface of Lake Michigan like little white ants, and the street was a gridlock of toy cars. Summer was a busy time for Chicagoans— criminals included.

I motioned for Crouch, and he heeled like a chastened puppy. Beat cops were getting younger every year; this one barely needed to shave. He had the cop stare, though—hard eyes and a perpetual scowl, always expecting to be lied to.

"I need you to do a door-to-door. Get statements from everyone on this floor. Find out who knew the victim, who might have seen anything."

Crouch frowned. "But she killed herself. The only way in the apartment is the one door, and it was locked from the inside, with the safety chain on. Plus there was a sofa pushed in front of it."

"I'm sure I don't need to remind you that suicides are treated as homicides in this town, Officer."

He rolled his eyes. I could practically read his thoughts. How did this dumb broad get to be Homicide Lieutenant? She sleep with the PC?

"Lieut, the weapon is still in her hand. Don't you think..."

I sighed. Time to school the rookie.

"How many cuts are on her wrist, Crouch?"

"One."

"Didn't they teach you about hesitation cuts at the Academy? A suicidal person usually has to work up the courage. Where was she found?"

"On the floor."

"Why not her bed? Or the bathtub? Or a comfy chair? If you were ending your life, would you do it standing in the middle of the living room?"

He became visibly flustered, but I wasn't through yet.

"How would you describe the temperature in this room?"

"It's freezing."

"And all she's wearing is a slip. Little cold for that, don't you think? Did you read the suicide note?"

"She didn't leave a note."

"They all leave notes. I've worked these streets for twenty years, and never saw a suicide where the vic didn't leave a note. But for some strange reason, there's no note here. Which is a shame because maybe her note would explain how she got the multiple contusions on her face and arm."

Crouch was cowed, but he managed to mumble, "The door—"

"Speaking of doors," I interrupted, "why are you still here when you were given an order to start the door-to-door? Move your ass."

Crouch looked at his shoes and then left the apartment. Herb raised an eyebrow.

"Kinda hard on the newbie, Jack."

"He wouldn't have questioned me if I had a penis."

"I think you have one now. You took his."

"If he does a good job, I'll give it back."

Herb turned to look at the body. He rubbed his mustache.

"It could still play as suicide," he said. "If she was hit by a sudden urge to die. Maybe she got some terrible news. She gets out of the shower, puts on a slip, cranks up the air conditioning, gets a phone call, immediately grabs the knife and with one quick slice..."

He made a cutting motion over his wrist.

"Do you buy it?" I asked.

Herb made a show of mulling it over.

"No," he consented. "I think someone knocked her out, sliced her wrist, turned up the air so the smell wouldn't get too bad, and then..."

"Managed to escape from a locked room."

I sighed, my shoulders sagging.

Herb's eyes scanned the view. "A window washer?"

I checked the window, but as expected it didn't open. Winds this high up weren't friendly.

"There's no other way in?" Herb asked.

"Just the one entryway."

I walked up to it. The safety chain hung on the door at eye level, its wall mounting and three screws dangling from it. The doorframe where it had been attached was splintered and cracked from Crouch's entrance. There were three screw holes in the frame that matched the mounting, and a fourth screw still remained, sticking out of the frame about an inch.

The hinges on the door were dusty and showed no signs of tampering. A black leather sofa was pushed off to the side, near the doorway. I followed the tracks that its feet had made in the carpet. The sofa had been placed in front of the door and then shoved aside.

I opened the door, holding the knob with two fingers. It moved easily, even though it was heavy and solid. I closed it, stumped.

"How did the killer get out?" I said, mostly to myself.

"Maybe he didn't get out. Maybe the killer is still in the apartment." Herb's eyes widened and his hand shot up, pointing over my shoulder. "Jack! Behind you!"

I rolled my eyes.

"Funny, Herb. I already searched the place."

I peeled off the gloves and stuck them back in my pocket.

"Well, then there are only three possibilities." Herb held up his hand, ticking off fingers. "One, Crouch and Johnson and the superintendent are all lying. Two, the killer was skinny enough to slip out of the apartment by going under the door. Or three, it was Houdini."

"Houdini's dead."

"Did you check? Get an alibi? "

"I'll send a team to the cemetery."

While we waited for the ME to arrive, Herb and I busied ourselves with tossing the place. Bank statements told us Janet Hellerman made a comfortable living and paid her bills on time. She was financing a late model Lexus, which we confirmed was parked in the lot below. Her credit card debt was minimal, with a recent charge for plane tickets. A call to Delta confirmed two seats to Montana for next week, one in her name and one in the name of Glenn Hale.

Herb called the precinct, requesting a sheet on Hale.

I checked the answering machine and listened to thirty-eight messages. Twenty were from Janet's distraught mother, wondering where she was. Two were telemarketers. One was from a friend named Sheila who wanted to get together for dinner, and the rest were real estate related.

Nothing from Hale. He wasn't on the caller ID either.

I checked her cell phone next, and listened to forty more messages; ten from mom, and thirty from home buyers. Hale hadn't left any messages, but there was a 'Glenn' listed on speed dial. The phone's call log showed that Glenn's number had called over a dozen times, but not once since last week.

"Look at this, Jack."

I glanced over at Herb. He set a pink plastic case on the kitchen counter and opened it up. It was a woman's toolkit, the kind they sold at department stores for fifteen bucks. Each tool had a cute pink handle and a corresponding compartment that it snugged into. This kit contained a hammer, four screwdrivers, a measuring tape, and eight wrenches. There were also two empty slots; one for needle nose pliers, and one for something five inches long and rectangular.

"The utility knife," I said.

Herb nodded. "She owned the weapon. It's looking more and more like suicide, Jack. She has a fight with Hale. He dumps her. She kills herself."

"You find anything else?"

"Nothing really. She liked to mountain climb, apparently. There's about forty miles of rope in her closet, lots of spikes and beaners, and a picture of her clinging to a cliff. She also has an extraordinary amount of teddy bears. There were so many piled on her bed, I don't know how she could sleep on it."

"Diary? Computer?"

"Neither. Some photo albums, a few letters that we'll have to look through."

Someone knocked. We glanced across the breakfast bar and saw the door ease open.

Mortimer Hughes entered. Hughes was a medical examiner. He worked for the city, and his job was to visit crime scenes and declare people dead. You'd never guess his profession if you met him on the street—he had the smiling eyes and infectious enthusiasm of a television chef.

"Hello Jack, Herb, beautiful day out." He nodded at us and set down a large tackle box that housed the many particular tools of his trade. Hughes opened it up and snugged on some plastic gloves and booties. He also brandished knee pads.

Herb and I paused in our search and watched him work. Hughes knelt beside the vic and spent ten minutes poking and prodding, humming tunelessly to himself. When he finally spoke, it was high-pitched and cheerful.

"She's dead," Hughes said.

We waited for more.

"At least four days, probably longer. I'm guessing from hypovolemic shock. Blood loss is more than forty percent. Her right zygomatic bone is shattered, pre-mortem or early post."

"Could she have broken her cheek falling down?" Herb asked.

"On this thick carpet? Possible—yes. Likely—no. Look at the blood pool. No arcs. No trails."

"So she wasn't conscious when her wrist was cut?"

"That would be my assumption, unless she laid down on the floor and stayed perfectly still while bleeding to death."

"Sexually assaulted?"

"Can't tell. I'll do a swab."

I chose not to watch, and Herb and I went back into the kitchen. Herb pursed his lips.

"It could still be suicide. She cuts her wrist, falls over, breaks her cheek bone, dies unconscious."

"You don't sound convinced."

"I'm not. I like the boyfriend. They're fighting, he bashes her one in the face. Maybe he can't wake her up, or he thinks he's killed her. Or he wants to kill her. He finds the toolbox, gets the utility knife, makes it look like a suicide."

"And then magically disappears."

Herb frowned. "That part I don't like."

"Maybe he flushed himself down the toilet, escaped through the plumbing."

"You can send Crouch out to get a plunger."

"Lieutenant?"

Officer Crouch had returned. He stood by the kitchen counter, his face ashen.

"What is it, Officer?"

"I was doing the door-to-door. No one answered at the apartment right across the hall. The superintendent thought that was strange– an old lady named Mrs. Flagstone lives there, and she never leaves her home. She even sends out for groceries. So the super opens up her door and...you'd better come look.

#

Mrs. Flagstone stared up at me with milky eyes. Her tongue protruded from her lips like a hunk of raw liver. She was naked in the bathtub, her face and upper body submerged in foul water, one chubby leg hanging over the edge. The bloating was extensive. Her white hair floated around her head like a halo.

"Still think it's a suicide?" I asked Herb.

Mortimer Hughes rolled up his sleeve and put his hand into the water. He pressed her chest and bubbles exploded out of her mouth and nose.

"Didn't drown. Her lungs are full of air."

He moved his hand higher, prodding the wrinkled skin on her neck.

"I can feel some damage to the trachea. There also appears to be a lesion around her neck. I want to get a sample of the water before I pull the drain plug."

Hughes dove into his box. Herb, Crouch, and I left him and went into the living room. Herb called in, requesting the forensics team.

"Any hits from the other tenants?" I asked the rookie.

He flipped open his pad. "One door over, at apartment 3010, the occupant, a Mr. Stanley Mankowicz, remembers some yelling coming from the victim's place about six days ago."

"Does he remember what time?"

"It was late, he was in bed. Mr. Mankowicz shares a wall with the vic, and has called her on several occasions to tell her to turn her television down."

"Did he call that night?"

"He was about to, but the noise stopped."

"Where's the super?"

"Johnson hasn't finished taking his statement."

"Call them both in here."

While waiting for them to arrive, I examined Mrs. Flagstone's door. Like Janet's, it had a safety chain, and like Janet's, it had been ripped from the wall and the mounting was hanging from the door. I found four screws and some splinters on the floor. There were no screws in the door frame.

A knock, and I opened the door. Officer Johnson and the super. Johnson was older than his partner, bigger, with the same dead eyes. The superintendent was a Pakistani man named Majid Patel. Mr. Patel had dark skin and red eyes and he clearly enjoyed all of this attention.

"I moved to this country ten years ago, and I have never seen a dead body before. Now I have seen two in the same day. I must call and tell my mother. I call my mother when anything exciting happens."

"We'll let you go in a moment, Mr. Patel. I'm Lt. Jack Daniels, this is Detective Herb Benedict. We just have a few..."

"Your name is Jack Daniels? But you are not a man."

"You're very observant," I deadpanned. "Did you know Janet Hellerman?"

Patel winked at me. Was he flirting?

"It must be hard, Lt. Jack Daniels, to be a pretty woman with a funny name in a profession so dominated by male chauvinist pigs." Patel offered Herb a look. "No offense."

Herb returned a pleasant smile. "None taken. If you could please answer the Lieutenant's question."

Patel grinned, crooked teeth and spinach remnants.

"She was a real estate lawyer. Young and good looking. Always paid her rent on time. My brother gave her a deal on her apartment, because she had nice legs." Patel had no reservations about openly checking out mine. "Yours are very nice too, Jack Daniels. For an older lady. Are you single?"

"She's single." Herb winked at me, gave me an elbow. I made a mental note to fire him later.

"Your brother?" I asked Patel.

"He's the building owner," Officer Johnson chimed in. "It's the family business."

"Did you know anything about Janet's personal life?"

"She had a shit for a boyfriend, a man named Glenn. He had an affair and she dumped him."

"When was this?"

"About ten days ago. I know because she asked me to change the lock on her door. She had given him a key and he wouldn't return it."

"Did you change the lock?"

"I did not. Ms. Hellerman just mentioned it to me in the elevator once. She never filled out the work order request."

"Does the building have a doorman?"

"No. We have security cameras."

"I'll need to see tapes going back two weeks. Can you get them for me?"

"It will not be a problem."

Mortimer Hughes came out of the bathroom. He was holding a closed set of tweezers in one hand, his other hand cupped beneath it.

"I dug a fiber out of the victim's neck. Red, looks synthetic."

"From a rope?" I asked.

Hughes nodded.

"Mr. Patel, we'll be down shortly for those tapes. Crouch, Johnson, help Herb and I search the apartment. Let's see if we can find the murder weapon."

We did a thorough toss, but couldn't find any rope. Herb, however, found a pair of needle nose pliers in a closet. Pliers with pink handles.

"They were neighbors," Herb reasoned. "Janet could have lent them to her."

"Could have. But we both doubt it. Call base to see if they found anything on Hale."

Herb dialed, talked for a minute, then hung up.

"Glenn Hale has been arrested three times, all assault charges. Did three months in Joliet."

I wasn't surprised. All evidence pointed to the boyfriend, except for the damned locked room. Maybe Herb was right and the killer just slipped under the door and...

Epiphany.

"Call the lab team. I want the whole apartment dusted. Then get an address and a place of work on Hale and send cars. Tell them to wait for the warrant."

Herb raised an eyebrow. "A warrant? Shouldn't we question the guy first?"

"No need," I said. "He did it, and I know how."

#

Feeling, a bit foolishly, like Sherlock Holmes, I took everyone back into Janet's apartment. They began hurling questions at me, but I held up my hand for order.

"Here's how it went," I began. "Janet finds out Glenn is cheating, dumps him. He comes over, wanting to get her back. She won't let him in. He uses his key, but the safety chain is on. So he busts in and breaks the chain."

"But the chain was on when we came in the first time," Crouch complained.

Herb hushed him, saving me the trouble.

"They argue," I went on. "Glenn grabs her arm, hits her. She falls to the floor, unconscious. Who knows what's going through his mind? Maybe he's afraid she'll call the police, and he'll go to jail– he has a record and this state has zero tolerance for repeat offenders. Maybe he's so mad at her he thinks she deserves to die. Whatever the case, he finds Janet's toolkit and takes out the utility knife. He slits her wrist and puts the knife in her other hand."

Five inquisitive faces hung on my every word. It was a heady experience.

"Glenn has to know he'd be a suspect," I raised my voice, just a touch for dramatic effect. "He's got a history with Janet, and a criminal record. The only way to throw off suspicion is to make it look like no one else could have been in the room, to show the police that it had to be a suicide."

"Jack," Herb admonished. "You're dragging it out."

"If you figured it out, then you'd have the right to drag it out too."

"Are you really single?" Patel asked. He grinned again, showing more spinach.

"If she keeps stalling," Herb told him, "I'll personally give you her number."

I shot Herb with my eyes, then continued.

"Okay, so Glenn goes into Janet's closet and gets a length of climbing rope. He also grabs the needle nose pliers from her toolbox and heads back to the front door. The safety chain has been ripped out of the frame, and the mounting is dangling on the end. He takes a single screw," I pointed at the screw sticking in the door frame, "and puts it back in the doorframe about halfway."

Herb nodded, getting it. "When the mounting ripped out, it had to pull out all four screws. So the only way one could still be in the doorframe is if someone put it there."

"Right. Then he takes the rope and loops it under a sofa leg. He goes out into the hall with the rope, and closes the door, still holding both ends of the rope. He tugs the rope through the crack under the door, and pulls the sofa right up to the door from the other side."

"Clever," Johnson said.

"I must insist you meet my mother," Patel said.

"But the chain..." Crouch whined.

I smiled at Crouch. "He opens the door a few inches, and grabs the chain with the needle nose pliers. He swings the loose end over to the door frame, where it catches and rests on the screw he put in halfway."

I watched the light finally go on in Crouch's eyes. "When Mr. Patel opened the door, it looked like the chain was on, but it really wasn't. It was just hanging on the screw. The thing that kept the door from opening was the sofa."

"Right. So when you burst into the room, you weren't the one that broke the safety chain. It was already broken."

Crouch nodded rapidly. "The perp just lets go of one end of the rope and pulls in the other end, freeing it from the sofa leg. Then he locks the door with his own key."

"But poor Mrs. Flagstone," I continued, "must have seen him in the hallway. She has her safety chain on, maybe asks him what he's doing. So he bursts into her room and strangles her with the climbing rope. The rope was red, right Herb?"

Herb grinned. "Naturally. How did you know that?"

"I guessed. Then Glenn ditches the pliers in the closet, makes a half-assed attempt to stage Mrs. Flagstone's death like a drowning, and leaves with the rope. I bet the security tapes will concur."

"What if he isn't seen carrying the rope?"

No problem. I was on a roll.

"Then he either ditched it in a hall, or wrapped it around his waist under his shirt before leaving."

"I'm gonna go check the tapes," Johnson said, hurrying out.

"I'm going to call my mother," Patel said, hurrying out.

Herb got on the phone to get a warrant, and Mortimer Hughes dropped to his hands and knees and began to search the carpeting, ostensibly for red fibers—even thought that wasn't his job.

I was feeling pretty smug, something I rarely associated with my line of work, when I noticed Officer Crouch staring at me. His face was projecting such unabashed admiration that I almost blushed.

"Lieutenant– that was just...amazing."

"Simple detective work. You could have figured it out if you thought about it."

"I never would have figured that out." He glanced at his shoes, then back at me, and then he turned and left.

Herb pocketed his cell and offered me a sly grin.

"We can swing by the DA's office, pick up the warrant in an hour. Tell me, Jack. How'd you put it all together?"

"Actually, you gave me the idea. You said the only way the killer could have gotten out of the room was by slipping under the door. In a way, that's what he did."

Herb clapped his hand on my shoulder.

"Nice job, Lieutenant. Don't get a big head. You wanna come over for supper tonight? Bernice is making pot roast. I'll let you invite Mr. Patel."

"He'd have to call his mother first. Speaking of mothers..."

I glanced at the body of Janet Hellerman, and again felt the emotional punch. The Caller ID in the kitchen gave me the number for Janet's mom. It took some time to tell the whole story, and she cried through most of it. By the end, she was crying so much that she couldn't talk anymore.

I gave her my home number so she could call me later.

The lab team finally arrived, headed by a Detective named Perkins. Soon both apartments were swarming with tech heads— vacuuming fibers, taking samples, spraying chemicals, shining ALS, snapping pictures and shooting video.

I filled in Detective Perkins on what went down, and left him in charge of the scene.

Then Herb and I went off to get the warrant.

Whelp Wanted

Harry McGlade dates back to 1985, when I was 15. I've been a mystery fan since I was nine years old, and I thought it would be a fun genre to parody. On a summer afternoon at my friend Jim Coursey's house, we sat at his Apple IIe (with the green phosphorus monitor) and giggled like fiends writing one stupid PI cliché after another. I picked the name Harry McGlade out of a phone book. For the next dozen years, I wrote over a hundred McGlade short stories. None of them were any good, but they did garner me my very first rejection letters, including one in 1989 from Playboy. This story was sold to the now-defunct Futures Mysterious Anthology Magazine. I wrote it just after my first novel came out in 2004.

I was halfway through a meatball sandwich when a man came into my office and offered me money to steal a dog.

A lot of money.

"Are you an animal lover, Mr. McGlade?"

"Depends on the animal. And call me Harry."

He offered his hand. I stuck out mine, and watched him frown when he noticed the marinara stains. He abruptly pulled back, reaching instead into the inner pocket of his blazer. The suit he wore was tailored and looked expensive, and his skin was tanned to a shade only money can buy.

"This is Marcus." His hand extended again, holding a photograph. "He's a Shar-pei."

Marcus was one of those unfortunate Chinese wrinkle dogs, the kind that look like a great big raisin with fur. He was light brown, and his face had so many folds of skin that his eyes were completely covered.

I bet the poor pooch walked into a lot of walls.

"Cute," I said, because the man wanted to hire me.

"Marcus is a champion show dog. He's won four AKC competitions. Several judges have commented that he's the finest example of the breed they've ever seen."

I wanted to say something about Marcus needing a good starch and press, but instead inquired about the dog's worth.

"With the winnings, and stud fees, he's worth upwards of ten thousand dollars."

I whistled. The dog was worth more than I was.

"So, what's the deal, Mr..."

"Thorpe. Vincent Thorpe. I'm willing to double your usual fee if you can get him back."

I took another bite of meatball, wiped my mouth on my sleeve, and leaned back in my swivel chair. The chair groaned in disapproval.

"Tell me a little about Marcus, Mr. Thorpe. Curly fries?"

"Pardon me?"

I gestured to the bag on my desk. "Did you want any curly fries? Potatoes make me bloaty."

He shook his head. I snatched a fry, bloating be damned.

"I've, um, raised Marcus since he was a pup. He has one of the best pedigrees in the sport. Since Samson passed away, there has quite literally been no competition."

"Samson?"

"Another Shar-pei. Came from the same littler as Marcus, owned by a man named Glen Ricketts. Magnificent dog. We went neck and neck several times."

"Hold on, a second. I'd like to take notes."

I pulled out my notepad and a pencil. On the first piece of paper, I wrote, "Dog."

"Do you know who has Marcus now?"

"Another breeder named Abigail Cummings. She borrowed Marcus to service her Shar-pei, Julia. When I went to pick him up, she insisted she didn't have him, and claimed she didn't know what I was talking about."

I jotted this down. My fingers made a grease spot on the page.

"Did you try the police?"

"Yes. They searched her house, but didn't find Marcus. She's insisting I made a mistake."

"Did Abigail give you money to borrow Marcus? Sign any contracts?"

"No. I lent him to her as a favor. And she kept him."

"How do you know her?"

"Casually, from the American Kennel Club. Her Shar-pei, Julia, is a truly magnificent bitch. You should see her haunches."

I let that one go.

"Why did you lend out Marcus if you only knew her casually?"

"She called me a few days ago, promised me the pick of the litter if I lent her Marcus. I never should have done it. I should have just given her a straw."

"A straw?"

"Of Marcus's semen. I milk him by..."

I held up my palm and scribbled out the word 'straw.' It was more info than I wanted. "Let's move on."

Thorpe pressed his lips together so tightly they lost color. His eyes got sticky.

"Please, Harry. Marcus is more than just a dog to me. He's my best friend."

I didn't doubt it. You don't milk a casual acquaintance.

"Maybe you could hire an attorney."

"That takes too long. If I go through legal channels, it could be months before my case is called. And even then, I'd need some kind of proof that she had him, so I'd have to hire a private investigator anyway."

I scraped away a coffee stain on my desk with my thumbnail.

"I'm sorry for your loss, Mr. Thorpe. But hiring me to bust into someone's home and steal a dog...I'm guessing that breaks all sorts of laws. I could have my license revoked, I could go to jail—"

"I'll triple your fee."

"I take cash, checks, or major credit cards."

#

Night Vision Goggles use a microprocessor to magnify ambient light and allow a user to see in almost total blackness.

They're also pricey as hell, so I had to make due with a flashlight and some old binoculars.

It was a little past eleven in the evening, and I was sitting in the bough of a tree, staring into the backyard of Abigail Cummings. I'd been there for almost two hours. The night was typical for July in Chicago; hot, sticky, and humid. The black ski mask I wore was so damp with sweat it threatened to drown me.

Plus, I was bloaty.

I let the binocs hang around my neck and flashed the light at my notepad to review my stake-out report.

9:14pm—Climbed tree.

9:40pm—Drank two sodas.

10:15pm—Foot fell asleep.

Not too exciting so far. I took out my pencil and added, "11:04pm— really regret drinking those sodas."

To keep my mind off of my bladder, I spent a few minutes trying to balance the pencil on the tip of my finger. It worked, until I dropped the pencil.

I checked my watch. 11:09. I attempted to write "dropped my pencil" on my notepad, but you can guess how that turned out.

I was all set to call it a night, when I saw movement in the backyard.

It was a woman, sixty-something, her short white hair glowing in the porch light.

Next to her, on a leash, was Marcus.

"Is someone in my tree?"

I fought panic, and through Herculean effort managed to keep my pants dry.

"No," I answered.

She wasn't fooled.

"I'm calling the police!"

"Wait!" My voice must have sounded desperate, because she paused in her race back to the house.

"I'm from the US Department of Foliage. I was taking samples of your tree. It seems to be infested with the Japanese Saganaki Beetle."

"Why are you wearing that mask?"

"Uh...so they don't recognize me. Hold on, I need to ask you a few sapling questions."

I eased down, careful to avoid straining myself. When I reached ground, the dog trotted over and amiably sniffed at my pants.

"I'm afraid I don't know much about agriculture."

From the tree, Ms. Cummings was nothing to look at. Up close, she made me wish I was still in the tree.

The woman was almost as wrinkly as the dog. But unlike her canine companion, she had tried to fill in those wrinkles with make-up. From the amount, she must have used a paint roller. The eye shadow alone was thick enough to stop a bullet. Add to that a voice like raking gravel, and she was quite the catch.

I tried to think of something to ask her, to keep the beetle ploy going. But this was getting too complicated, so I just took out my gun.

"The dog."

Her mouth dropped open.

"The what?"

"That thing on your leash that's wagging its tail. Hand it over."

"Why do you want my dog?"

"Does it matter?"

"Of course it does. I don't want you to shoot me, but I also don't want to hand over my dog to a homicidal maniac."

"I'm not a homicidal maniac."

"You're wearing a ski mask in ninety degree weather, hopping from one foot to the other like some kind of monkey."

"I had too much soda. Give me the damn leash."

She handed me the damn leash. So far so good.

"Okay. You just stand right here, and count to a thousand before you go back inside, or else I'll shoot you."

"Aren't you leaving?"

"Yeah."

"Not to second-guess you, Mr. Dognapper, but how can you shoot me, if you've already gone?"

Know-it-all.

"I think you need a bit more blush on your cheeks. There are some folks in Wisconsin who can't see it from there."

Her lips down turned. With all the lipstick, they looked like two cartoon hot dogs.

"This is Max Factor."

"I won't tell Max if you don't. Now start counting."

I was out of there before she got to six.

#

After I got back to my office, I took care of some personal business, washed my hands, and called the client. He agreed to come right over.

"Mr. McGlade, I can't tell you how...oh, yuck."

"Watch where you're stepping. Marcus decided to mark his territory."

Thorpe made an unhappy face, then he took off his shoe and left it by the door.

"Mr. McGlade, thank you for...yuck."

"He's marked a couple spots. I told you to watch out."

He removed the other shoe.

"Did you bring the money?"

"I did, and I—wait a second!"

"You might as well just throw away the sock, because those stains..."

"That's not Marcus!"

I looked at the dog, who was sniffing around my desk, searching for another place to make a deposit.

"Of course it's your dog. Look at that face. He's a poster boy for Retin-A."

"That's not a he. It's a she."

"Really?" I peeked under the dog's tail and frowned. "I'll be damned."

"You took the wrong dog, Mr. McGlade. This is Abigail's bitch, Julia."

"It's an honest mistake, Mr. Thorpe. Anyone could have made it."

"No, not anyone, Mr. McGlade. Most semi-literate adults know the difference between boys and girls. Would you like me to draw you a picture?"

"Ease up, Thorpe. When I meet a new dog, I don't lift up a hind leg and stick my face down there to check out the plumbing."

"This is just...oh, yuck."

"The garbage can is over there."

Thorpe removed his sock, and I wracked my brain to figure out how this could be salvaged.

"Any chance you want to keep this dog instead? You said she was a magnificent broad."

"Bitch, Mr. McGlade. It's what we call female dogs."

"I was trying to put a polite spin on it."

"I want Marcus. That was the deal."

"Okay, okay, let me think."

I thought.

Julia had her nose in the garbage can, sniffing Thorpe's sock. If I could only switch dogs somehow.

That was it.

"I'll switch dogs somehow," I said.

"What are you talking about?"

"Like a hostage trade. I'll call up Ms. Cummings, and trade Julia for Marcus."

"Do you think it'll work?"

"Only one way to find out."

I picked up the phone.

#

"Ms. Cummings? I have your dog."

"I know. I watched you steal him an hour ago."

For someone who looked like a mime, she was sure full of comments.

"If you'd like your dog back, we can make a deal."

"Is my little Poopsie okay? Are you taking care of her?"

"She's fine. I can see why you call her Poopsie."

"Does Miss Julia still have the trots? Poor thing."

I stared at the land mines dotting my floor. "Yeah. I'm all broken up about it."

"Make sure she eats well. Only braised liver and the leanest pork."

Julia was currently snacking on a tuna sandwich I'd dropped under the desk sometime last week.

"I'll do that. Look, I want to make a trade."

I had to play it cool here, if she knew I knew about Marcus, she'd know Thorpe was the one who hired me.

"What kind of trade?"

"I don't want a female dog. I want a male."

"Did Vincent Thorpe hire you?"

Dammit.

"Uh, never heard of him."

"Mr. Thorpe claims I have his dog, Marcus. But the last time I saw Marcus was at an AKC show last April. I have no idea where his dog is."

"That's not how he tells it."

Nice, Harry. I tried to regroup.

"Look, Cummings, you have twelve hours to come up with a male dog. I also want sixty dollars, cash."

Thorpe nudged me and mouthed, "Sixty dollars?"

I put my hand over the mouthpiece. "Carpet cleaning."

"I don't know if I can find a male dog in just 12 hours, Mr. Dognapper."

"Then I turn Julia into a set of luggage."

I heard her gasp. "You horrible man!"

"I'll do it, too. She's got enough hide on her to make two suitcases and a carry-on. The wrinkled look is hot this year."

I scratched Julia on the head, and she licked my chin. Her breath made me teary-eyed.

"Please don't hurt my dog."

"I'll call you tomorrow morning with the details. If you contact the police, I'll mail you Julia's tail."

"I...I already called the police. I called them right after you left."

Hell. "Well, don't call the police again. I have a friend at the Post Office who gives me a discount rate. I'm there twice a week, mailing doggie parts."

I hit the disconnect.

"Did it work?" Thorpe asked.

"Like a charm. Go home and get some rest. In about twelve hours, you'll have your dog back."

#

The trick was finding an exchange location where I wouldn't be conspicuous in a ski mask. Chicago had several ice rinks, but I didn't think any of them allowed dogs.

I decided on the alley behind the Congress Hotel, off of Michigan Avenue. I got there two hours early to check the place out.

Time crawled by. I kept track of it in my notepad.

> 9:02am—Arrive at scene. Don't see any cops. Pull on ski mask and wait.
>
> 9:11am—It sure is hot.
>
> 9:33am—Julia finds some rotting fruit behind the dumpster. Eats it.
>
> 10:01am—Boy, is it hot.
>
> 10:20am—I think I'm getting a heat rash in this mask. Am I allergic to wool?
>
> 10:38am—Julia finds a dead rat. Eats it.
>
> 10:40am—Sure is a hot one.

11:02am—Play fetch with the dog, using my pencil.

Julia ate the pencil. I was going to jot this down on the pad, but you can guess how that went.

"Julia!"

The dog jerked on the leash, tugging me to my feet. Abigail Cummings had arrived. She wore a pink linen pants suit, and more make-up than the Rockettes. All of them, combined. I fought the urge to carve my initials in her cheek with my fingernail.

Dog and dog owner had a happy little reunion, hugging and licking, and I was getting ready to sigh in relief when I noticed the pooch Abigail had brought with her.

"I'm no expert, but isn't that a Collie?"

"A Collie/Shepherd mix. I picked him up at the shelter."

"That's not Marcus."

Abigail frowned at me. "I told you before, Mr. Dognapper. I don't have Vincent Thorpe's dog."

Her bottom lip began to quiver, and her eyes went glassy. I realized, to my befuddlement, that I actually believed her.

"Fine. Give me the mutt."

Abigail handed me the leash. I stared down at the dog. It was a male, but I doubted I could fool Thorpe into thinking it was Marcus. Even if I shaved off all the fur and shortened the legs with a saw.

"What about my money?" I asked.

She dug into her purse and pulled out a check.

"I can't take a check."

"It's good. I swear."

"How am I supposed to remain incognito if I deposit a check?"

Abigail did the lip quiver thing again.

"Oh my goodness, I didn't even think of that. Please don't make Julia into baggage."

More tears.

"Calm down. Don't cry. You'll ruin your...uh...make-up."

I offered her a handkerchief. She dabbed at her eyes and handed it back to me.

It looked like it had been tie-dyed.

"I think I have two or three dollars in my purse," she rasped in her smoker voice. "Is that okay?"

What the hell. I took it.

"I'll take those Tic-Tacs, too."

She handed them over. Wint-O-Green.

"Can we go now?"

"Go ahead."

She turned to leave the alley, and a thought occurred to me.

"Ms. Cummings! When the police came to visit you to look for Marcus, did you have an alibi?"

She glanced over her shoulder and nodded vigorously.

"That's the point. The day Vincent said he brought the dog to my house, I wasn't home. I was enjoying the third day of an Alaskan Cruise."

#

Vincent Thorpe was waiting for me when I got back to my office. He carefully scanned the floor before approaching my desk.

"That's not Marcus! That's not even a Shar-pei!"

"We'll discuss that later."

"Where's Marcus?"

"There have been some complications."

"Complications?" Thorpe leaned in closer, raised an eyebrow. "What happened to your face?"

"I think I'm allergic to wool."

"It looks like you rubbed your cheeks with sandpaper."

I wrote, "I hate him" on my notepad.

"Look, Mr. Thorpe, Abigail Cummings doesn't have Marcus. But I may have an idea who does."

"Who?"

"First, I need to ask you a few questions..."

#

My face was too sore for the ski mask again, so I opted for a nylon stocking.

It was hot.

I shifted positions on the branch I was sitting on, and took another look through the binoculars.

Nothing. The backyard was quiet. But thirty feet away, next to a holly bush, was either a small, brown anthill, or evidence that there was a dog on the premises.

I took out my pencil and reviewed my stake-out sheet.

9:46pm—Climbed tree.

9:55pm—My face hurts.

10:07pm—It really hurts bad.

10:22pm—I think I'll go see a doctor.

10:45pm—Maybe the drug store has some kind of cream.

I added, "11:07pm—Spotted evidence in backyard. Remember to pick up some aloe vera on the way home."

Before I had a chance to cross my Ts, the patio door opened.

I didn't even need the binoculars. A man, mid-forties with short, brown hair, was walking a dog that was obviously a Shar-pei.

Though my track-team days were far behind me (okay, non-existent), I still managed to leap down from the tree without hurting myself.

The man yelped in surprise, but I had my gun out and in his face before he had a chance to move.

"Hi there, Mr. Ricketts. Kneel down."

"Who are you? What do..."

I cocked the gun.

"Kneel!"

He knelt.

"Good. Now lift up that dog's back leg."

"What?"

"Now!"

Glen Ricketts lifted. I checked.

It was Marcus.

"Leash," I ordered.

He handed me the leash. My third dog in two days, but this time it was the right one.

Now for Part Two of the Big Plan.

"Do you know who I am, Glen?"

He shook his head, terrified.

"Special Agent Phillip Pants, of the American Kennel Club. Do you know why I'm here?"

He shook his head again.

"Don't lie to me, Glen! Does the AKC allow dognapping?"

"No," he whimpered.

"Your dog show days are over, Ricketts. Consider your membership revoked. If I so much catch you in the pet food isle at the Piggly Wiggly, I'm going to take you in and have you neutered. Got it?"

He nodded, eager to please. I gave Marcus a pat on the head, and then turned to leave.

"Hold on!"

Glen's eyes were defeated, pleading.

"What?"

"You mean I can't own a dog, ever again?"

"Not ever."

"But...but...dogs are my life. I love dogs."

"And that's why you should have never stole someone else's."

He sniffled, loud and wet.

"What am I supposed to do now?"

I frowned. Grown men crying like babies weren't my favorite thing to watch. But this joker had brought it upon himself.

"Buy a cat," I told him.

Then I walked back to my car, Marcus in tow.

#

"Marcus!"

I watching, grinning, as Vincent Thorpe paid no mind to his expensive suit and rolled around on my floor with his dog, giggling like a caffeinated school boy.

"Mr. McGlade, how can I ever repay you?"

"Cash is good."

He disentangled himself from the pooch long enough to pull out his wallet and hand over a fat wad of bills.

"Tell me, how did you know it was Glen Rickets?"

"Simple. You said yourself that he was always one of your closest competitors, up until his dog died earlier this year."

"But what about Ms. Cummings? I talked to her on the phone. I even dropped the dog off at her house, and she took him from me. Wasn't she involved somehow?"

"The phone was easy—Ms. Cummings has a voice like a chainsaw. With practice, anyone can imitate a smoker's croak. But Glen really got clever for the meeting. He picked a time when Ms. Cummings was out of town, and then he spent a good hour or two with Max Factor."

"Excuse me?"

"Cosmetics. As you recall, Abigail Cummings wore enough make-up to cause back-problems. Who could tell what she looked like under all that gunk? Glen just slopped on enough to look like a circus clown, and then he impersonated her."

Thorpe shook his head, clucking his tongue.

"So it wasn't actually Abigail. It was Glen all along. Such a nice guy, too."

"It's the nice ones you have to watch."

"So, now what? Should I call the police?"

"No need. Glen won't be bothering you, or any dog owner, ever again."

I gave him the quick version of the backyard scene.

"He deserves it, taking Marcus from me. But now I have you back, don't I, boy?"

There was more wrestling, and he actually kissed Marcus on the mouth.

"Kind of unsanitary, isn't it?"

"Are you kidding? A dog's saliva is full of antiseptic properties."

"I was speaking for Marcus."

Thorpe laughed. "Friendship transcends species, Mr. McGlade. Speaking of which, where's that Collie/Shepherd mix that Abigail gave you?"

"At my apartment."

"See? You've made a new friend, yourself."

"Nope. I've got a six o'clock appointment at the animal shelter. I'm getting him gassed."

Thorpe shot me surprised look.

"Mr. McGlade! After this whole ordeal, don't you see what amazing companions canines are? A dog can enrich your life! All you have to do is give him a chance."

I mulled it over. How bad could it be, having a friend who never borrowed money, stole your girl, or talked behind your back?

"You know what, Mr. Thorpe? I may just give it a shot."

When I got home a few hours later, I discovered my new best friend had chewed the padding off of my leather couch.

I made it to the shelter an hour before my scheduled appointment.

Street Music

Street Music is my favorite story of any I've written. Phineas Trout was the hero of my first novel, an unpublished mystery called Dead On My Feet, written back in 1992. It was unabashedly hardboiled, and it helped me land my first agent. The book never sold, probably because it was unabashedly hardboiled. Phin starred in two more unpublished novels, and then I relegated him to the role of sidekick in the Jack Daniels series, which did wind up selling. I'm intrigued by the idea of a hero dying of cancer, and how having no hope left could erode a man's morality. I wrote this story right after selling Whiskey Sour, and soon after sold it to Ellery Queen.

Mitch couldn't answer me with the barrel of my gun in his mouth, so I pulled it out.

"I don't know! I swear!"

If that was the truth, I had no use for it. After three days of questioning dozens of hookers, junkies, and other fine examples of Chicago's populace, Mitch was my only link to Jasmine. I was seriously jonesing; I hadn't done a line since Thursday. Plus, the pain in my side felt like a baby alligator was trying to eat its way out of my pancreas.

I gave Mitch's chin a little tap with the butt of the Glock.

"I really don't know!"

"She's one of yours, Mitch. I thought big, tough pimps like you ran a tight ship."

His black face was shiny with sweat and a little blood. Sure, he was scared. But he wasn't stupid. Telling me Jasmine's whereabouts would put a dent in his income.

I raised the gun back to hit him again.

"She went rogue on me, man! She ditched!"

I paused. If Jasmine had left Mitch, his reluctance to talk about it made some sense. Mack Daddies don't like word to get out that they're losing their game.

"How much money do you have on you?"

"About four hundos. It's yours, man. Front pants pocket."

"I'm not putting my hand in there. Take it out."

Mitch managed to stop shaking long enough to retrieve a fat money clip. I took the cash, and threw the clip—a gold emblem in the shape of a female breast–onto the sidewalk.

"You letting me go?" Mitch asked.

"You're free to pimp another day. Go run to the bus station, see if you can find some other fresh meat to bust out."

When I let go of his lapels, his spine seemed to grow back. He adjusted the collar on his velour jump suit and made sure his baseball hat was tilted to the correct odd angle.

"Ain't like that. I treat my girls good. Plenty of sweet love and all the rock they can smoke."

"Leave. Now. Before I decide to do society a favor."

He sneered, spun on his three hundred dollar sneakers, and did his pimp strut away from me.

I probably should have killed him; I had too many enemies already. But, tough as I am, shooting fourteen-year-old kids in the back isn't my style.

The four hundred was enough to score some coke, but not very much. I thought about calling Manny, my dealer, and getting a sample to help kill the pain, but every minute I wasted gave Jasmine a chance to slip farther away.

Pain relief would have to wait. I pressed my hand to my left side and exited the alley and wondered where the hell I should look next.

I'd already checked Jasmine's apartment, her boyfriend's apartment, her parent's house, her known pick-up spots, and three local crack houses.

To rule out other options, I had to call in a marker.

It was September, about seventy with clear skies, so I took a walk down the block. The first payphone I came to had gum jammed in the coin slot. The second one smelled like a urinal, but I made do.

"Violent Crimes, Daniels."

"Hi, Jack. Phineas Troutt."

"Phin? Haven't seen you at the pool hall lately. Afraid I'll kick your ass?"

My lips twisted in a tight grin. Jacqueline Daniels was a police Lieutenant who busted me a few years back. We had an on-again-off-again eight ball game Monday nights. I'd missed a few.

"I'm sort of preoccupied with something."

"Chemo again?"

"No, work. Listen, you know what I do, right?"

"You're a freelance thug."

"I prefer the term problem solver. I keep it clean."

"I'm guessing that's because we haven't caught you in the act, yet."

"And you never will. Look, Jack, I need a favor."

"I can't do anything illegal, Phin. You know that."

"Nothing shady. I just have to rule some stuff out. I'm looking for a woman. Hooker. Name is Janet Cumberland, goes by the street nick Jasmine. Any recent arrests or deaths with that name?"

There was a pause on the line. I could only guess Jack's thoughts.

"Give me half an hour," she decided. "Got a number where I can call you back?"

I killed time at a hot dog stand, sipping black coffee mixed with ten crushed Tylenol tablets; they worked faster when they were pre-dissolved.

The phone rang eighteen minutes later.

"No one at the morgue matching that name, and her last arrest was three months ago."

"Do you have a place of residence?"

Jack read off the apartment number I'd already checked.

"How about known acquaintances?"

"She's one of Mitch D's girls. Been arrested a few times with another prostitute named Georgia Williamson, street name is Ajax. Kind of an odd name for a hooker."

"She one of Mitch's, too?"

"Lemme check. No, looks like she's solo."

"Got an addy?"

Jack gave it to me.

"There's also a note in Janet's file, says her parents are looking for her. That your angle? Even if you find her, the recit rate with crack is over 95 percent. They'll stick her in rehab and a week later she'll be on the street again."

"Thanks for the help, Jack. Next time we play pool, beer's on me."

"You're on, Phin. How's the—"

"Hurts," I interrupted. "But my doc says it won't for much longer."

"The tumor is shrinking? That's great news!"

I didn't correct her. The tumor was growing like a weed. I wouldn't be in pain much longer because I didn't have much longer.

Which is why I had to find Jasmine, and fast.

She had to die first.

#

Georgia Williams, aka Ajax, lived on 81st and Stoney, in a particularly mean part of Chicago's South Side. Night was rolling in, bringing with it the bangers, junkies, ballers, wanna-bes, and thugs. None of them were thrilled to see a white guy on their turf, and some flashed their iron as I drove by.

Ajax's place wasn't easy to find, and asking for directions didn't strike me as a smart idea. Maybe in neighborhoods this bad, whole buildings got stolen.

Finally, I narrowed it down to a decrepit apartment without any street number. I parked in front, set the alarm on my Bronco, and made sure I had one in the chamber.

"You lost, white boy?"

I ignored the three gang members—Gangster Disciples according to their colors—and headed for the building. The front door had a security lock, but it was long broken. There was a large puddle of something in front of the staircase, which I walked around.

Ajax lived in 206. I took the stairs two at a time, followed a hall decorated with graffiti and vomit, and found her door.

"Georgia Williams? Chicago PD!"

Another door opened opposite me, fearful old eyes peeking out through the crack.

"Is Ms. Williams home?" I asked the neighbor.

The door closed again.

I kicked away a broken bottle that was near my feet, and knocked again.

"Georgia Williams! Open the door!"

"You got ID?"

A woman's voice, cold and firm. I held a brass star, $12.95 on eBay, up to the peephole.

"Where's your partner?" asked the voice.

"Watching the car. We're looking for a friend of yours. Jasmine. She's in big trouble."

"She sure is."

"Can I come in?"

I heard a deadbolt snick back. Then another. The door swung inward, revealing a black girl of no more than sixteen. She wore jeans, a white blouse. Her face was garishly made-up. Stuck to her hip was a sleeping infant.

"Can't be long. Gotta go to work."

Ajax stepped to the side, and I entered her apartment. Expecting squalor, I was surprised to find the place clean and modestly furnished. The ceiling had some water damage, and one wall was losing its plaster, but there were nice curtains and matching furniture and even some framed art. This was the apartment of someone who hadn't given up yet.

"I'll be straight with you, Georgia. If we don't find Jasmine soon, it's very likely she'll be killed. You know about Artie Collins?"

She nodded, once.

"If you know where she is, it's in her best interest to tell me."

"Sorry, cop. I don't know nothing."

I took out my Glock, watched her eyes get big.

"Do you have a license for this firearm I found on your premises, Georgia?"

"Aw, this is—"

I got in her face, sneering.

"I'll tell you what this is. Six months in County, minimum. With your record, the judge won't even think twice. And say goodbye to your baby; when I get done wrecking this place, DCFS will declare you so unfit you won't be allowed within two hundred yards of anyone under aged ten."

Her lips trembled, but there were no tears.

"You bastards are all the same."

"I want Jasmine, Ajax. She's dead if I don't find her."

I gave her credit for toughness. She held out. I had to topple a dresser and put my foot through her TV before she broke down.

"Stop it! She's with her boyfriend!"

"Nice try. I already checked Melvin Kincaid."

"Not Mel. She found a new guy. Named Buster something."

"Buster what?"

"I dunno."

I chucked a vase at the wall. The baby in her arms was wiggling, hysterical.

"I don't have his last name! But I got a number."

Georgia went for her purse on the bed, but I shoved the Glock in her face.

"I'll look."

The purse was the size of a cigarette pack, with rhinestone studs and spaghetti straps. A hooker purse. I didn't figure there could be much of a weapon in there, and was once again surprised. A .22 ATM spilled onto the bed.

"I'm sure this has a license."

Georgia didn't answer. I rifled through the packs of mint gum and condoms until I found a matchbook with a phone number written on the back.

"This it?"

"Yeah."

"Can't you shut that kid up?"

Georgia cooed the baby, rocking it back and forth, while I picked up her .22 and removed the bullets. I tossed the gun back on the bed, and put the lead and the matchbook in my pocket.

She got my evil face when I walked past her.

"If you warn her I'm coming, I'll know it was you."

"I won't say a damn thing, officer."

"I know you won't."

I fished out three of the hundreds I took from Mitch D, and shoved them into her hand. It was a lot more than the TV was worth.

"By the way, why do they call you Ajax?"

She shrugged.

"I've robbed a few tricks."

"Meaning?"

"Ajax cleans out the johns."

When I got back outside, the three Disciples had multiplied into six, and they were standing in front of my truck.

"This is a nice truck, white boy. Can we have it?"

My Glock 21 held thirteen forty-five caliber rounds. More than enough. But Jack was the one who gave me this address, and if I killed any of these bozos she'd eventually get the word.

Dying of cancer was bad enough. Dying of cancer in prison was not on my to-do list.

Stuck in my belt, nestled along my spine, was a combat baton. Sixteen inches long, made of a tightly coiled steel spring. Because it could bend, it didn't break bones.

But it did hurt like crazy.

The Disciples had apparently expected me to tremble in fear, because I clocked three of them across the heads before they went into attack mode.

The first one to draw was a thin kid who watched too many rap videos. He pulled a 9mm out of his baggy pants and thrust it at me sideways, with the back of his hand facing skyward.

Not only did this mess up your aim, but your grip was severely compromised. I gave him a tap across the back of the knuckles, and the gun hit the pavement. A second smack in the forehead opened up a nice gash. As with his buddies, the blood running into his eyes made him blind and worthless. I turned on the last two.

One had a blade. He held it underhanded, tip up, showing me he knew how to use it. After two feints, he thrust it at my face.

I turned, catching the tip on my cheek, and gave him an elbow to the nose. When he stumbled back, he also got a tap across the eyebrows.

The last guy was fifty yards away, sprinting for reinforcements.

I climbed in my Bronco and hauled out of there before they arrived.

#

"Hi, Jack, I need one more favor."

"You already owe me a night of beer."

"I'll also spring for pizza. I need an address to go with this number."

"Lemme have it."

I read it to her, hoping Georgia was honest with me. I didn't want to pay another visit to Stoney Island.

"Buster McDonalds. Four-four-two-three Irving Park, apartment seven-oh-six."

"Thanks again, Jack."

"Listen, Phin, I asked around about Janet Cumberland. The word on the street is that Artie Collins put a contract out on her."

"I'll be careful."

There was a long pause on the line. I cut off her thought.

"I don't work for mobsters, Jack. I don't kill people for money."

"Watch yourself, Phin."

She hung up.

I stopped at a drive-thru, filled up on grease, and had ten more aspirin. My side ached to the touch. I had stronger stuff, doctor prescribed, but that dulled the senses and took away my edge. I thought about scoring some coke, but the hundred I had left wouldn't buy much, and time was winding down.

I had to find Jasmine.

Buster's neighborhood was several rungs above Ajax's as far as quality of life went. No junkies shooting up in the alleys, hookers on the corners, or roving gangs of teens with firearms.

There were, however, lots of kids drunk out of their minds, moving in great human waves from bar to bar. The area was a hot spot for night life, and Friday night meant the partying was mandatory.

Even the hydrants were taken, so I parked in an alley, blocking the entrance. I took the duffle bag from the passenger seat and climbed out into the night air.

The temp had dropped, and I imagined I could smell Lake Michigan, even though it was miles away. There were voices, shouting, laughing, cars honking. I stood in the shadows.

The security door on Buster's apartment had a lock that was intact and functioning, unlike Ajax's. I spotted someone walking out and caught the door before it closed, and then I took the elevator to the seventh floor.

The cop impersonation wouldn't work this time; Jasmine was on the run and wouldn't open the door for anybody.

But I had a key.

It was another online purchase. There were thirty-four major lock companies in the US, and they made ninety-five percent of all the locks in America. These lock companies each had a few dozen models, and each of the models had a master key that opened up every lock in the series.

Locksmiths could buy these master keys. So could anyone with a credit card who knew the right website.

The lock on Buster's apartment was a Schlage. I took a large key ring from my duffel bag and got the door open on the third try.

Jasmine and Buster were on a futon, watching TV. I was on him before he had a chance to get up.

When he reached for me, I grabbed his wrist and twisted. Then, using his arm like a lever, I forced him face down into the carpeting.

"Buster!"

I didn't have time to deal with Jasmine yet, so she got a kick in the gut. She went down. I took out roll of duct tape and secured Buster's wrists behind him. When that was done, I wound it around his legs a few times.

"Jazz, run!"

His mouth was next.

Jasmine had curled up in the corner of the room, hugging her knees and rocking back and forth. She was a little thing, no older than Ajax, wearing sweatpants and an extra large t-shirt. Her black hair was pulled back and fear distorted her features.

I made it worse by showing her my Glock.

"Tell me about Artie Collins."

She shrunk back, making herself smaller.

"You're going to kill me."

"No one is killing anyone. Why does Artie want you dead?"

"The book."

"What book?"

She pointed to the table next to the futon. I picked up a ledger, scanned a few pages.

Financial figures, from two of Artie's clubs. I guessed that these were the ones the IRS didn't see.

"Stupid move, lady. Why'd you take these from him?"

"He's a pig," she spat, anger overriding terror. "Artie doesn't like it straight. He's a real freak. He did things to me, things no one has ever done."

"So you stole this?"

"I didn't know what it was. I wanted to hurt him, it was right there in the dresser. So I took it."

Gutsy, but dumb. Stealing from one of the most connected guys in the Midwest was a good way to shorten your life expectancy.

"Artie is offering ten thousand dollars for you. And there's a bonus if it's messy."

I put the book in the duffle bag, and then removed a knife.

#

Artie Collins was a slug, and everyone knew it. He had his public side; the restaurants, the riverboat gambling, the night clubs, but anyone worth their street smarts knew he also peddled kiddie porn, smack cut with rat poison, and owned a handful of cops and judges.

Standing before me, he even looked like a slug, from his sweaty, fat face, to the sharkskin suit in dark brown, of all colors.

"I don't know you," he said.

"Better that way."

"I like to know who I'm doing business with."

"This is a one time deal. Two ships in the night."

He seemed to consider that, and laughed.

"Okay then, Mystery Man. You told my boys you had something for me."

I reached into my jacket. Artie didn't flinch; he knew his men had frisked me earlier and taken my gun. I took out a wad of Polaroids and handed them over.

Artie glanced through them, smiling like a carved pumpkin. He flashed one at me. Jasmine naked and tied up, the knife going in.

"That's a good one. A real Kodak moment."

I said nothing. Artie finished viewing my camera work and carefully stuck the pics in his blazer.

"These are nice, but I still need to know where she's at."

"The bottom of the Chicago river."

"I meant, where she was hiding. She had something of mine."

I nodded, once again going into my jacket. When Artie saw the ledger I thought he'd crap sunshine.

"She told me some things when I was working on her."

"I'll bet she did," Artie laughed.

He gave the ledger a cursory flip through, then tossed it onto his desk. I took a breath, let it out slow. The moment stretched. Finally, Artie waggled a fat, hot dog finger at me.

"You're good, my friend. I could use a man of your talents."

"I'm freelance."

"I offer benefits. A 401K. Dental. Plus whores and drugs, of course. I'd pay some good money to see you work a girl over like you did to that whore."

"You said you'd also pay good money for whoever brought you proof of Jasmine's death."

He nodded, slowly.

"You sure you don't want to work for me?"

"I don't play well with others."

Artie made a show of walking in a complete circle around me, checking me out. This wasn't going down as easy as I'd hoped.

"Brave man, to come in here all by yourself."

"My partner's outside."

"Partner, huh? Let's say, for the sake of argument, I had my boys kill you. What would your partner do? Come running into my place, guns blazing?"

He chuckled, and the two goons in the room with us giggled like stoned teenagers.

"No. He'd put the word out on the street that you're a liar. Then the next time you need a little favor from the outside, your reputation as a square guy would be sullied."

"Sullied!" Artie laughed again. He had a laugh like a frog. "That's rich. Would you work for a man with a sullied reputation, Jimmy?"

The thug named Jimmy shrugged, wisely choosing not to answer.

"You're right, of course." Artie said when the chuckles faded. "I have a good rep in this town, and my word is bond. Max."

The other thug handed me a briefcase. Leather. A good weight.

"There was supposed to be a bonus for making it messy."

"Oh, it's in there, my friend. I'm sure you'll be quite pleased. You can count it, if you like."

I shook my head.

"I trust you."

I turned to walk out, but Artie's men stayed in front of the door.

If Artie was more psychotic than I guessed, he could easily kill me right there, and I couldn't do a damn thing to stop him. I lied about having a partner, and the line about his street rep was just ego stroking.

I braced myself, deciding to go for the guy on the left first.

"One more thing, Mystery Man," Artie said to my back. "You wouldn't have made any copies of that ledger, maybe to try and grease me for more money sometime in the future?"

I turned around, gave Artie my cold stare.

"You think I would mess with you?"

His eyes drilled into me. They no longer held any amusement. They were the dark, hard eyes of a man who has killed many people, who has done awful things.

But I'd done some awful things, too. And I made sure he saw it in me.

"No," Artie finally decided. "No, you wouldn't mess with me."

I tilted my head, slightly.

"A pleasure doing business with you, Mr. Collins."

The thugs parted, and I walked out the door.

#

When I got a safe distance away, I counted the money.

Fifteen thousand bucks.

I dropped by Manny's, spent two gees on coke, and did a few lines.

The pain in my side became a dim memory.

Unlike pills, cocaine took away the pain and let me keep my edge.

These days, my edge was all I had.

I didn't have to wait for someone to leave Buster's apartment this time; he buzzed me in.

"Jazz is in the shower," he told me.

"Did you dump the bag?"

"In the river, like you told me. And I mailed out those photocopies to the cop with the alcohol name."

He gave me a beer, and Jasmine walked into the living room, wrapped in a towel. Her face and collarbone were still stained red from the stage blood.

"What now?" she asked.

"You're dead. Get the hell out of town."

I handed her a bag filled with five thousand dollars. She looked inside, then showed it to Buster.

"Jesus!" Buster yelped. "Thanks, man!"

Jasmine raised an eyebrow at me. "Why are you doing this?"

"If you're seen around here, Artie will know I lied. He won't be pleased. Take this and go back home. Your parents are looking for you."

Jasmine's voice was small. The voice of a teenager, not a strung-out street whore.

"Thank you."

"Since you're so grateful, you can do me one a small favor."

"Anything."

"Your friend. Ajax. I think she wants out of the life. Take her with you."

"You got it, Buddy!" Buster pumped my hand, grinning ear to ear.

"Why don't you hang out for a while? We'll tilt a few."

"Thanks, but I have some things to do."

Jasmine stood on her tiptoes, gave me a wet peck on the cheek. Then she whispered in my ear.

"You could have killed me, kept it all. Why didn't you?"

She didn't get it, but that was okay. Most people went through their whole lives without ever realizing how precious life was. Jasmine didn't understand that.

But someday she might.

"I don't kill people for money," I told her instead.

Then I left.

#

All things considered, I did pretty good. The blood, latex scars, and fake knife cost less than a hundred bucks. Pizza and beer for Jack came out to fifty. The money I gave to Ajax wasn't mine in the first place, and I already owned the master keys, the badge, and the Polaroid camera.

The cash would keep me in drugs for a while.

It might even take me up until the very end.

As for Artie Collins…word on the street, his bosses weren't happy about his arrest. Artie wasn't going to last very long in prison.

I did another line and laid back on my bed, letting the exhilaration wash over me. It took away the pain.

All the pain.

Outside my window, the city sounds invaded. Honking horns. Screeching tires. A man coughing. A woman shouting. The el train rushing past, clackety-clacking down the tracks louder than a thunder clap.

To most people, it was background noise.

But to me, it was music.

The One That Got Away

Brilliance Audio does the books on tape for the Jack series, and every year they let me read an extra short story to include with the audio version. Sort of like a DVD bonus. This was included on the audio of Whiskey Sour. I thought it would be interesting to revisit the Gingerbread Man, the villain from that book, through the point-of-view of a victim.

A steel crossbeam, flaking brown paint.

Stained PVC pipes.

White and green wires hanging on nails.

What she sees.

Moni blinks, yawns, tries to turn onto her side.

Can't.

The memory comes, jolting.

Rainy, after midnight, huddling under an overpass. Trying to keep warm in hot pants and a halter top. Rent money overdue. Not a single john in sight.

When the first car stopped, Moni would have tricked for free just to get inside and warm up.

Didn't have to, though. The guy flashed a big roll of twenties. Talked smooth, educated. Smiled a lot.

But there was something wrong with his eyes. Something dead.

Freak eyes.

Moni didn't do freaks. She'd made the mistake once, got hurt bad. Freaks weren't out for sex. They were out for pain. And Moni, bad as she needed money, wasn't going to take a beating for it.

She reached around, felt for the door handle to get out.

No handle.

Mace in her tiny purse, buried in condoms. She reached for it, but the needle found her arm and then everything went blurry.

And now...

Moni blinks, tries to clear her head. The floor under her is cold. Concrete.

She's in a basement. Staring up at the unfinished ceiling.

Moni tries to sit up, but her arms don't move. They're bound with twine, bound to steel rods set into the floor. She raises her head, sees her feet are also tied, legs apart.

Her clothes are gone.

Moni feels a scream building inside her, forces it back down. Forces herself to think.

She takes in her surroundings. It's bright, brighter than a basement should be. Two big lights on stands point down at her.

Between them is a tripod. A camcorder.

Next to the tripod, a table. Moni can see several knives on top. A hammer. A drill. A blowtorch. A cleaver.

The cleaver is caked with little brown bits, and something else.

Hair. Long, pink hair.

Moni screams.

Charlene has long pink hair. Charlene, who's been missing for a week.

Street talk was she'd gone straight, quit the life.

Street talk was wrong.

Moni screams until her lungs burn. Until her throat is raw. She twists and pulls and yanks, crying to get free, panic overriding the pain of the twine rubbing her wrists raw.

The twine doesn't budge.

Moni leans to the right, stretching her neck, trying to reach the twine with her teeth.

Not even close. But as she tries, she notices the stains on the floor beneath her. Sticky brown stains that smell like meat gone bad.

Charlene's blood.

Moni's breath catches. Her gaze drifts to the table again, even though she doesn't want to look, doesn't want to see what this freak is going to use on her.

"I'm dead," she thinks. "And it's gonna be bad."

Moni doesn't like herself. Hasn't for a while. It's tough to find self-respect when one does the things she does for money. But even though she ruined her life with drugs, even though she hates the twenty-dollar-a-pop whore she's become, Moni doesn't want to die.

Not yet.

And not like this.

Moni closes her eyes. She breathes in. Breathes out. Wills her muscles to relax.

"I hope you didn't pass out."

Every muscle in Moni's body contracts in shock. The freak is looking down at her, smiling.

He'd been standing right behind Moni the whole time. Out of her line of sight.

"Please let me go."

His laugh is an evil thing. She knows, looking at his eyes, he won't cut her free until her heart has stopped.

"Keep begging. I like it. I like the begging almost as much as I like the screaming."

He walks around her, over to the table. Takes his time fondling his tools.

"What should we start with? I'll let you pick."

Moni doesn't answer. She thinks back to when she was a child, before all of the bad stuff in her life happened, before hope was just another four-letter word. She remembers the little girl she used to be, bright and full of energy, wanting to grow up and be a lawyer like all of those fancy-dressed women on TV.

"If I get through this," Moni promises God, "I'll quit the street and go back to school. I swear."

"Are you praying?" The freak grins. He's got the blowtorch in his hand. "God doesn't answer prayers here."

He fiddles with the camcorder, then kneels between her open legs. The torch ignites with the strike of a match. It's the shape of a small fire extinguisher. The blue flame shooting from the nozzle hisses like a leaky tire.

"I won't lie to you. This is going to hurt. A lot. But it smells delicious. Just like cooking bacon."

Moni wonders how she can possibly brace herself for the oncoming pain, and realizes that she can't. There's nothing she can do. All of the mistakes, all of the bad choices, have led up to this sick final moment in her life, being burned alive in some psycho's basement.

She clenches her teeth, squeezes her eyes shut.

A bell chimes.

"Dammit."

The freak pauses, the flame a foot away from her thighs.

The bell chimes again. A doorbell, coming from upstairs.

Moni begins to cry out, but he guesses her intent, bringing his fist down hard onto her face.

Moni sees blurry motes, tastes blood. A moment later he's shoving something in her mouth. Her halter top, wedging it in so far it sticks to the back of her throat.

"Be right back, bitch. The Fed-Ex guy is bringing me something for you."

The freak walks off, up the stairs, out of sight.

Moni tries to scream, choking on the cloth. She shakes and pulls and bucks but there's no release from the twine and the gag won't come out and any second he'll be coming back down the stairs to use that awful blowtorch...

The blowtorch.

Moni stops struggling. Listens for the hissing sound.

It's behind her.

She twists, cranes her neck around, sees the torch sitting on the floor only a few inches from her head.

It's still on.

Moni scoots her body toward it. Strains against the ropes. Stretches her limbs to the limit.

The top of her head touches the steel canister.

Moni's unsure of how much time she has, unsure if this will work, knowing she has less than a one-in-a-zillion chance but she has to try something and maybe dear god just maybe this will work.

She cocks her head back and snaps it against the blowtorch. The torch teeters, falls onto its side, and begins a slow, agonizing roll over to her right hand.

"Please," Moni begs the universe. "Please."

The torch rolls close–too close–the flame brushing Moni's arm and the horrible heat singeing hair and burning skin.

Moni screams into her gag, jerks her elbow, tries to force the searing flame closer to the rope.

The pain blinds her, takes her to a place beyond sensation, where her only thought, her only goal, is to make it stop make it stop MAKE IT STOP!

Her arm is suddenly loose.

Moni grabs the blowtorch, ignoring the burning twine that's still wrapped tightly around her wrist. She points the flame at her left hand, severs the rope. Then her feet.

She's free!

No time to dress. No time to hide. Up the stairs, two at a time, ready to dive out of a window naked and screaming and–

"What the hell?"

The freak is at the top of the stairs, pulling a wicked-looking hunting knife out of a cardboard box. He notices Moni and confusion registers on his face.

It quickly morphs into rage.

Moni doesn't hesitate, bringing the blowtorch around, swinging it like a club, connecting hard with the side of the freak's head, and then he's falling forward, past her, arms pinwheeling as he dives face-first into the stairs.

Moni continues to run, up into the house, looking left and right, finding the front door, reaching for the knob...

And pauses.

The freak took a hard fall, but he might still be alive.

There will be other girls. Other girls in his basement.

Girls like Charlene.

Cops don't help whores. Cops don't care.

But Moni does.

Next to the front door is the living room. A couch. Curtains. A throw rug.

Moni picks up the rug, wraps it around her body. Using the torch, she sets the couch ablaze, the curtains on fire, before throwing it onto the floor and running out into the street.

It's early morning. The sidewalk is cold under her bare feet. She's shaken, and her burned arm throbs, but she feels lighter than air.

A car stops.

A john, cruising. Rolls down the window and asks if she's for sale.

"Not anymore," Moni says.

She walks away, not looking back.

With a Twist

Another locked room mystery, this one even more complicated. What's fun about Jack is that I can put her in different sub genres without changing her character. She can function as Sherlock Holmes, or Spenser, or Kay Scarpetta, depending on the story. This won 2nd place in the Ellery Queen Reader's Choice Contest.

"His skull is shattered, and his spinal column looks like a Dutch pretzel." Phil Blasky straightened from his crouch and locked eyes with me, his expression neutral. "This man has fallen from a great height."

I glanced up from my notepad, not having written a word. "You're positive?"

"I've autopsied enough jumpers in my tenure as ME to know a pancake when I see one, Jack."

I stared at the body, arms and legs akimbo, splayed out on a living room carpet damp with bodily fluids. On impulse I looked up, focusing on a ceiling that couldn't be any higher than eight feet.

"Maybe he jumped off the couch." This from my partner, Detective First Class Herb Benedict. His left hand scratched his expansive stomach, his light blue shirt dotted with mustard stains. It was 11am, so how the mustard got there was anybody's guess.

I frowned at Herb, then located a patch of dry beige carpeting and knelt next to the corpse, careful not to stain my heels or pants. The victim was named Edward Wyatt, and this was his house. He was Caucasian, 67 years old, and as dead as dead can be. The smell wasn't too bad—this was a fresh one—but the wake would definitely be a closed casket.

"What do you make of the blood spatters, Phil?"

"Unremarkable star-configuration, arcing away from the nexus of the body in all directions. Droplets coating the walls and ceiling. Notice the double pattern—see the large spot here, next to the body? It has it's own larger radius of spatters."

"Meaning?"

"Meaning he bounced once, when he hit the carpet. Consistent with jumpers, leaving a primary then a secondary spatter."

Benedict cleared his throat. "You're telling us this is authentic? That he fell five stories into a living room?"

"I'm telling you it looks that way."

I've been with the Chicago Police Department for twenty years, half of those with the Violent Crimes unit, and have seen a few things. But this was flat-out weird. I almost ordered my team to do a house sweep for Rod Serling.

"Could somebody have dumped him here? After he died someplace else?"

"That seems reasonable, but I don't notice any tissue or fluid missing. If he were scraped off the street, there would be blood left behind. If anything, there's too much blood in this room."

I would have asked how it was possible for him to know that, but Phil knew more about dead people than Mick Jagger knew about rock and roll.

"Also," Phil motioned us closer, "take a look at this."

He crouched, holding some tweezers, and used a gloved hand to gently lift the corpse's head. After some prodding and poking, he removed a small fiber.

"Beige carpeting, deeply embedded in his flesh. The deceased has hundreds of these fibers in the skin, consistent with..."

I finished the sentence for him. "...falling from a great height."

"However improbable it seems. It's as if someone took off the roof, and he jumped out of a plane and landed in his living room. And don't forget about the doors."

I felt a headache coming on. The house had two entry points, the front door and the rear door. Each had been dead-bolted from the inside—no outside entry was possible. The locks were privacy locks, similar to the ones on hotel rooms; there were no keyholes, just a latch. The first officers on the scene had to break through a window to get in; the windows had all been locked from the inside.

"Lt. Daniels?" A uniform, name of Perez, motioned me over to a corner of the room. "There's a note."

I watched my step, making my way to the room-length book shelf, crammed full of several hundred paperbacks. Their spines were splashed with blood, but I could make out some authors: Carr, Chandler, Chesterton. Perez pointed to a pristine sheet of white typing paper, tacked to the shelf between Sladek and Stout. The handwriting on it was done in black marker. I snugged on a pair of latex gloves I keep in my blazer pocket, and picked up the note.

God doesn't understand. Eternal peace I desire. The only way out is death. Answers come to those who seek. Can't get through another day. Let me rest. Until we meet in heaven. Edward.

I pondered the message for a moment, then returned to Benedict and Blasky.

"What about a steamroller?" Herb was asking. "That would crush a body, right?"

"It wouldn't explain the spatters. Also, unless there's a steamroller in the closet, I don't see how..."

I interrupted. "I'm looking around, Herb. When the techies get here, I want video of everything."

"That a suicide note?" Herb pointed his chin at the paper I held.

"Yeah. Strange, though. Take a peek and let me know if you spot the anomaly."

"Anomaly? You've been watching too many of those cop shows on TV."

I winked at him. "I'll let you know if I find the steamroller."

Notebook in hand, I went to explore the house. It was a modest two bedroom split-level, in a good neighborhood on the upper north side. Nine-one-one had gotten an anonymous call from a nearby payphone, someone stating that he'd walked past the house and smelled a horrible stench. The officers who caught the call claimed to hear gunshots, and entered through a window. They discovered the body, but found no evidence of any gun or shooter.

I checked the back door again. Still locked, the deadbolt in place. The door was old, its white paint fading, contrast to the new decorative trim around the frame.

I checked the linoleum floor and found it clean, polished, pristine.

Running my finger along the door frame, I picked up dust, dirt, and some white powder. I sniffed. Plaster. The hinges were solid, tarnished with age. The knob was heavy brass, and the deadbolt shiny steel. Both in perfect working order.

I turned the deadbolt and opened the door. It must have been warped with age, because it only opened 3/4 of the way and then rubbed against the kitchen floor. I walked outside.

The backyard consisted of a well-kept vegetable garden and twelve tall bushes that lined the perimeter fence, offering privacy from the neighbors. I examined the outside of the door and found nothing unusual. The door frame had trim that matched the interior. The porch was clean. I knelt on the welcome mat and examined the strike panel and the lock mechanisms. Both were solid, normal.

I stood, brushed some sawdust from my knee, and went back into the house.

The windows seemed normal, untampered with. There was broken glass on the floor by the window where the uniforms had entered. Other than being shattered, it also appeared normal.

The front door was unlocked; after breaching the residence through the window, the uniforms had opened the door to let the rest of the crew inside. I examined the door, and didn't find anything unusual.

The kitchen was small, tidy. A Dell puzzle magazine rested on the table, next to the salt and pepper. Another sat by the sink. The dishwasher contained eight clean mason jars, with lids, and a turkey baster. Nothing else. No garbage in the garbage can. The refrigerator was empty except for a box of baking soda. The freezer contained three full trays of ice cubes.

I checked cabinets, found a few glasses and dishes, but no food. The drawers held silverware, some dishtowels, and a full box of Swedish Fish cherry gummy candy.

I left the kitchen for the den, sat at the late Edward Wyatt's desk, and inched my way through it. There was a bankbook for a savings account. It held $188,679.42—up until last month when the account had been emptied out.

I kept digging and found a file full of receipts dating back ten years. Last month, the victim had apparently toured Europe, staying in London, Paris, Rome, and Berlin. Bills for fancy restaurants abounded. The most recent purchases included several hundred dollars at a local hardware store, a dinner for two at the 95th Floor that cost over six-hundred dollars, a one week stay at the Four Seasons hotel in Chicago, a digital video recorder and an expensive new stereo, and a bill for wall-to-wall carpeting; the beige shag Mr. Wyatt was currently staining had been installed last month.

I also found several grocery lists, and the handwriting seemed to match the handwriting on the suicide note.

Next to the desk, on a cabinet, sat a Chicago phonebook. It was open to BURGLAR ALARMS.

The den also had a cabinet which contained some games (Monopoly, chess, Clue, backgammon) and jigsaw puzzles, including an old Rubik's Cube. I remember solving mine, back in the 1980s, by pulling the stickers off the sides. This one had also been solved, and the stickers appeared intact.

I left the den and found the door to the basement. It was small, unfinished. The floor was bare concrete, and a florescent lamp attached to an overhead beam provided adequate light. A utility sink sat in a corner, next to a washer and dryer. On the other side was a workbench, clean and tidy. The drawers contained the average assortment of hand tools; wrenches, hammers, screwdrivers, saws, chisels. Atop the workbench was an electric reciprocating saw that looked practically new.

A closet was tucked away in the corner. Inside I found an old volleyball net, a large roll of carpet padding, a croquet set, some scraps of decorative trim, and half a can of blue paint. Also, hanging on a makeshift rack, were three badminton rackets, an extra-large super-soaker squirt gun, and a plastic lawn chair.

After snooping until there was nothing left to snoop, I met Herb back in the living room.

"Find anything?" Herb asked.

I described through my search, ending with the Swedish Fish.

"That was the only food?" Herb asked.

"Seems to be."

"Are we taking it as evidence?"

"I'm not sure yet. Why?"

"I love Swedish Fish."

"If I poured chocolate syrup on the corpse, would you eat that too?"

"You found chocolate syrup?"

I switched gears. "You figure out the note?"

Herb smiled. "Yeah. Funny how the note is perfectly clean when everything around it, and behind it, is soaked in blood."

"Find anything else?"

"I tossed the bedrooms upstairs, found some basics; clothes, shoes, linen. Bathroom contained bathroom stuff; towels, toiletries, a lot of puzzle magazines. Another bookshelf—non-fiction this time. Some prescription meds in the cabinet." Benedict checked his pad. "Diflucan, Abarelix, Taxotere, and Docetexel."

"Cancer drugs," Phil Blasky said. He held Wyatt's right arm. "That explains this plastic catheter implanted in his vein and this rash on his neck. This man has been on long term chemotherapy."

A picture began to form in my head, but I didn't have all the pieces yet.

"Herb, did you find any religious paraphernalia? Bibles, crucifixes, prayer books, things like that?"

"No. There were some books upstairs, but mostly philosophy and logic puzzles. In fact, there was a whole shelf dedicated to Free-Thinking."

"As opposed to thinking that costs money?"

"That's a term atheists use."

Curiouser and curiouser.

"I found receipts for a new stereo and camcorder. Were they upstairs?" I asked.

"The stereo was, set-up in the bedroom next to that big bay window. I didn't see any camcorders."

"Let me see that note again."

The suicide letter had been placed in a clear plastic bag. I read it twice, then had to laugh. "Quite a few religious references for a Free-Thinker."

"If he was dying of cancer, maybe he found God."

"Or maybe he found a way to die on his terms."

"Meaning?"

"The terms of a man who loved mysteries, games, and puzzles. Look at the first letter of each sentence."

Herb read silently, his lips moving. "G-E-T-A-C-L-U-E. Cute. You know, I became a cop because it required very little lateral thinking."

"I thought it was because vendors gave you free donuts."

"Shhh. Hold on...I'm forming a hypothesis."

"I'll alert the media."

Phil Blasky snorted. "You guys have a drink minimum for this show?"

Herb ignored us. "Wyatt obviously had some help, because the note was placed on top of the blood. But was his help in the form of assisted suicide? Or murder?"

"It doesn't matter to us—they're treated the same way."

"Exactly. So if this is a game for us to figure out, and the clues have been staged, will the clues lead us to what really happened, or to what Wyatt or the killer would like us to believe really happened?"

The word 'game' made me remember the cabinet in the den. I returned to it, finding the Parker Brothers classic board game, Clue. Inside the box, instead of cards, pieces, and a game board, was a cryptogram magazine.

"I'm going out to the car to get my deermilker cap," Herb said.

"It's deerstalker. While you're out there, call the Irregulars."

I removed the magazine and flipped through it, noting that all of the puzzles had been solved. Nothing else appeared unusual. I went through it again, slower, and noticed that page 20 had been circled.

"Herb, grab all puzzle magazines you can find. I'll meet you back here in five."

I did a quick search of the first floor and gathered up eight magazines. Each had a different page number circled. Herb waddled down the stairs a moment later.

"I've got twelve of them."

"Did he circle page numbers?"

"Yeah."

We took the magazines over to the dining room table and spread them out. Herb made a list of the page number circled in each issue.

"Let's try chronological order," I said. "The earliest issue is February of last year. Write down the page numbers beginning with that one."

I watched Herb jot down 7, 19, 22, 14, 26, 13, 4, 19, 12, 16, 13, 22, 4, 7, 12, 12, 14, 6, 24, and 19.

Herb rubbed his mustache. "No number higher than twenty-six. Could be an alphabet code." He hummed the alphabet, stopping at the seventh letter. "Number seven is G."

"Yeah, but nineteen is S and twenty-two is V. What word starts with GSV?"

"Maybe it's reverse chronological order. Start with the latest magazine."

I did some quick calculating. "That would be SXF. Not too many words begin like that."

"Are you hungry? I'm getting hungry."

"We'll eat after we figure this out."

"How about reverse alphabet code? Z is one, Y is two, and so on."

I couldn't do that in my head, and had to write down the alphabet and match up letters to numbers. Then I began to decode.

"You nailed it, Herb. The message is T-H-E-M-A-N-W-H-O-K-N-E-W-T-O-O-M-U-C-H. The Man Who Knew Too Much."

"That Hitchcock movie. Maybe he's got a copy lying around."

We searched, and didn't find a single video or DVD. My hands were pruning in the latex gloves. I snapped the gloves off and stuffed them in my pocket. The air felt good.

"Was it based off a book?" Herb asked. "The guy's got plenty of books."

"Could have been. Let me ask the expert." I pulled out my cell and called the smartest mystery expert I knew; my mother.

"Jacqueline! I'm so happy to hear from you. It's about time I get out of bed."

I felt a pang of alarm. "Mom, it's almost noon. Are you okay?"

"I'm fine, dear."

"But you've been alone in bed all day..."

"Did I say I was alone?" There was a slapping sound, and my mother said, "Behave, it's my daughter."

I felt myself flush, but worked through it.

"Mom, do you remember that old Hitchcock movie? The Man Who Knew Too Much?"

"The Leslie Banks original, or the Jimmy Stewart remake?"

"Either. Was it based off a book?"

"Not that I'm aware of. I can check, if you like. I have both versions."

"Can you? It's important."

Herb nudged me. "Can I have that Swedish Fish candy?"

I nodded, and Herb waddled off.

"Jacqueline? On the Leslie Banks version, the back of the box lists the screenwriter, but doesn't mention it is based on a book. And...neither does the Jimmy Stewart version."

Damn.

"Can you give me the screenwriter's name?"

"Two folks, Charles Bennett and D.B. Wyndham-Lewis. Why is this so important?"

"It's a case. I'll tell you about it later. I was hoping The Man Who Knew Too Much was a book."

"It is a book. By G.K. Chesterton, written in the early 1920s. But that had nothing to do with the movie."

"Chesterton? Thanks, Mom."

"Chesterton was a wonderful author. He did quite a few locked-room mysteries. Not too many writers do those anymore."

"I'll call you tonight. Be good."

"I most certainly won't."

I put away the phone and went to the blood-stained bookshelf. The Chesterton book was easy to find. I put the gloves back on and picked it up. Wedged between pages sixty-two and sixty-three was a thin, plastic flash video card, a recent technology that was used instead of film in digital video cameras. And camcorders...

I met Herb in the kitchen. He had his mouth full of red gummy candy. I held up my prize.

"I found a video card."

Herb said something that might have been, "Really?" but I couldn't be sure with his teeth glued together.

"Is your new laptop in your car?"

He nodded, chewing.

"Do you have a card reader?"

He nodded again, shoving the candy box into his pants pocket and easing though the back door.

Two minutes later Herb's laptop was booting up. I pushed the flash card into his reader slot, and the appropriate program opened the file and began to play the contents.

On Herb's screen, a very-much-alive Edward Wyatt smiled at us.

"Hello," the dead man said. "Congratulations on reaching this point. I thought it fitting, having spent my life enjoying puzzles, to end my life with a puzzle as well. Though I commend you for your brainpower thus far, I regret to say that this video won't be providing you with any clues as to how this seemingly impossible act was committed. But I will say it has been done of my own, free will. My oncologist has given me less than a month to live, and

I'm afraid it won't be a pleasant month. I've chosen to end things early."

"Pause it," I said.

Herb pressed a button. "What?"

"Go back just a few frames, in slow motion."

Herb did. I pointed at the screen. "See that? The camera moved. Someone's holding it."

Herb nodded. "Assisted suicide. I wonder if he moved the camera on purpose, to let us know he had help."

"Let it finish playing."

Herb hit a button, and Wyatt began again.

"Undoubtedly, by this point you know I've had help."

Benedict and I exchanged a look.

"Of course," Wyatt continued, "I wouldn't want to put my helper in any legal jeopardy. This friend graciously helped me fulfill my last wish, and I'd hate for this special person to be arrested for what is entirely my idea, my wishes, my decision, and my fault. But I also know a little about how the law works, and I know this person might indeed become a target of Chicago's finest. Steps have been taken to make sure this person is never found. These steps are already in motion."

Herb paused the recording and looked at me. "I'm fine stopping right here. He says it was suicide, I believe him, let's clear the case and grab a bite to eat."

I folded my arms. "You're kidding. How did the body get inside when everything was locked? How could he have jumped to his death in his living room? Who's the helper? Don't you want answers to these questions?"

"Not really. I don't like mysteries."

"You're fired."

Herb ignored me. I fire him several times a week. He let the recording play.

"However," Wyatt went on, "all good mysteries have a sense of closure.

With me dead, and my helper gone, how will you know if you've figured out everything? There's a way. If you're a sharpie, and you've found all the clues, there will be confirmation. Good luck. And don't be discouraged...this is, after all, supposed to be fun."

Benedict snorted his opinion on the matter. The recording ended, and I closed my eyes in thought.

"Herb—the stereo upstairs. Was it on or off?"

"Off."

"Fully off? Or on standby?"

"I'll check."

Benedict wandered out of the kitchen, and I went back into the basement. I found a hammer in the workbench drawer and brought it to the back door. Once again, when I opened the door, it caught on the linoleum flooring. The floor remained shiny, even where the door touched it.

The lack of scuff marks struck me as a pretty decent clue.

Since the door looked old, but the decorative trim around the frame appear new, I decided to remove a section of trim. After a full thirty seconds of searching for a nail to pull, I realized there were no nails holding the trim on.

How interesting.

Using the claw end of the hammer, I wedged off a piece of side trim. And in doing so, I solved the locked-room part of the mystery.

Three gunshots exploded from the floor above, shattering my smugness. I tugged my .38 from my shoulder holster and sprinted up the stairs, flanked by Perez.

"Herb!"

Three more gunshots, impossibly loud. Coming from the room at the end of the hall. I crouched in the doorway, my pistol coming up.

"Jack! All clear!" Herb stood by the stereo, a CD clutched in one hand, the other grasping his chest. "Damn, you almost gave me a heart attack."

I put two and two together quickly enough, but Officer Henry Perez wasn't endowed with the same preternatural detecting abilities.

"Where's the gun?" he croaked, arms and legs locked in full Weaver stance. "Who's got the gun?"

"Easy, Officer." I put a hand on his elbow and eased his arms down. "There is no gun."

Perez's face wrinkled up. "No gun? That sounded just like..."

Herb finished his sentence, "...the gunshots you heard when you arrived on the scene. I know. It's all right here."

Herb held up the CD.

"It's a recording of gunshots," I told Perez. "It was used to get you to break into the house. Probable cause. Or else you never would have gone in—the 911 call talked about a bad smell, but the corpse is fresh and there is no smell."

Perez seemed reluctant to holster his weapon. I ignored him, holding out my hand for the CD. It was a Maxell recordable CD-R. On the front, in written black marker, was the number 209. I held the disc up to the light, checking for prints. It looked clean.

"Maybe this is one of those clues the dear, departed Edward Wyatt mentioned in his video." Herb said. "You ready to get some lunch?"

"I figured out how the doors were locked from the inside," I said.

We went downstairs and I showed Herb the fruits of my labors, prying off another piece of trim.

"Smart. What made you think of it, Jack?"

"The trim is glued on, rather than nailed. Which made me wonder why, and what it covered up."

"Impressive, Oh Great One. Did you also happen to notice the number?"

"What number?"

"Written on the back of the trim, in black marker." Herb pointed at the number 847.

"What did Wyatt say in his recording? About being a sharpie? What's the most popular black marker?"

"A Sharpie." Herb grunted his disapproval. "Wyatt's lucky he's dead, because if he were still alive I'd smack him around for making us jump through these hoops."

"Are you saying you'd rather be interviewing a domestic battery?"

"I'm saying my brain hurts. I'm going to need to watch a few hours of prime time to dumb myself back down. Isn't that reality show on tonight? The one where the seven contestants eat live bugs on a tropical island to marry a millionaire who's really a janitor? My IQ drops ten points each time I watch that show."

I stared at the black marker writing. "Eight four seven is a local area code. The two zero nine could be a prefix."

"Almost a phone number. Maybe there's another clue with the last four digits."

We went back to the game of Clue, but nothing was written on or inside the box. Another ten minutes were wasted going through the pile of puzzle magazines.

"Okay, what have we figured out so far?" I said, thinking out loud. "We figured out the gunshots that brought us to the scene, and we figured out the locked room part. But we still don't know how he fell to his death in the living room."

"He must have jumped off a building somewhere else, and then his partner brought the body here and staged the scene."

I rubbed my eyes, getting a smudge of eyeliner on my gloves.

"It's a damn good staging. ME said the blood spatters indicate he fell into that room. Plus there are carpet fibers embedded in his face."

"Maybe," Herb got a gleam in his eye, "he jumped onto that carpet at another location, then both the carpet and the body were put back into the room."

"The entire living room is carpeted, Herb."

"Maybe the helper cut out a section, then put it back in."

We went back into the living room, wound plastic food wrap around our shoes and pants, and spent half an hour crawling over the damp carpet, looking for seams that meant it had been cut out. It was a dead end.

"Damn it." Herb stripped off some bloody cling wrap. "I was sure that's how he did it."

I shrugged. My neck hurt from being on all fours, and some of the blood had gotten through the plastic and stained my pants. "Maybe the fibers embedded in the body won't match the fibers from this carpet."

Herb sighed. "And maybe the blood found squirted all over the room won't match, either. But we both know that everything will match. This guy was so meticulous..."

"Hold it! You said 'squirted.'"

"It's a perfectly good word."

"I think I know why the living room looks that way. Come into the kitchen."

I opened the dishwasher, showing Herb the mason jars and turkey baster. Herb remained dubious.

"That turkey baster wouldn't work. Not powerful enough."

"But what about one of those air-pump squirt guns? The kind that holds a gallon of water, and can shoot a stream twenty feet?"

I led Herb into the basement closet, holding up the squirt gun I'd seen earlier. Written on the handle, in black marker, was the word 'Charlie.'"

"Okay, so we've got two three-digit numbers, and a name. Now what? We still don't know how the fibers got embedded in the victim."

Herb rubbed his chin, thinking or doing a fair imitation of it. "Maybe the helper embedded the fibers by hand after death?"

"Phil would have caught that. I think Wyatt actually leapt to his death and landed on carpeting."

"I've got it," Herb said. He explained.

"Herb, that's perfect! But there's no way you can put black marker on something that isn't here. What else do we have?

"Got me. That revelation taxed my mental abilities for the month."

"The only other obvious clue is the Swedish Fish candy."

Herb pulled the box out of his pocket. The package, and contents, seemed normal. So normal that Herb ate another handful.

I racked my brain, trying to find something we'd missed. So far, all the clues made sense except for that damn candy.

"I'm going back upstairs," Herb said. "Want to order a pizza?"

"You're kidding."

"I'm not kidding. I have to eat something. We might be here for the rest of our lives."

"Herb, you can't have a pizza delivered to a crime scene."

"How about Chinese food? I haven't had Mu Shu Pork since Thursday. You want anything?"

"No."

"You sure?"

"I'm sure."

"You're not getting any of mine."

"Get me a small order of beef with pea pods."

"That sounds good. How about a large order and we split it?"

"What about the Mu Shu pork?"

Herb patted his expansive belly. "I'll get that too. You think I got this fat just looking at food?" He turned, heading for the stairs. "Where's Wyatt's phone book?"

"It's on his desk." Insight struck. "Herb! That might be another clue!"

"Chinese food?"

"The phone book! It's open to a page."

I squeezed past my portly partner and raced up the stairs. The phone book was where I left it, BURGLAR ALARMS covering the left-hand page. I went through each of the listings, put there was no black marker. I checked the other page, and didn't see anything unusual. But on the very top of the right hand page was spillover from the previous entry. A listing called CHARLIE'S, with the phone number 847-209-7219.

When I noted what subject came alphabetically before BURGLAR ALARMS in the phonebook, I grinned like an idiot. Then I pulled out my cell and called the number. After four rings and a click, a male voice answered.

"This is Charlie."

"This is Lieutenant Jack Daniels of the Chicago Police Department."

"That was fast. Edward would have been pleased."

"You helped murder him?"

"No. He killed himself. I helped set up all of the other stuff, but I had nothing to do with killing him. I've got proof, too. Footage of him jumping to his death."

"Off of your crane. Or platform. What is it you use?"

"A hundred foot platform. He went quick—in less than four seconds. He preferred it to the agony of cancer."

Herb sidled up to me, putting his ear next to the phone.

"How did Wyatt find you?" I asked Charlie.

"The want ads. He saw I was selling my business. I guess that's how he came up with this whole idea. Pretty clever, don't you think? He bought me out, plus paid me to assist in setting up the scene. Nice guy. I liked him a lot."

"You know, of course, we'll have to arrest you."

"I know. Which is why my office phone forwarded this call to my cell. I'm on my way out of the country. Edward paid me enough to lay low for a while."

"One hundred and eighty-eight thousand dollars." I remembered the number from the empty bank account.

"No, not nearly. Edward lived very well for the last month of his life. He spent a lot of money. And good for him—what good is a life savings if you can't have some fun with it?"

"Not much," Herb said.

I shushed him.

"Can I assume, Lieutenant, that you've figured everything out? Found all the clues? If you know everything, I'm supposed to give you a reward. Edward has this list of questions. Are you ready?"

Not knowing what else to say, I agreed.

"Okay, question number one; how were the doors locked from the inside?"

"You removed the entire door and frame while the door was already locked. Edward, or you, used a reciprocating saw to cut around the door frame. Then one of you glued new trim to the inside of the frame. When the door was pulled back into place, the trim covered the inside cut marks. Then you nailed the frame in place from the outside, and put more trim around the edges to cover the outside cut."

"What gave it away?"

"Sawdust on the outside matt, a receipt from the hardware store, a new electric saw in the basement, and extra trim in the closet. Plus, the door didn't open all the way."

"Edward purposely left all the clues except that last one. The door was heavy, and I couldn't fit it back in the hole perfectly. Question number two; how did it appear Edward jumped to his death in his living room?"

"He'd been drawing his own blood for a few weeks, using the catheter in his arm, and saving it in the refrigerator in mason jars. Then he used a turkey baster to fill a super soaker squirt gun with his blood, and sprayed the living room. I assume he read enough mysteries to know how to mimic blood spatters. He even faked the bounce that happens when a jumper hits."

"Excellent. How did the carpet fibers get on the body?"

"He visited Charlie's Bungee Jumping Emporium in Palatine and did a swan dive onto a pile of carpet remainders. We found carpet padding in the basement, but no remainders, and usually the installers give you all the extra pieces. A clue by omission."

"Very good. Question number three; where did the gunshots come from?"

"The stereo upstairs. That was also a new purchase. The stereo faced the window, so you must have hit the PLAY button from the street, using the remote."

"I did. The remote is in a garbage can next to the payphone I called from, if anyone wants it back. Did you find anything else interesting?"

I explained the suicide note, the Clue game, and the puzzle magazines.

"How about the Swedish Fish candy?" he asked.

"We have no idea what that means."

"That was Edward's favorite clue. I'd tell you, but I'm sure you'll figure it out eventually. Anyway, there's a surprise for you in John Dickson Carr's book The Three Coffins. Don't bother calling me back—I'm throwing away this phone as soon as I hang up. Good-bye, Lieutenant."

And he was gone.

We found the Carr book without difficulty. In the pages were a folded cashier's check, and another flash card. We played the card on Herb's computer.

Edward Wyatt, standing atop a large bungee platform, smiled at the camera, winked, and said, "Congratulations on figuring it out. In order to make absolutely, positively sure that there's no doubt I'm doing this of my own free will, without assistance or coercion, I give you this proof."

He jumped. The camera followed him down onto a pile of beige carpet remainders. I winced when he bounced.

"So that's it?" Herb whined. "We spend our entire afternoon, without any food, on a plain, old suicide?"

"I don't think this one qualifies as plain or old. Plus, a twenty grand check for the KITLOD Fund is a nice return for our time."

"I think I'd rather be killed in the line of duty than forced to go through one of these again. And he didn't tell you the reason for the Swedish Fish?"

"No. It doesn't seem to fit at all. Almost as if..." I began to laugh.

"What's funny?"

"Don't you get it? Wyatt planted a box of little red candy fish, knowing it would confuse us. It was meant to throw us off the trail."

"I still don't get it."

"You need to read more mysteries, Herb."

"So, you're not going to tell me?"

"You'll figure it out. Now let's go grab that Chinese food." I smiled, pleased with myself. "Preferably a place that sells herring."

Epitaph

I've been a longtime David Morrell fan, so when he co-founded the International Thriller Writers organization and asked me to join, I complied even though I'm not much of a joiner. I'm glad I did, because they published an anthology called Thriller, edited by James Patterson, and I won a wild card spot among the many bestselling authors in the collection. This story was later nominated for a British Dagger award, but what excited me most was to share the covers with F. Paul Wilson's Repairman Jack, Phin's literary ancestor.

There's an art to getting your ass kicked.

Guys on either side held my arms, stretching me out crucifixion-style. The joker who worked me over swung wildly, without planting his feet or putting his body into it. He spent most of his energy swearing and screaming when he should have been focusing on inflicting maximum damage.

Amateur.

Not that I was complaining. What he lacked in professionalism, he made up for in mean.

He moved in and rabbit-punched me in the side. I flexed my abs and tried to shift to take the blow in the center of my stomach, rather than the more vulnerable kidneys.

I exhaled hard when his fist landed. Saw stars.

He stepped away to pop me in the face. Rather than tense up, I relaxed, trying to absorb the contact by letting my neck snap back.

It still hurt like hell.

I tasted blood, wasn't sure if it came from my nose or my mouth. Probably both. My left eye had already swollen shut.

"Hijo calvo de una perra!"

You bald son of a bitch. Real original. His breath was ragged now, shoulders slumping, face glowing with sweat.

Gang-bangers these days aren't in very good shape. I blame TV and junk food.

One final punch—a half-hearted smack to my broken nose—and then I was released.

I collapsed face-first in a puddle that smelled like urine. The three Latin Kings each took the time to spit on me. Then they strolled out of the alley, laughing and giving each other high-fives.

When they got a good distance away, I crawled over to a Dumpster and pulled myself to my feet. The alley was dark, quiet. I felt something scurry over my foot.

Rats, licking up my dripping blood.

Nice neighborhood.

I hurt a lot, but pain and I were old acquaintances. I took a deep breath, let it out slow, did some poking and prodding. Nothing seemed seriously damaged.

I'd been lucky.

I spat. The bloody saliva clung to my swollen lower lip and dribbled onto my T-shirt. I tried a few steps forward, managed to keep my balance, and continued to walk out of the alley, onto the sidewalk, and to the corner bus stop.

I sat.

The Kings took my wallet, which had no ID or credit cards, but did have a few hundred in cash. I kept an emergency fiver in my shoe. The bus arrived, and the portly driver raised an eyebrow at my appearance.

"Do you need a doctor, buddy?"

"I've got plenty of doctors."

He shrugged and took my money.

On the ride back, my fellow passengers made heroic efforts to avoid looking at me. I leaned forward, so the blood pooled between my feet rather than stained my clothing any further. These were my good jeans.

When my stop came up, I gave everyone a cheery wave goodbye and stumbled out of the bus.

The corner of State and Cermak was all lit up, twinkling in both English and Chinese. Unlike NY and LA, each of which had sprawling Chinatowns, Chicago has more of a Chinablock. Blink while you're driving west on 22nd and you'll miss it.

Though Caucasian, I found a kind of peace in Chinatown that I didn't find among the Anglos. Since my diagnosis, I've pretty much disowned society. Living here was like living in a foreign country—or a least a square block of a foreign country.

I kept a room at the Lucky Lucky Hotel, tucked away between a crumbling apartment building and a Chinese butcher shop, on State and 25th. The hotel did most of its business at an hourly rate, though I couldn't think of a more repulsive place to take a woman, even if you were renting her as well as the room. The halls stank like mildew and worse and the plaster snowed on you when you climbed the stairs and obscene graffiti lined the halls and the whole building leaned slightly to the right.

I got a decent rent; free—as long as I kept out the drug dealers. Which I did, except for the ones who dealt to me.

I nodded at the proprietor, Kenny-Jen-Bang-Ko, and asked for my key. Kenny was three times my age, clean-shaven save for several black moles on his cheeks that sprouted long, white hairs. He tugged at these hairs while contemplating me.

"How is other guy?" Kenny asked.

"Drinking a forty of malt liquor that he bought with my money."

He nodded, as if that was the answer he'd been expecting. "You want pizza?"

Kenny gestured to a box on the counter. The slices were so old and shrunken they looked like Doritos.

"I thought the Chinese hated fast food."

"Pizza not fast. Took thirty minutes. Anchovy and red pepper."

I declined.

My room was one squeaky stair flight up. I unlocked the door and lumbered over to the bathroom, looking into the cracked mirror above the sink.

Ouch.

My left eye had completely closed, and the surrounding tissue bulged out like a peach. Purple bruising competed with angry red swelling along my cheeks and forehead. My nose was a glob of strawberry jelly, and blood had crusted black along my lips and down my neck.

It looked like Jackson Pollack kicked my ass.

I stripped off the T-shirt, peeled off my shoes and jeans, and turned the shower up to scald.

It hurt, but got most of the crap off.

After the shower I popped five Tylenol, chased them with a shot of tequila, and spent ten minutes in front of the mirror, tears streaming down my face, forcing my nose back into place.

I had some coke, but wouldn't be able to sniff anything with my sniffer all clotted up, and I was too exhausted to shoot any. I made do with the tequila, thinking that tomorrow I'd have that codeine prescription refilled.

Since the pain wouldn't let me sleep, I decided to do a little work.

Using a dirty fork, I pried up the floorboards near the radiator and took out a plastic bag full of what appeared to be little gray stones. The granules were the size and consistency of aquarium gravel.

I placed the bag on the floor, then removed the Lee Load-All, the scale, a container of gunpowder, some wads, and a box of empty 12 gauge shells.

Everything went over to my kitchen table. I snapped on a fresh pair of latex gloves, clamped the loader onto my counter top, and spent an hour carefully filling ten shells. When I finished, I loaded five of them into my Mossberg 935, the barrel and stock of which had been cut down for easier concealment.

I liked shotguns—you had more leeway when aiming, the cops couldn't trace them like they could trace bullets, and nothing put the fear of god into a guy like the sound of racking a shell into the chamber.

For this job, I didn't have a choice.

By the time I was done, my nose had taken the gold medal in throbbing, with my eye coming close with the silver. I swallowed five more Tylenol and four shots of tequila, then laid down on my cot and fell asleep.

With sleep came the dream.

It happened every night, so vivid I could smell Donna's perfume. We were still together, living in the suburbs. She was smiling at me, running her fingers through my hair.

"Phin, the caterer wants to know if we're going with the split pea or the wedding ball soup."

"Explain the wedding ball soup to me again."

"It's a chicken stock with tiny veal meatballs in it."

"That sounds good to you?"

"It's very good. I've had it before."

"Then let's go with that."

She kissed me; playful, loving.

I woke up drenched in sweat.

If someone had told me that happy memories would one day be a source of incredible pain, I wouldn't have believed it.

Things change.

Sun peeked in through my dirty window, making me squint. I stretched, wincing because my whole body hurt—my whole body except for my left side, where a team of doctors severed the nerves during an operation called a chordotomy. The surgery had been purely palliative. The area felt dead, even though the cancer still thrived inside my pancreas. And elsewhere, by now.

The chordotomy offered enough pain relief to allow me to function, and tequila, cocaine, and codeine made up for the remainder.

I dressed in some baggy sweatpants, my bloody gym shoes (with a new five dollar bill in the sole), and a clean white T-shirt. I strapped my leather shotgun sling under my armpits, and placed the Mossberg in the holster. It hung directly between my shoulder blades, barrel up, and could be freed by reaching my right hand behind me at waist-level.

A baggy black trench coat went on over the rig, concealing the shotgun and the leather straps that held it in place.

I pocketed the five extra shells, the bag of gray granules, a Glock 21 with two extra clips of .45 rounds, and a six inch butterfly knife. Then I hung an iron crowbar on an extra strap sewn into the lining of my coat, and headed out to greet the morning.

Chinatown smelled like a combination of soy sauce and garbage. It was worse in the summer, when stenches seemed to settle in and stick to your clothes. Though not yet seven in the morning, the temperature already hovered in the low 90s. The sun made my face hurt.

I walked up State, past Cermak, and went east. The Sing Lung Bakery had opened for business an hour earlier. The manager, a squat Mandarin Chinese named Ti, did a double-take when I entered.

"Phin! Your face is horrible!" He rushed around the counter to meet me, hands and shirt dusty with flour.

"My mom liked it okay."

Ti's features twisted in concern. "Was it them? The ones who butchered my daughter?"

I gave him a brief nod.

Ti hung his head. "I am sorry to bring this suffering upon you. They are very bad men."

I shrugged, which hurt. "It was my fault. I got careless."

That was an understatement. After combing Chicago for almost a week, I'd discovered the bangers had gone underground. I got one guy to talk, and after a bit of friendly persuasion he gladly offered some vital info; Sunny's killers were due to appear in court on an unrelated charge.

I'd gone to the Daly Center, where the prelim hearing was being held, and watched from the sidelines. After matching their names to faces, I followed them back to their hidey-hole.

My mistake had been to stick around. A white guy in a Hispanic neighborhood tends to stand out. Having just been to court, which required walking through a metal detector, I had no weapons on me.

Stupid. Ti and Sunny deserved someone smarter.

Ti had found me through the grapevine, where I got most of my business. Phineas Troutt, Problem Solver. No job too dirty, no fee too high.

I'd met him in a parking lot across the street, and he laid out the whole sad, sick story of what these animals had done to his little girl.

"Cops do nothing. Sunny's friend too scared to press charges."

Sunny's friend had managed to escape with only ten missing teeth, six stab wounds, and a torn rectum. Sunny hadn't been as lucky.

Ti agreed to my price without question. Not too many people haggled with paid killers.

"You finish job today?" Ti asked, reaching into his glass display counter for a pastry.

"Yeah."

"In the way we talk about?"

"In the way we talked about."

Ti bowed and thanked me. Then he stuffed two pastries into a bag and held them out.

"Duck egg moon cake, and red bean ball with sesame. Please take."

I took.

"Tell me when you find them."

"I'll be back later today. Keep an eye on the news. You might see something you'll like."

I left the bakery and headed for the bus. Ti had paid me enough to afford a cab, or even a limo, but cabs and limos kept records. Besides, I preferred to save my money for more important things, like drugs and hookers. I try to live every day as if it's my last.

After all, it very well might be.

The bus arrived, and again everyone took great pains not to stare. The trip was short, only about two miles, taking me to a neighborhood known as Pilsen, on Racine and 18th.

I left my duck egg moon cake and my red bean ball on the bus for some other lucky passenger to enjoy, and then stepped out into Little Mexico.

It smelled like a combination of salsa and garbage.

There weren't many people out—too early for shoppers and commuters. The stores here had Spanish signs, not bothering with English translations: zapatos, ropa, restuarante, tiendas de comestibles, bancos, teléfonos de la célula. I passed the alley where I'd gotten the shit kicked out of me, kept heading north, and located the apartment building where my three amigos were staying. I tried the front door.

They hadn't left it open for me.

Though the gray paint was faded and peeling, the door was heavy aluminum, and the lock solid. But the jamb, as I'd remembered from yesterday's visit, was old wood. I removed the crowbar from my jacket lining, gave a discreet look in either direction, and pried open the door in less time than it took to open it with a key, the frame splintering and cracking.

The Kings occupied the basement apartment to the left of the entrance, facing the street. Last night I'd counted seven—five men and two women—including my three targets. Of course, there may be other people inside that I'd missed.

This was going to be interesting.

Unlike the front door, their apartment door was a joke. They apparently thought being gang members meant they didn't need decent security.

They thought wrong.

I took out my Glock and tried to stop hyperventilating. Breaking into someone's place is scary as hell. It always is.

One hard kick and the door burst inward.

A guy on the couch, sleeping in front of the TV. Not one of my marks. He woke up and stared at me. It took a millisecond to register the gang tattoo, a five pointed crown, on the back of his hand.

I shot him in his forehead.

If the busted door didn't wake everyone up, the .45 did, sounding like thunder in the small room.

Movement to my right. A woman in the kitchen, in panties and a Dago-T, too much make-up and baby fat.

"Te vayas!" I hissed at her.

She took the message and ran out the door.

A man stumbled into the hall, tripping and falling to the thin carpet. One of mine, the guy who held my right arm while I'd been worked over. He clutched a stiletto. I was on him in two quick steps, putting one in his elbow and one through the back of his knee when he fell.

He screamed falsetto.

I walked down the hall in a crouch, and a bullet zinged over my head and buried itself in the ceiling. I kissed the floor, looked left, and saw the shooter in the bathroom; the guy who held my other arm and laughed every time I got smacked.

I stuck the Glock in my jeans and reached behind me, unslinging the Mossberg.

He fired again, missed, and I aimed the shotgun and peppered his face.

Unlike lead shot, the gray granules didn't have deep penetrating power. Instead of blowing his head off, they peeled off his lips, cheeks, and eyes.

He ate linoleum, blind and choking on blood.

Movement behind me. I fell sideways and rolled onto my back. A kid, about thirteen, stood in the hall a few feet away. He wore Latin Kings colors; black to represent death, gold to represent life.

His hand ended in a pistol.

I racked the shotgun, aimed low.

If the kid were old enough to be sexually active, he wasn't anymore.

He dropped to his knees, still holding the gun.

I was on him in two steps, driving a knee into his nose. He went down and out.

Three more guys burst out of the bedroom.

Apparently I'd counted wrong.

Two were young, muscular, brandishing knives. The third was the guy who'd worked me over the night before. The one who called me a bald son of a bitch.

They were on me before I could rack the shotgun again.

The first one slashed at me with his pig-sticker, and I parried with the barrel of the Mossberg. He jabbed again, slicing me across the knuckles of my right hand.

I threw the shotgun at his face and went for my Glock.

He was fast.

I was faster.

Bang bang and he was a paycheck for the coroner. I spun left, aimed at the second guy. He was already in mid-jump, launching himself at me with a battle cry and switchblades in both hands.

One gun beats two knives.

He took three in the chest and two in the neck before he dropped.

The last guy, the guy who broke my nose, grabbed my shotgun and dove behind the couch.

Chck chck. He ejected the shell and racked another into the chamber. I pulled the Glock's magazine and slammed a fresh one home.

"Hijo calvo de una perra!"

Again with the bald son of a bitch taunt. I worked through my hurt feelings and crawled to an end table, tipping it over and getting behind it.

The shotgun boomed. Had it been loaded with shot, it would have torn through the cheap particle board and turned me into ground beef. Or ground hijo calvo de una perra. But at that distance, the granules didn't do much more than make a loud noise.

The banger apparently didn't learn from experience, because he tried twice more with similar results, and then the shotgun was empty.

I stood up from behind the table, my heart a lump in my throat and my hands shaking with adrenalin.

The King turned and ran.

His back was an easy target.

I took a quick look around, making sure everyone was down or out, and then went to retrieve my shotgun. I loaded five more shells and approached the downed leader, who was sucking carpet and whimpering. The wounds in his back were ugly, but he still made a feeble effort to crawl away.

I bent down, turned him over, and shoved the barrel of the Mossburg between his bloody lips.

"You remember Sunny Lung," I said, and fired.

It wasn't pretty. It also wasn't fatal. The granules blew out his cheeks, and tore into his throat, but somehow the guy managed to keep breathing.

I gave him one more, jamming the gun further down the wreck of his face.

That did the trick.

The second perp, the one I'd blinded, had passed out on the bathroom floor. His face didn't look like a face anymore, and blood bubbles were coming out of the hole where his mouth would have been.

"Sunny Lung sends her regards," I said.

This time I pushed the gun in deep, and the first shot did the trick, blowing through his throat.

The last guy, the one who made like Pavarotti when I took out his knee, left a blood smear from the hall into the kitchen. He cowered in the corner, a dishrag pressed to his leg.

"Don't kill me, man! Don't kill me!"

"I bet Sunny Lung said the same thing."

The Mossberg thundered twice; once to the chest, and once to the head.

It wasn't enough. What was left alive gasped for air.

I removed the bag of granules from my pocket, took out a handful, and shoved them down his throat until he stopped breathing.

Then I went to the bathroom and threw up in the sink.

Sirens wailed in the distance. Time to go. I washed my hands, and then rinsed off the barrel of the Mossberg, holstering it in my rig.

In the hallway, the kid I emasculated was clutching himself between the legs, sobbing.

"There's always the priesthood," I told him, and got out of there.

#

My nose was still clogged, but I managed to get enough coke up there to damper the pain. Before closing time I stopped by the bakery, and Ti greeted me with a somber nod.

"Saw the news. They said it was a massacre."

"Wasn't pretty."

"You did as we said?"

"I did, Ti. Your daughter got her revenge. She's the one that killed them. All three."

I fished out the bag of granules and handed it to her father. Sunny's cremated remains.

"Xie xie," Ti said, thanking me in Mandarin. He held out an envelope filled with cash.

Ti looked uncomfortable, and I had drugs to buy, so I took the money and left without another word.

An hour later I'd filled my codeine prescription, picked up two bottles of tequila and a skinny hooker with track marks on her arms, and had a party back at my place. I popped and drank and screwed and snorted, trying to blot out the memory of the last two days. And of the last six months.

That's when I'd been diagnosed. A week before my wedding day. My gift to my bride-to-be was running away so she wouldn't have to watch me die of cancer.

Those Latin Kings this morning, they got off easy. They didn't see it coming.

Seeing it coming is so much worse.

Taken to the Cleaners

Harry is my favorite character to write for. I love the idea of an idiotic, selfish jerk as a protagonist. He's too obnoxious and unsympathetic to carry a book on his own, but I think he makes a great foil for Jack, so he appears in every novel. Some readers hate him. Some readers adore him. This story sold to The Strand Magazine in 2005.

"I want you to kill the man that my husband hired to kill the man that I hired to kill my husband."

If I had been paying attention, I still wouldn't have understood what she wanted me to do. But I was busy looking at her legs, which weren't adequately covered by her skirt. She had great legs, curvy without being heavy, tan and long, and she had them crossed in that sexy way that women cross their legs, knee over knee, not the ugly way that guys do it, with the ankle on the knee, though if she did cross her legs that way it would have been sexy too.

"Mr. McGlade, did you hear what I just said?"

"Hmm? Yeah, sure I did, baby. The man, the husband, I got it."

"So you'll do it?"

"Do what?"

"Kill the man that my husband—"

I held up my hand. "Whoa. Hold it right there. I'm just a plain old private eye. That's what is says on the door you just walked through. The door even has a big magnifying glass silhouette logo thingy painted on it, which I paid way too much money for, just so no one gets confused. I don't kill people for money. Absolutely, positively, no way." I leaned forward a little. "But, for the sake of argument, how much money are we talking about here?"

"I don't know where else to turn."

The tears came, and she buried her face in her hands, giving me the opportunity to look at her legs again. Marietta Garbonzo had found me through the ad I placed in the Chicago phone book. The ad used the expensive magnifying glass logo, along with the tagline, Harry McGlade Investigators: We'll Do Whatever it Takes. It brought in more customers than my last tagline: No Job Too Small, No Fee Too High, or the one prior to that, We'll Investigate Your Privates.

Mrs. Garbonzo had never been to a private eye before, and she was playing her role to the hilt. Besides the short skirt and tight blouse, she had gone to town with the hair and make-up; her blonde locks curled and sprayed, her lips painted deep, glossy red, her purple eye shadow so thick that she managed to get some on her collar.

"My husband beats me, Mr. McGlade. Do you know why?"

"Beats me," I said, shrugging. Her wailing kicked in again. I wondered where she worked out. Legs like that, she must work out.

"He's insane, Mr. McGlade. We've been married for a year, and Roy always had a temper. I once saw him attack another man with a tire iron. They were having an argument, Roy went out to the car, grabbed a crow bar from the trunk, then came back and practically killed him."

"Where do you work out?"

"Excuse me?"

"Exercise. Do you belong to a gym, or work out at home?"

"Mr. McGlade, I'm trying to tell you about my husband."

"I know, the insane guy who beats you. Probably shouldn't have married a guy who used a tire iron for anything other than changing tires."

"I married too young. But while we were dating, he treated me kindly. It was only after we married that the abuse began."

She turned her head away and unbuttoned her blouse. My gaze shifted from her legs to her chest. She had a nice chest, packed tight into a silky black bra with lace around the edges and an underwire that displayed things to a good effect, both lifting and separating.

"See these bruises?"

"Hmm?"

"It's humiliating to reveal them, but I don't know where else to go."

"Does he hit you anywhere else? You can show me, I'm a professional."

The tears returned. "I hired a man to kill him, Mr. McGlade. I hired a man to kill my husband. But somehow Roy found out about it, and he hired a man to kill the man I hired. So I'd like you to kill his man so my man can kill him."

I removed the bottle of whiskey from my desk that I keep there for medicinal purposes, like getting drunk. I unscrewed the cap, wiped off the bottle neck with my tie, and handed it to her.

"You're not making sense, Mrs. Garbonzo. Have a swig of this."

"I shouldn't. When I drink I lose my inhibitions."

"Keep the bottle."

She took a sip, coughing after it went down.

"I already paid the assassin. I paid him a lot of money, and he won't refund it. But I'm afraid he'll die before he kills my husband, so I need someone to kill the man who is after him."

"Shouldn't you tell the guy you hired that he's got a hit on him?"

"I called him. He says not to worry. But I am worried, Mr. McGlade."

"As I said before, I don't kill people for money."

"Even if you're killing someone who kills people for money?"

"But I'd be killing someone who is killing someone who kills people for money. What prevents that killer from hiring someone to kill me because he's killing someone who is killing someone that I...hand me that bottle."

I took a swig.

"Please, Mr. McGlade. I'm a desperate woman. I'll do anything."

She walked around the desk and stood before me, shivering in her bra, her breath coming out in short gasps through red, wet lips. Her hands rested on my shoulders, squeezing, and she bent forward.

"My laundry," I said.

"What?"

"Do my laundry."

"Mr. McGlade, I'm offering you my body."

"And it's a tempting offer, Mrs. Garbonzo. But that will take, what, five minutes? I've got about six loads of laundry back at my place, they take an hour for each cycle."

"Isn't there a dry cleaner in your neighborhood?"

"A hassle. I'd have to write my name on all the labels, on every sock, on the elastic band of my whitey tighties, plus haul six bags of clothes down the street. You want me to help you? I get five hundred a day, plus expenses. And you do my laundry."

"And you'll kill him?"

"No. I don't kill people for money. Or for laundry. But I'll protect your guy from getting whacked."

"Thank you, Mr. McGlade."

She leaned down to kiss me. Not wanting to appear rude, I let her. And so she didn't feel unwanted, I stuck my hand up her skirt.

"You won't tell the police, will you Mr. McGlade?"

"Look, baby, I'm not your priest and I'm not your lawyer and I'm not your shrink. I'm just a man. A man who will keep his mouth shut, except when I'm eating. Or talking, or sleeping, because sometimes I sleep with my mouth open because I have the apnea."

"Thank you, Mr. McGlade."

"I'll take the first week in advance, Visa and MasterCard are fine. Here are my spare keys."

"Your keys?"

"For my apartment. It's in Hyde Park. I don't have a hamper, so I leave my dirty clothes all over the floor. Do the bed sheets too—those haven't been washed since, well, ever. Washer and dryer are in the basement of the building, washer costs seventy-five cents, dryer costs fifty cents for each thirty minutes, and the heavy things like jeans and sweaters take about a buck fifty to dry. Make yourself at home, but don't touch anything, sit on anything, eat any of my food, or turn on the TV."

I gave her my address, and she gave me a check and all of her info. The info was surprising.

"You hired a killer from the personal ads in Famous Soldier Magazine?"

"I didn't know where else to go."

"How about the police? A divorce attorney?"

"My husband is a rich and powerful man, Mr. McGlade. You don't recognize his name?"

I flipped though my mental Rolodex. "Roy Garbonzo? Is he the Roy Garbonzo that owns Happy Roy's Chicken Shack?"

"Yes."

"He seems so happy on those commercials."

"He's a beast, Mr. McGlade."

"The guy is like a hundred and thirty years old. And on those commercials, he's always laughing and signing and dancing with that claymation chicken. He's the guy that's abusing you?"

"Would you like to see the proof again?"

"If it isn't too much trouble."

She grabbed my face in one hand, squeezing my cheeks together.

"Happy Roy is a vicious psycho, Mr. McGlade. He's a brutal, misogynist pig who enjoys inflicting pain."

"He's probably rich too."

Mrs. Garbonzo narrowed her eyes. "He's wealthy, yes. What are you implying?"

"I like his extra spicy recipe. Do you get to take chicken home for free? You probably have a fridge stuffed full of it, am I right?"

She released my face and buttoned up her blouse.

"I have to go. My husband gets paranoid when I go out."

"Maybe because when you go out, you hire people to kill him."

She picked up her purse and headed for the door. "I expect you to call me when you've made some progress."

"That includes ironing," I called after her. "And hanging the stuff up. I don't have any hangers, so you'll have to buy some."

After she left, I turned off all the office lights and closed the blinds, because what I had to do next, I had to do in complete privacy.

I took a nap.

When I awoke a few hours later, I went to the bank, cashed Mrs. Garbonzo's check, and went to start earning my money.

My first instinct was to dive head-first into the belly of the beast and confront Mrs. Garbonzo's hired hitman help. My second instinct was to get some nachos, maybe a beer or two.

I went with my second instinct. The nachos were good, spicy but not so much that all you tasted was peppers. After the third beer I hopped in my ride and headed for the assassin's headquarters, which turned out to be in a well-to-do suburb of Chicago called Barrington. The development I pulled into boasted some amazingly huge houses, complete with big lawns and swimming pools and trimmed bushes that looked like corkscrews and lollipops. I double-checked the address I'd scribbled down, then pulled into a long circular driveway and up to a home that was bigger than the public school I attended, and I came from the city where they grew schools big.

The hitman biz must be booming.

I half expected some sort of maid or butler to answer the door, but instead I was greeted by a fifty-something woman, her facelift sporting a deep tan. I appraised her.

"If you stay out in the sun, the wrinkles will come back."

"Then I'll just have more work done." Her voice was steady, cultured. "Are you here to clean the pool?"

"I'm here to speak to William Johansenn."

"Billy? Sure, he's in the basement."

She let me in. Perhaps all rich suburban women were fearless and let strange guys into their homes. Or perhaps this one simply didn't care. I didn't get a chance to ask, because she walked off just as I entered.

"Lady? Where's the basement?"

"Down the hall, stairs to the right," she said without turning around.

I took a long, tiled hallway past a powder room, a den, and a door that opened to a descending staircase. Heavy metal music blared up at me.

"Billy!" I called down.

My effort was fruitless—with the noise, I couldn't even hear myself. The lights were off, and squinting did nothing to penetrate the darkness.

Surprising a paid assassin in his own lair wasn't on the list of 100 things I longed to do before I die, but I didn't see much of a choice. I beer-belched, then went down the stairs.

The basement was furnished, though furnished didn't seem to be the right word. The floor had carpet, and the walls had paint, and there seemed to be furniture, but I couldn't really tell because everything was covered with food wrappers, pop cans, dirty clothing, and discarded magazines. It looked like a 7-Eleven exploded.

William "Billy" Johansenn was asleep on a waterbed, a copy of Creem open on his chest. He had a galaxy of pimples dotting his forehead and six curly hairs sprouting from his chin.

He couldn't have been a day over sixteen.

I killed the stereo. Billy continued to snore. Among the clutter on the floor were several issues of Famous Soldier, along with various gun and hunting magazines. I poked through his drawers and found a cheap Rambo knife, a CO2 powered BB gun, and a dog-eared copy of the infamous How to be a Hitman book from Paladin Press.

I gave the kid a shake, then another. The third shake got him to open his eyes.

"Who the hell are you?" he said, defiant.

"I'm your wake-up call."

I slapped the kid, making his eyes cross.

"Hey! You hit me!"

"A woman hired you to kill her husband."

"I don't know what you're—"

He got another smack. "That's for lying."

"You can't hit me," he whined. "I'll sue you."

I hit him twice more; once because I didn't like being threatened by punk kids, and once because I didn't like lawyers. When I pulled my palm back for threesies, the kid broke.

"Please! Stop it! I admit it!"

I released his t-shirt and let him blubber for a minute. His blue eyes matched those of the woman upstairs. Not many professional killers lived in their mother's basement, and I wondered how Marietta Garbonzo could have been this naive.

"I'm guessing you never met Mrs. Garbonzo in person."

"I only talked to her on the phone. She sent the money to a P.O. Box. That's how the pros do it."

"So how did she get your home address?"

"She wouldn't give me the money without my address. She said if I didn't trust her, why should she trust me?"

Here was my proof that each new generation of teenagers was stupider than the last. I blame MTV.

"How much did she give you?"

He smiled, showing me a mouth full of braces. "Fifty large."

"And how were you going to do it? With your BB gun?"

"I was going to follow him around and then...you know...shove him."

"Shove him?"

"He's an old guy. I was thinking I'd shove him down some stairs, or into traffic. I dunno."

"Have you shoved a lot of old people into traffic, Billy boy?"

He must not have liked the look in my eyes, because he shrunk two sizes.

"No! Never! I never killed anybody!"

"So why put an ad in the magazine?"

"I dunno. Something to do."

I considered hitting him again, but didn't know what purpose it would serve.

I hit him anyway.

"Ow! My lip's caught in my braces!"

"You pimple-faced little moron. Do you have any idea what kind of trouble you're in right now? Not only did you accept money to commit a felony, but now you've got a price on your head. Did Mrs. Garbonzo tell you about the guy her husband hired to kill you?"

He nodded, his Adam's apple wiggling like a fish.

"Are-are you here to kill me?"

"No."

"But you've got a gun." He pointed to the butt of my Magnum, jutting out of my shoulder holster.

"I'm a private detective."

"Is that a real gun?"

"Yes."

"Can I touch it?"

"No."

"Come on. Lemme touch it."

This is what happens when you spare the rod and spoil the child.

"Look kid, I know that you're a loser that nobody likes, and that you're a virgin and will probably stay one for the next ten years, but do you want to die?"

"Ten years?"

"Answer the question."

"No. I don't want to die."

I sighed. "That's a start. Where's the money?"

"I've got a secret place. In the wall."

He rolled off the bed, eager, and pried a piece of paneling away from the plaster in a less-cluttered corner of the room. His hand reached in, and came out with a brown paper shopping bag.

"Is it all there?"

Billy shook his head. "I spent three hundred on a wicked MP3 player."

"Hand over the money. And the MP3 player."

Billy showed a bit of reluctance, so I smacked him again to help with his motivation.

It helped. He also gave me fresh batteries for the player.

"Now what?" he sniffled.

"Now we tell your parents."

"Do we have to?"

"You'd prefer the cops?"

He shook his head. "No. No cops."

"That blonde upstairs with the face like a snare drum, that your mom?"

"Yeah."

"Let's go have a talk with her."

Mrs. Johansenn was perched in front of a sixty inch television, watching a soap.

"Nice TV. High definition?"

"Plasma."

"Nice. Billy has something he wants to tell you."

Billy stared at his shoes. "Mom, I bought an ad in the back of Famous Soldier Magazine, and some lady gave me fifty thousand dollars to kill her husband."

Mrs. Johansenn hit the mute button on the remote, shaking her head in obvious disappointment.

"Billy, dammit, this is too much. You're a hired killer?"

"Sorry," he mumbled.

"You're father is going to have a stroke when he hears this."

"Do we have to tell Dad?"

"Are you kidding?"

"I gave the money back."

"Who are you?" Billy's mom squinted at me.

"I'm Harry McGlade. I'm a private eye. I was hired to find Billy. Someone is trying to kill him."

Mrs. Johansenn rolled her eyes. "Oh, this gets better and better. I need to call Sal."

"You husband?"

"My lawyer."

"Ma'am, a lawyer isn't going to do much to save Billy's life, unless he's standing between him and a bullet."

"So what then, the police?"

"Not the cops, Mom! I don't want to go to jail!"

"He won't survive in prison," I said. "The lifers will pass him around like a bong at a college party. They'll trade him for candy bars and cigarettes."

"I don't want to be traded for candy bars, Mom!"

Mrs. Johansenn frowned, forming new wrinkles. "Then what should we do, Mr. McGlade?"

I paused for a moment, then I grinned.

"I get five-hundred a day, plus expenses."

#

I celebrated my recent windfall with a nice dinner at a nice restaurant. I was more of a burger and fries guy than a steak and lobster guy, but the steak and lobster went down easy, and after leaving a 17% tip I headed to Evanston to visit the Chicken King.

Roy Garbonzo's estate made the Johansenn's look like a third world mud hut. He had his own private access road, a giant wrought iron perimeter fence, and a uniformed guard posted at the gate. I was wondering how to play it when the aforementioned uniformed guard knocked on my window.

"I need to see Roy Garbonzo," I told him. "My son choked to death on a Sunny Meal toy."

"He's expecting you, Mr. McGlade."

The gate rolled back, and I drove up to the mansion. It looked like five mansions stuck together. I parked between two massive Doric columns and pressed the buzzer next to the giant double doors. Before anyone answered, a startling thought flashed through my head.

How did the guard know my name?

"It's a set up," I said aloud. I yanked the Magnum out of my shoulder holster and dove into one of the hydrangea bushes flanking the entryway just as the knob turned.

I peeked through the lavender blooms, finger on the trigger, watching the door swing open. A sinister-looking man wearing a tuxedo stepped out of the house and peered down his nose at me.

"Would Mr. McGlade care for a drink?"

"You're a butler," I said.

"Observant of you, sir."

"You work for Roy Garbonzo."

"An excellent deduction, sir. A drink?"

"Uh—whiskey, rocks."

"Would you care to have it in the parlor, sir, or would you prefer to remain squatting in the Neidersachen?"

"I thought it was a hydrangea."

"It's a hydrangea Neidersachen, sir."

"It's pretty," I said. "But I think I'll take that drink inside."

"Very good, sir."

I extricated myself from the Neidersachen, brushed off some clinging leaves, and followed Jeeves through the tiled foyer, through the carpeted library, and into the parlor, which had wood floors and an ornate Persian rug big enough to park a bus on.

"Please have a seat, sir. Mr. Garbonzo will be with your shortly. Were you planning on shooting him?"

"Excuse me?"

"You're holding a gun, sir."

I glanced down at my hand, still clenched around my Magnum.

"Sorry. Forgot."

I holstered the .44 and sat in a high-backed leather chair, which was so plush I sank four inches. Waddles returned with my whiskey, and I sipped it and stared at the paintings hanging on the walls. One in particular caught my interest, of a nude woman eating grapes.

"Admiring the Degas?" a familiar voice boomed from behind.

I turned and saw Happy Roy the vicious misogynist psycho, all five foot two inches of him, walking up to me. He wore an expensive silk suit, but like most old men the waist was too high, making him seem more hunched over than he actually was. On his feet were slippers, and his glasses had black plastic frames and looked thick enough to stop a bullet.

"Her name is Degas?" I asked. "Silly name for a chick."

He held out his hand and I shook it, noticing his knuckles were swollen and bruised.

"Degas is the painter, Mr. McGlade. My business advisors thought it was a good investment. Do you like it?"

"Not really. She's got too much in back, not enough up front, and her face is a double-bagger."

"A double-bagger?"

"I'd make her wear two bags over her head, in case one fell off."

The Chicken King laughed. "I always thought she was ugly too. Apparently, this little lady was the ideal beauty hundreds of years ago."

"Or maybe Degas just liked ugly, pear-shaped chicks. How did you know I was coming, Mr. Garbonzo?"

He sat in the chair across from me, sinking in so deep he had trouble seeing over his knees.

"Please, call me Happy Roy. I've been having my wife followed, Mr. McGlade. The man I hired tailed her to your office. Does that surprise you?"

"Why should I be surprised? I remember that she came to my office."

"What I meant was, are you surprised I'm having my wife followed?"

I considered it. "No. She's young, beautiful, and you look like a Caucasian version of one of the California Raisins."

"I remember those commercials. That's where I got the idea for the claymation chicken in the Chicken Shack spots. Expensive to produce, those commercials."

"Enough of the small talk. I want you to call off your goon."

"My goon?"

"The person your wife hired to whack you, he's a teenage kid living in the suburbs. He's not a real threat."

"I'm aware of that."

"So you don't need to have that kid killed."

"Mr. McGlade, I'm not having anyone killed. I'm Happy Roy. I don't kill people. I promote world peace through deep fried poultry. I simply told my wife that I hired a killer, even though I didn't."

"You lied to her?"

Happy Roy let out a big, dramatic sigh. "When I found out she wanted me dead, I was justifiably annoyed. I confronted her, we got into an argument, and I told her that I'd have her assassin killed. I was trying to get her to call it off on her own."

I absorbed this information, drinking more whiskey. When the whiskey ran out, I sucked on an ice cube.

"Tho wmer mmmpt wooor—"

"Excuse me? I can't understand you with that ice in your mouth."

I spit out the ice. "She said you abuse her. That you're insane."

"The only thing insane about me is my upcoming promotion. Buy a box of chicken, get a second box for half price."

I wondered if I should tell him about the bruises she had, but chose to keep silent.

"What about divorce?"

"I love Marietta, Mr. McGlade. I know she's too young for me. I know she's a devious, back-stabbing maneater. That just makes her more adorable."

"She wants you dead."

"All spouses have their quirks."

I leaned forward, an effort because my butt was sunk so low in the chair.

"Happy Roy, I have no doubt that Marietta will kill you if she can.

When this doesn't pan out, she'll try something else. Eventually, she'll hook up with a real assassin."

Happy Roy's eye became hooded, dark. "She's my wife, Mr. McGlade. I'll deal with her my way."

"By beating her?"

"This conversation is over. I'll have my butler show you to the door."

I pried myself out of the chair. "You're disgustingly rich, powerful, and not a bad looking guy for someone older than God. Let Marietta go and find some other bimbo to play with."

"Good bye, Mr. McGlade. Feel free to keep working for my wife."

"Are you trying to pay me off, so I drop this case?"

"No. Not at all."

"If you were thinking about paying me off, how much money would we be talking?"

"I'm not trying to pay you off, Mr. McGlade."

I got in the smaller man's face. "You might be able to afford fat Degas and huge estates, but I'm a person, Happy Roy. And no matter how rich you get, you'll never be able to buy a human being. Because it's illegal, Happy Roy. Buying people is illegal."

"I'm not trying to buy you!"

"I'll find my own way out."

I stormed out of the parlor, through the library, into the dining room, into another parlor, or maybe it was a den, and then I wound up in the kitchen somehow. I tried to back track, wandered into the dining room, and then found myself back in one of the parlors, but I couldn't tell if it was the first parlor or the second parlor. I didn't see that painting of the naked heifer, but Happy Roy may have taken it down just to confuse me.

"Hello?" I called out. "I'm a little lost here."

No one answered.

I went back into the dining room, then the kitchen, and took another door which led down a hallway which led to a bathroom, which was fine because I needed to go to the bathroom anyway.

When the lizard had been adequately drained, I discovered some very interesting prescription drugs, just lying there, in the medicine cabinet.

And then it all made sense.

Forty minutes later I found the front door and headed back to my apartment.

Time to drop the truth on Little Miss Marietta.

#

At first, I thought I had the wrong place. Everything was so...clean. Not only were all of my clothes picked up, but the apartment had been vacuumed—a real feat since I didn't think I owned a vacuum cleaner.

"Mrs. Garbonzo? You here?"

I walked into the bedroom. The bed had been made, and the closet door was open, revealing over a dozen shirts on hangers.

In the kitchen, the sink was empty of dishes for the first time since I rented the place fifteen years ago. There was even a fresh smell of lilacs and orange zest in the air.

The door opened and I swung around, hand going to my gun. Mrs. Garbonzo entered, carrying a plastic laundry basket overflowing with my socks. She flinched when she saw me.

"Mr. McGlade. I didn't expect you back so soon."

"Surprised, Marietta? I thought you might be."

"Did you take care of the guy?"

"Sit down. We need to talk."

She set the basket down on my kitchen counter, and seductively perched herself on one of my breakfast bar stools. Her blouse had been untucked from her skirt, the shirt tails tied in a knot around her flat stomach.

"You lied to me, Marietta."

"Lied?" She batted her eyelashes. "How?"

There was a bottle of window cleaner next to the sink that I'd never seen before. I picked it up.

"How about opening up that shirt and letting me squirt you with this?"

"Is that what turns you on? Spraying women with glass cleaner?"

I grabbed her blouse and pulled, tearing buttons.

"I was thinking more along the lines of washing off those fake bruises. They're so fake, the purple has even rubbed off on your collar. See?"

I shot two quick streams at the marks, then used my sleeve to wipe them off.

They didn't wipe off.

I tried again, to similar effect.

Marietta sneered at me. "Are you finished?"

"So what's that purple stuff on your collar?"

"Eye shadow." She pointed at her eyes. "That's why it matches my eye shadow."

"Big deal. So you gave yourself those bruises. Or paid someone to give them to you. I met your husband today, Mrs. Garbonzo. All ninety pounds of him. He couldn't beat up a quadriplegic."

"My husband abuses me, Mr. McGlade."

"Yeah, I saw his swollen knuckles. At first, I thought they were swollen from hitting you. But he didn't hit you, did he Marietta? Roy has rheumatoid arthritis. I saw his medication. His knuckles are swollen because of his disease, and they undoubtedly cause him great pain. So much pain, he'd never be able to hit you."

Marietta put her hands on her hips.

"He beats me with a belt, Mr. McGlade."

"A belt?"

"These bruises are from the buckle. It also causes welts. See?"

She turned around, lifting her blouse. Angry, red scabs stretched across her back.

I gave them a spritz of the window cleaner, just to be sure.

"Ow!"

"Sorry. Had to check."

Marietta faced me. "I've paid you, I've done your laundry, and I've cleaned your apartment. Did you take care of the assassin for me?"

"Your husband didn't hire an assassin."

"Is that what he told you?"

"I know it for a fact. The guy you hired is a sixteen-year-old pimply-faced kid. He couldn't whack anyone. He couldn't even whack a mole."

I smiled at my pun.

Marietta made a face. "I thought he sounded young on the phone. He really won't do it?"

"He lives in his parent's basement."

The tears came. "I gave him a lot of money. Everything I've been able to hide from Roy during six years of marriage."

I thought about mentioning I got the money back, but decided against it.

"Look, Marietta, just divorce the guy."

"I can't. He threatened to kill me if I divorced him."

"You can run away. Hire a lawyer."

She sniffled. "Pre-nup."

"Pre-nup?"

"I signed a pre-nuptial agreement. If I divorce Roy, I don't get a penny. And after six years of abuse, I deserve more than that." She licked her lips. "But if he dies, I get it all."

"Don't you think killing the guy is a little extreme?"

She threw herself at me, teary-eyed and heaving. "Please, Harry. You have to help me. I'll give you half—half of the entire chicken empire. Help me kill the son of a bitch."

"Marietta..."

"I cleaned your place, you promised you'd help." She added a little grinding action to her hug. "Please kill him for me."

I looked around the kitchen. She did do a pretty good job. I wondered, briefly, if I'd make a decent Chicken King.

"I'll tell you what, Marietta. I don't do that kind of thing. But I know someone who can help. Do you want me to make a phone call?"

"Yes. Oh, yes."

I pried myself out of her grasp and picked up the phone, dialing the number from memory.

"Hi, partner. It's me. Look, I've got a woman here who wants to kill her husband. I told her I'm not interested, but I thought maybe you'd be able to set something up. Say, tomorrow, around noon? You can meet her at the Hilton. Rent a room under the name Lipshultz. No, schultz, with a U-L. Okay, she'll be there."

I hung up. "Got it all set for you, sugar."

She squeezed me tight and kissed my neck. "Thanks, Harry. Thank you so much. Is there anything I can do to repay you?" Her breath was hot in my ear. "Anything at all?"

"You can start by folding those socks. And maybe some dusting. Yeah, dusting would be good."

She smiled wickedly and caressed my cheek. "I was thinking of something a little more intimate."

"I was thinking about dinner."

"Dinner would be wonderful."

"I'm sure it will be. Have the place dusted by the time I get back."

#

Marietta Garbonzo called me the next night, around eight in the evening.

"You son of a bitch! You set me up! You didn't call a hitman! You called a cop!"

"You can't go around murdering people, sweetheart. It's wrong on so many levels."

"But what about all of the washing? The cleaning? The dusting? And what about after dinner? What we did? How could you betray me after that?"

"You expect me to throw away all of my principles because we spent five minutes doing the worm? It was fun, but not worth twenty to life."

"You bastard. When I get out of here I'll..."

I hung up and went back to the Sharper Image catalog I'd been thumbing through. I had my eye on one of those massaging easy chairs. That would set me back two grand. Earlier that day, I bought a sixty inch plasma TV. The money I took from William "Billy" Johansenn was being put to good use.

I plopped down in front of the TV, found the wrestling channel, and settled in to watch two hours of pay-per-view sports entertainment. The Iron Commie had Captain Frankenbeef in a suplex when I felt the gun press against the back of my head.

"Hello, Mr. McGlade."

"Happy Roy?"

"Yes. Stand up, slowly. Then turn around."

I followed instructions. Happy Roy held a four barreled COP .357, a nasty weapon that could do a lot of damage at close range.

"How'd you get in?" I asked.

"You gave a key to my wife, you moron. I took it from her last night, when she got home." His face got mean. "After you slept with her."

"Technically, we didn't do any sleeping."

The gun trembled in Happy Roy's hand.

"She's in jail now, Mr. McGlade. Because of you."

"She wanted to kill you, Happy Roy. You should thank me."

"You idiot!" Spittle flew from his lips. "I wanted to kill her myself. With my own two hands. Now I have to get her out of jail before I can do it. Do you have any idea what Johnny Cochrane charges an hour?"

"Whatever it is, you can afford it."

Happy Roy's voice cracked. "I'm practically broke. Those damn claymation commercials are costing me a fortune, and no one is buying the tie-in products. I've got ten thousand Happy Roy t-shirts, moldering away in a warehouse. Plus the burger chains with their processed chicken strips are forcing me into bankruptcy."

"Those new Wendy's strips are pretty good."

"Shut up! Put your hands over your head. No quick moves."

"What about your mansion? Can't you sell that?"

"It's a rental."

"Really? Do you mind if I ask what you pay a month?"

"Enough! We're going for a ride, Mr. McGlade. I'm going to introduce you to one of our extra large deep fryers, up close and personal."

"You told me I could keep working with your wife."

"I said you could work with her, not set her up!"

"Six of one, half a dozen of..."

"I'm the Chicken King, goddammit! I'm an American icon! Nobody crosses me and gets away with it!

I'd had enough of the Chicken King's crazy ranting, so I reached for the gun. Happy Roy tried to squeeze the trigger, but I easily yanked it away before he had the chance.

"Let me give you a little lesson in firearms, Happy Roy. A COP .357 has a twenty pound trigger pull. Much too hard to fire for a guy with arthritis."

Happy Roy reached for his belt, fighting with the buckle. "You bastard! I'll beat the fear of Happy Roy into you, you son of a bitch! No one crosses..."

I tapped him on the head with his gun, and the Chicken King collapsed. After checking for a pulse, I went for the phone and dialed my Lieutenant friend.

"Hi, Jack. Me again. Marietta Garbonzo's husband just broke into my place, tried to kill me. Yeah, Happy Roy himself. No, he doesn't look so happy right now. Can you send someone by? And can you make it quick? He's bleeding all over my carpet, and I just had it cleaned. Thanks."

I hung up and stared down at the Chicken King, who was mumbling something into the carpet.

"You say something, Happy Roy?"

"I should have stayed single."

"No kidding," I said. "Relationships can be murder."

Body Shots

Amazon.com introduced a program in 2005 called Amazon Shorts, where customers could download short stories for 49 cents. I wrote this story specifically for Amazon. It was an attempt to really take Jack to the brink, by making the situation get worse and worse no matter how hard she tried to fix things. It's as dark as Jack has gotten, so far...

"And can you mega-size that meal deal?"

I reach over from the passenger seat and give my partner, Sergeant Herb Benedict, a poke in the ribs, except I don't actually feel his ribs because they're encased in a substantial layer of fat—the result of many years of mega-sizing his fast food meals.

"What?" he asks. "You want me to mega-size your fat-free yogurt?"

"No. You told me to point it out whenever I saw you overeating."

"How am I overeating?"

"You just mega-sized a triple bacon cheeseburger and a chocolate shake."

Herb shrugs, multiple chins wiggling.

"So? It's just one meal."

"The mega-size french fries come in a carton bigger than your head. The shake is the size of a rain barrel."

"Be realistic here, Jack. It's only 49 cents. You can't buy anything for 49 cents these days."

"How about another heart attack? How much is that—"

My words are cut off by two quick pops from the drive-thru speaker. Though October, Chicago has been blessed with unseasonably warm weather, and my passenger window is wide open, the sound reaching me through there as well. It's coming from the restaurant.

Only one thing makes a sound like that.

Herb hits the radio. "This is Car 118, officer needs assistance. Shots fired at the Burger Barn on Kedzie and Wabash."

I beat Herb out of the car, pulling my star from the pocket of my jacket and my .38 from my shoulder holster. I'm wearing flats and a beige skirt. A cool wind kicks up and brings goosebumps to my legs. The shoes are Kate Spade. The jacket and skirt are Donna Karan. The holster is Smith and Wesson.

As I near the building, I can make out screams, followed by another gunshot. A spatter of blood and tissue blossoms on the inside of the drive-thru window, blocking my view of the interior.

I hold up my pinky—my signal to Herb that there are casualties—and hurry past the window in a crouch, stopping before the glass doors. I tug the lanyard out of the badge case and loop it over my head. On one knee, I crane my neck around the brick jamb and peek into the restaurant.

I spot a single perp, Caucasian male, mid-thirties. I can't make out his hair color because he's wearing a black football helmet complete with face gear. Jeans, black combat boots, and a gray trench coat complete the ensemble. And under the trench coat...

An ammo belt.

Two strips of leather crisscross his chest, bandolero style. Instead of bullets in the webbing, I count eight clips. Four more clips are stuck into his waistband. I assume they're for the 9mm Beretta in his hand, currently pointed at a family cowering under a plastiform table.

A mother and two kids.

Before my mind can register what is happening, he fires six times. The bullets tear through the table and into the mother's back. Blood sprays onto the children she's been shielding, and then erupts from the children in fireworks patterns.

I tear my eyes away from the horror and scan for more hostiles, but see only potential victims—at least twenty. Behind me, I hear footfalls and Herb's labored breathing.

"At least four down. One perp, heavily armed."

"You want to be old yeller?"

I shake my head and swallow. "I want the shot."

"On three."

Herb flashes one, two, three fingers, then I shove through the door first, rolling to the side, coming up in a shooting position just as Herb yells, "POLICE! DROP THE WEAPON!"

The gunman swings toward Herb, I let out a slow breath and squeeze—angle up to discourage ricochets, aiming at the body mass, no ricochet because the shot is true, squeeze, the perp recoiling and stepping back once, twice, dropping the green duffle bag that's slung over his shoulder, squeeze, screams from everywhere at once, Herb's gun going off behind me, squeeze, watching the impact but not seeing blood—

Vest.

I scream, "Vest!" and roll to the side as the gunman takes aim, firing where I was, orange tile chips peppering the side of my face like BBs.

I come up in a kneeling position behind a rectangular trash can enclosure, look at Herb and see that he's out of the line of fire, gone to ground.

I stick my head around the garbage island, watch as the perp vaults the counter, shooting a teenaged cashier who's hugging the shake machine and sobbing. The back of the teen's head opens up and empties onto the greasy floor.

"Everybody out!" I yell.

There's a stampede to the door, and I glance back and see Herb get tackled by a wall of people, then I take a deep breath and bolt for the counter.

The gunman appears, holding a screaming employee dressed in a Burger Barn uniform, using the kid as a human shield. Her face is streaked with tears, and there's a dark patch in the front of her jeans where she's wet herself. The Beretta is jammed against her forehead.

The perp says, "Drop the gun, Jack."

His voice is a low baritone, and it's eerily calm. His blue eyes lock on mine, and they hold my gaze. He doesn't seem psychotic at all, which terrifies me.

How does he know my name?

I stand up, adopt a Weaver stance, aiming for the face shot.

The gunman doesn't wait for me. He fires.

There's a sudden explosion of blood and tissue and the girl's eyes roll up and the perp ducks behind some fryers before her body hits the floor.

Too fast. This is all happening too fast.

I chance a look at the door, don't see Herb among the panicking people. I can't wait—there are probably more employees in the back. I dig into my blazer pocket and find some loose bullets, jamming them into my revolver. When I leap over the counter, my gun is at full cock.

No one by the grill. I glance left, see a body slumped next to the drive-thru window. Glance right, see a dead man on his back, most of his face gone. Stare forward, see a long stainless steel prep table. There's a young guy hiding under it. I tug him out and push him toward the counter, mouthing at him to "Run."

Movement ahead. The freezer door opens, and my finger almost pulls the trigger. It's another employee. Behind him, the perp.

The perp is grinning.

"Let's try this again," he says. "Drop the gun or I shoot."

I can't drop my gun. I'm not allowed to. It's one of the first things they teach you at the police academy.

"Let's talk this through," I say, trying to keep my voice steady.

"No talk."

He fires, and I watch another kid die in front of me.

I aim high, putting two rounds into the gunman's helmet, where they make dents and little else. He's already running away, pushing through the emergency exit, the alarm sounding off.

I tear after him, slipping on blood, falling to my hands and knees but holding onto my weapon. I crawl forward, my feet scrambling for purchase through the slickness, and then I'm opening the door, scanning the parking lot left and right.

He's standing ten feet away, aiming his Beretta at me.

I throw myself backward and feel the wind of the shots pass my face.

"Jack!" Herb, from the front of the restaurant.

"He went out the back!"

My hands, slippery with blood and sweat, are shaking like dying birds. I force myself to do a slow count to five, force my bunched muscles to relax, then nudge open the back door.

He's waiting for me.

He fires again, the bullet tugging at my shoulder pad, stinging like I've been whacked with a cane. I scoot backward on my ass, turn over, and crawl for the counter, more shots zinging over me before the back door closes under its own weight, having to climb over the girl he just killed, the scent of blood and death running up my nostrils and down the back of my throat.

I lean against the counter, pull back my jacket, feeling the burn, glancing at my wound and judging it superficial.

A soft voice, muffled, to my right.

"Hey!"

I see the green duffle bag that the perp dropped.

"Hello? Are you there, Jacqueline?"

The voice is coming from the bag. I go to it, tug back the zipper.

Gun. Another Beretta. Loose bullets, more than a hundred. And a walkie-talkie.

"Jack," the walkie barks.

How the hell does he know my name?

"Can you hear me, Jacqueline?"

I look around, find some napkins on a table, pick up the radio and hit the talk button.

"Who is this?"

"I'm doing this for you, Jacqueline. This is all for you. Do you remember Washington?"

Thoughts rush at me. Seven dead so far. He knows me. The perp has over a hundred bullets left. I don't know this guy. I've never been to Washington, the state or the capitol. He knows me. Someone I arrested before? Who is he?

I press talk. "If it's me you want, come and get me."

"I can't right now," the walkie says. "I'm late for class."

I race for the front doors. When I step onto the sidewalk, I see the perp darting through traffic and running full sprint down the sidewalk.

Heading for Thomas Jefferson Middle School.

I don't hear any sirens. Too soon. Look left and right, and don't see Herb.

I rush back into the restaurant, drop the radio into the perp's bag, grab the handle and run after him.

Three steps into the street I'm clipped by a bike messenger.

He spins me around, and I land on my knees, watching as he skids down the tarmac on his helmet, a spray of loose bullets from the gunman's bag jingling after him like dropped change. A car honks. There's a screech of tires. I manage to make it to my feet, still holding the bag, still holding my gun, too distracted to sense if I'm hurt or not.

The school.

I cross the rest of the street, realize I've somehow lost a shoe, my bare right foot slapping against the cold concrete, pedestrians jumping out of my path.

An alarm up ahead, so piercing I feel it in my teeth. The metal detector at the school entrance. It's followed by two more gunshots.

"Jack!"

Herb, from across the street.

"Cars in the parking lot!" I yell, hoping he'll understand. Guy in a football helmet and ammo belts didn't walk in off the street. Must have driven.

The school rushes up at me. I push through the glass doors, the metal detector screaming, a hall monitor slumped dead in her chair, blood pooling black on the rubber mat.

I drop the bag, pocket the Beretta and a handful of brass, hit talk on the radio.

"Where are you?"

Static. Then, coming through the speaker, children's screams.

Followed by gunshots.

I run, trying to follow the echo, trying to pinpoint the cries for help, passing door after door, rushing up a staircase, hearing more gunshots, seeing the muzzle flashes coming from a classroom, going in low and fast.

"Drop the gun," he says.

His Beretta is aimed at the head of a seven-year-old girl.

A sob gets caught in my throat, but I refuse to cry because tears will cloud my vision.

I can't watch anyone else die.

I drop my gun.

The perp begins to twitch, his face wet behind the football helmet.

"Do you have children, Jack?"

I'm not able to talk, so I just shake my head.

"Neither do I," he says. "Isn't...isn't it a shame?"

He pats the girl on the head, crouches down to whisper.

"You did good, sweetheart. I don't need you anymore."

I scream my soul raw when he pulls the trigger.

The little girl drops away, her pink dress now a shocking red, and I launch myself at him just as he turns his weapon on the children cowering in the corner of the room and opens fire.

One.

Two.

Three.

He manages four shots before I body-tackle him, both hands locking on his gun arm, pushing it up and away from the innocents, my head filled with frightened cries that might be from the children but might also be mine.

I grip his wrist and tug hard, locking his elbow, dropping down and forcing him to release the gun. It clatters to the ground.

His free hand tangles itself in my hair and pulls so hard my vision ignites like a flashbulb. I lose my grip and fall to my knees, and he jerks me in the other direction, white hot pain lacing across my scalp as a patch of hair rips free.

I drive an uppercut between his legs, my knuckles bouncing off a plastic supporter, then I'm being pushed away and he's leaping for the door.

My jacket is twisted up, and I can't find my pocket even though I feel the weight of the gun, and finally my hand slips in and I tug a Beretta free and bury three shots into his legs as he runs into the hallway.

I chance a quick look at the children, see several have been hit, see blood on the wall covering two dozen construction paper jack-o-lantern pictures, then I crawl after the perp with the gun raised.

He's waiting for me in the hall, sitting against the wall, bleeding from both knees. I hear him sobbing.

"You weren't supposed to drop your gun," he says.

My breath is coming quick, and I blow it out through my mouth. I'm shaking so bad I can't even keep a bead on him. I blink away tears and repeat over and over, "he's-unarmed-don't-shoot-he's-unarmed-don't shoot-he's-unarmed-don't shoot..."

Movement to my left.

Herb, barreling down the hall. He stops and aims.

"You okay?" Herb asks.

I think I nod.

"Hands in the air!" he screams at the perp.

The perp continues to moan. He doesn't raise his hands.

"Put your hands in the air now!"

The sob becomes a howl, and the perp reaches into his trench coat.

Herb and I empty our guns into him. I aim at his face.

My aim his true.

The perp slumps over, streaking the wall with red. Herb rushes up, pats down the corpse.

"He's clean," Herb says. "No weapons."

I can hear the sirens now. I manage to lower my gun as the paramedics storm the stairs. Kids flood out of the classroom, teachers hurrying them down the hall, telling them not to look.

Many of them look anyway.

I feel my vision narrow, my shoulders quake. I'm suddenly very cold.

"Are you hurt?" Herb asks, squatting down next to me. I'm covered with the blood of too many people.

I shake my head.

"I found the car," Herb says. "Registered to a William Phillip Martingale, Buffalo Grove Illinois. He left a suicide note on the windshield. It said, 'Life no longer matters.'"

"Priors?" I ask, my voice someone else's.

"No."

And something clicks. Some long ago memory from before I was a cop, before I was even an adult.

"I think I know him," I say.

William Phillip Martingale. Billy Martingale. In my fifth grade class at George Washington Elementary School.

"When we were kids. He asked me to the Valentine's Day dance." The words feel like stale bread crust stuck in my throat. "I turned him down. I already had a date."

"Jesus," Herb says.

But there was more. No one liked Billy. He had a bad front tooth, dark gray. Talked kind of slow. Everyone teased him. Everyone including me.

I crawl past the paramedics, over to the perp, probing the ruin of his face, finding that bad tooth he'd never bothered to get fixed.

The first body is wheeled out of the classroom, the body bag no larger than a pillow.

I begin to cry, and I don't think I'll ever be able to stop.

Suffer

Another Phin story. Phin comes from a long tradition of anti-heroes, and was influenced by Mickey Spillane's Mike Hammer, Max Allan Collins' Quarry, and Richard Stark's Parker. But he's mostly a direct descendant of F. Paul Wilson's Repairman Jack, with decidedly less humanity. I wrote this story at the request of the editor for the anthology Chicago Noir. He rejected it. So I sold it to EQMM and wrote another Phin story for him, Epitaph. He rejected that as well, and I sold that to James Patterson for the ITW Thriller anthology. I'm happy how things worked out.

"I want you to kill my wife."

The man sitting across from me, Lyle Tibbits, stared into my eyes like a dog stares at the steak you're eating. He was mid to late thirties, a few inches taller than my six feet, wearing jeans and a button down shirt that pinched his thick wrists.

I sipped some coffee and asked why he wanted his wife dead.

"Do you care?" he asked.

I shrugged. "No. As long as I get paid."

Lyle smiled, exposing gray smoker's teeth.

"I didn't think it mattered. When I called you, I heard you did anything for money."

I rubbed my nose. My nostrils were sore from all the coke I'd been snorting lately, and I'd been getting nosebleeds.

"Any particular way you want it done?"

He looked around Maxie's Coffee Shop—his choice for the meeting place—and leaned forward on his forearms, causing the table to shift and the cheap silverware to rattle.

"You break into my house, discover her home alone, then rape and kill her."

Jaded as I was, this made me raise an eyebrow.

"Rape her?"

"The husband is always a suspect when the wife dies. Either he did it, or he hired someone to do it. The rape will throw the police off. Plus, I figured, with your condition, you won't care about leaving evidence."

He made a point of glancing at my bald head.

"Who gave you my number?" I asked.

"I don't want to say."

I thought about the Glock nestled between my belt and my spine, knew I could get him to tell me if I needed to. We were on Damon and Diversey in Wicker Park, which wasn't the nicest part of Chicago. I could follow him out of the diner and put the hurt to him right there on the sidewalk, and chances were good we'd be ignored.

But truth be told, I didn't really care where he got my number, or that he knew I was dying of cancer. I was out of money, which meant I was out of cocaine. The line I'd done earlier was wearing off, and the pain would return soon.

"I get half up front, half when it's done. The heat will be on you after the job, and you won't have a chance to get the money to me. So you'll put the second half in a locker at the train station, hide the key someplace public, and then give me the info when I'm done. Call from a payphone so the number isn't traced. You fuck me, and I'll find you."

"You can trust me."

Like your wife trusts you? I thought. Instead I said, "How would you like me to do it?"

"Messy. The messier the better. I want her to suffer, and suffer for a long time."

"You've obviously been living in marital bliss."

"You have to hurt her, or else we don't have a deal."

I made a show of thinking it over, even though I'd already made my decision. I assumed this was a way to cash in on life insurance, but what life insurance policy paid extra for torture and rape?

"You have the money on you?" I asked.

"Yeah."

"Pass it under the table."

He hesitated. "Trust goes both ways, you know."

"I could just walk away."

Like hell I could. I needed a snort worse than Wimpy needed his daily hamburger. But I'm a pretty decent bluffer.

Lyle handed me the paper bag he'd brought with him. I set it on the booth next to me and peeked inside. The cash was rubber-banded in stacks of tens and twenties. I stuck my fingers in and did a quick count.

Six grand, to take a human life.

Not bad for a few hours work.

"When?" I asked.

"Tomorrow night, after 10pm. I'll be out, and she'll be home alone. I'll leave the front door open for you. I'm at 3626 North Christiana, off of Addison. Remember, rape and pain."

He seemed to be waiting for a reply so I said, "Sure."

"And Mr. Troutt..." Lyle smiled again, flashing gray. "Have fun with it."

#

After the diner meeting, I called a guy about securing some fake ID.
Then I called my dealer and scored enough coke to keep me high for a while.
I also bought some tequila and refilled my codeine prescription.

Back at my ratty apartment, Earl and I had a party.

Earl is what I call the tumor growing on my pancreas. Giving my killer
a name makes it a little easier to deal with. Each day, Earl eats a little more
of my body. Each day, I try to prevent Earl from doing that. There's chemo,
and radiation, and occasional surgery. And in the off-times, there's illegal
drugs, pharmaceuticals, and alcohol.

Earl was winning.

Luckily, being a drug abuser has some excellent side benefits, such as
not caring about anything, erasing all emotion, and helping to forget the past.

Just a few months ago I had a well paying job in the suburbs, a beautiful
fiancée, and a life most would be envious of. Earl changed all that. Now, not
even the roaches in my tenement building were envious of me.

I drank, and popped, and snorted, until the pain was gone. Until reality
was gone. Until consciousness was gone.

Earl woke me up the next morning, gnawing at my left side with jagged,
rabid teeth.

I peeled myself from the floor, stripped off the jeans and underwear I'd
soiled, and climbed into a shower slick with mildew. I turned the water as hot
as it would go, and the first blast came out rusty and stung my eyes. I had no
soap, so I used shampoo to scrub my body. I didn't eat well, if I remembered
to eat at all, and I could count the ribs on my hairless chest. I made a note to
eat something today. Who would hire a thug that weighed ninety pounds?

After the shower I found some fresh jeans and a white t-shirt. I did a
line, choked down three painkillers, and dug out an old Chicago phone book.

"Walker Insurance."

"I had a couple questions about life insurance."

"I'll transfer you to one of our agents."

I took my cell over the fridge and listened to a Musak version of Guns N Roses while rummaging through the ice box. Nothing in there but frost.

"This is Brad, can I help you?"

"I'm thinking of taking out a life insurance policy on my wife. We live in a nice neighborhood, but she has this unrealistic fear—call it a phobia—of being raped and killed. I'm sure that would never happen, but do you have policies that cover that?"

"Accidental death includes murder, but not suicide."

"And rape?"

"Well, I've heard of some countries like India and Africa that offer rape insurance, but there's nothing like that in the US. But if she's afraid of being attacked, a good life insurance policy can help bring some peace of mind."

"What if she doesn't like the idea of insurance? Could I insure her without her knowing it?"

"For certain types of insurance, the person covered doesn't need to sign the policy. You can insure anyone you want. Would you like to schedule an appointment to talk about this further?"

I thought about asking him if he covered people dying of cancer, but I resisted and hung up. My next call was to the 26th District of the Chicago Police Department.

"Daniels."

"Hi, Jack. It's Phineas Troutt."

"Haven't seen you at the pool hall lately. What's up?"

"I need a favor. I'm looking for paper on a guy named Lyle Tibbits."

"And I should help you because?"

"Because you're a friend. And because he owes me money. And because I probably won't live to see Christmas."

Jack arrested me a few years back, but she'd been cool about it, and we had an on-again-off-again eight ball game on Monday nights. I'd missed a few lately, too stoned to leave my apartment. But I'd helped Jack out a few times, and she owed me, and she knew it.

"Let's see what Mr. Computer has to say. Lyle Tibbits. Prior arrest for—it looks like trafficking kiddie porn. Did a nickel's worth at Joliet. Paroled last year."

"Anything about a wife or kids?"

"Nope."

"Address?"

"Roscoe Village, on Belmont."

She gave me the numbers, and I wrote them down.

"Nothing on Addison?"

"Nope."

"Can you give me his vitals?"

Jack ran through his birth date, social security number, mother's maiden name, and some other choice info cops are privy to.

"You coming this Monday?" she asked when the litany ended. "I finally bought my own cue."

"A Balabushka?"

"A custom stick on my salary? More like Wal-Mart."

"I'll try to make it. Thanks, Jack."

"Take care, Phin."

I tucked the Glock into my pants, pocketed my set of master keys and a pair of S & W handcuffs, and hit the street. It was cool for July, in the low seventies, the sun screened by clouds or smog or both. I grabbed some sweet and sour chicken at a local shop, and then spent an hour at a place on Cermak filling out paperwork. When I finished, I hopped in a cab and took it to Roscoe Village.

Lyle's apartment had a security door, which I opened on the fourth try.

One of my first acts as a criminal had been to rob a locksmith, earning me a set of sixty master keys. They opened ninety percent of the locks in the US. It was much easier than learning how to use picks and tension wrenches, which is something I didn't have the time to learn anyway.

The halls were empty, befitting midday. I found Lyle's apartment number and knocked twice, holding my pistol behind my back.

No answer.

I got through this door on the second try, set the security chain so no one could pop in on me, and began my search.

In the living room were six double DVD recorders, all which seemed to be running. In a box next to the TV were a hundred plastic clamshell boxes, and a spindle of blank recordable DVD-Rs. In the corner of the room were three digital camcorders and a PC. I powered up the computer, spent ten minutes trying to get his password, then gave up and turned it off.

The kitchen revealed a smorgasbord of junk food—he had enough sugar in here to put an elephant into a diabetic coma. On the counter, next to the phone, was a receipt for a glazier, the total more than five hundred bucks. Stuck to the fridge with a banana-shaped magnet was a picture of Lyle drinking a beer. I put the picture in my pocket.

In the bedroom, I found an extensive collection of porno DVDs. Bondage, watersports, S/M, D/s, extreme spanking, and even a kink new to me; latex vacuum mummification. All legal.

I found his illegal stuff in a padlocked trunk, in the back of the bedroom closet. The lock opened with the seventh key I tried.

Child porn. Movies with titles like "See Billy Cry" and "Maxie's Birthday Surprise." Some of the covers had pictures.

I tried not to look.

There were also a few other illegal movies, along with a bag full of cash. Over twenty grand worth.

I took the money, locked the trunk back up, and left the apartment.

Satisfied that I knew who I was dealing with, I bided my time until 10pm.

Then I could finish the job.

#

As promised, Lyle had left the door open for me.

The house was dark and quiet, just like the neighborhood. I walked down Christiana and up the porch stairs without encountering a soul. Once inside, I locked the door behind me and held my breath, listening for sounds of life.

Nothing.

The lights were on in the living room, and I held my Glock before me and did a quick search of the first floor. The furnishings leaned towards the feminine side; pink drapes and flower patterns on the couch. On the end table, copies of Glamour and Cosmo. In the kitchen, a half-eaten container of lowfat yogurt sat on the counter, a spoon alongside it. I checked the back door, found it locked, and then crept over to the staircase.

The stairs were carpeted, but they squeaked with my weight. I paused after every two steps, ears open. I didn't hear a damn thing.

The second floor revealed an empty bathroom, an empty guest room, and a bedroom.

The bedroom was occupied.

A woman was tied to the bed, naked and spread-eagled. She was white, late twenties, her blond hair tangled up in the red leather ball gag buckled around her mouth. Leather straps around her ankles and wrists twisted around the four bedposts. Her eyes were wide with terror, and she screamed when she saw me, the sound lost in her throat.

There was a note next to her head.

        Give it to her. And leave the gag in, or

she'll wake the neighbors.

The room was unusually well-lit. Besides the ceiling light, there were lamps on either side of the bed, one in the corner next to the mirrored closet, and an extra work-light—the portable kind that clips to things—attached to the bed canopy.

"Hello," I said to the woman.

She screamed again.

"Shh. I'll be with you in just a minute."

I took two steps backwards, toward the closet, and then spun around, facing the mirrored sliding door. My free hand pulled back the handle while my business hand jammed the Glock into the closet, into the chest of Lyle Tibbits.

Lyle yelped, dropping the camcorder and trying to push me away. I brought the gun up and clipped him in the teeth with the butt.

He fell forward, spitting blood and enamel. I gave him another chop on the back of the head, and he ate the floor.

"Dontkillmedontkillme!"

I put my foot on his neck and applied some weight, glancing back to check the rest of the closet. Empty. The mirror was one-way, and I could see the bed through the door's glass. The original mirror rested against the rear wall.

"Who is she, Lyle?"

He yelled something, the carpet muffling his words. I eased up some of the pressure from my foot.

"I just met her last week!"

"She's not your wife."

"No! She's just some chick I'm dating!"

"And you hired me to rape and kill her so you could videotape it. I saw the other films back at your apartment. Does snuff sell for more than kiddie porn?"

Lyle wiggled, trying to crane his neck around to look at me.

"It's worth a fortune! I'll cut you in, man! It's enough money for both of us!"

I glanced at the woman, tied up on the bed.

"How much money?" I asked.

"I've got over half a mil in advance orders! We'll be rich, man!"

"That's a lot of money, Lyle. But I'm not greedy. I don't need that much."

"How much do you want? Name the price!"

"You're worth eighty grand to me."

"Eighty grand? No problem! I can—"

I knelt on his back, cutting off his breath. Pressing the Glock to the back of his head, I yanked the handcuffs out of my pocket.

"Put your left hand behind your back, Lyle."

He complied. I yanked his arm back in a submission hold, slapped on the cuffs, then climbed off.

"Let's go into the bathroom, Lyle."

I was a bit too eager helping him to his feet, because I hyper-extended his arm and felt it snap at the elbow.

Lyle howled loud enough to hurt my ears, and I gave his broken arm a twist and told him to shut the hell up. In the bathroom, I chained him to the drainage pipe under the sink, then I went back into the bedroom.

"You're safe," I told the woman. "No one can hurt you now. I'm going to call the police. Are you okay to talk to them?"

She nodded, frantic. I took off her gag.

"He was gonna kill me."

"I know." I picked up the phone next to the bedside and dialed 911, then placed it on the bed next to her mouth.

I walked out of the room as she began talking.

#

I was in a drugged haze when Jack called on my cell.

"Missed you on Monday."

"Sorry. Been busy."

"Remember that guy you called me about? Lyle Tibbits? He got picked up a few days ago."

"Is that a fact?"

"It seems as if Mr. Tibbits was planning on making a snuff film, but someone came and rescued the snuffee."

I wiped some blood off my nose. "Sounds like she got lucky."

"She said it was a bald man."

"Poor guy. It's tough being bald. Society discriminates."

"It would help the case if this mysterious bald man came forward and testified."

"If I see him, I'll let him know. But you probably don't need him. If you check out Lyle's apartment, you might find plenty of reasons to lock him up for good."

"We did that already. Mr. Tibbits will be eligible for parole when he's four hundred years old."

"So why the call?"

"The woman who was saved wants to thank her hero. In person."

An image flashed through my head of Linda, my fiancée. I'd left her because I didn't want her to see me suffer and die.

No one should be subjected to that. To me.

"That's not possible," I told Jack.

"I'll let her know. Pool Monday?"

"I'll try to make it. Jack?"

"Yeah?"

"They holding Tibbits over at Cook County?"

"Yeah. Why?"

"General population?"

"I think so. He's in for kidnapping and attempted murder. The State's Attorney is putting together the illegal porn case."

"Thanks, Jack."

I staggered to the bathroom and rinsed the blood and powder off my face. Then I threw on some clothes, left my apartment, and staggered to the corner news vendor. The daily paper set me back a buck. I sat on the curb and read the police blotter until I found what I needed. Then I picked up three cartons of Marlboros and took a cab to Cook County Jail on 26th and California.

I spent two hours waiting before I was able to see Jerome Johnston. He was black, twenty-two years old, a member of the Gangsta Disciples. Jerome was being held for first degree murder.

"Who the hell are you, cracker?" he said upon meeting me in the visitation room.

"I've got a deal for you, Jerome. A good deal." I handed him the three cartons of smokes that the guards had already searched. "This is for your valuable time."

"What do you want?"

"There's a white boy in your division. Name of Lyle Tibbits. He's a baby raper. Likes to have sex with five-year-old boys and girls." I stared hard into Jerome's lifeless eyes. "I want you to spread the word. Anyone who takes care of him will get twenty cartons of cigarettes. He'll be an easy mark—he's got a broken arm. Here's a picture."

I handed him the photo I'd taken from Lyle's apartment.

"How do you know me?" Jerome asked.

"I don't. Just read about your drive-by in the paper. Thought you'd be the right man for the job. Are you, Jerome?"

Jerome looked at the picture, then back at me. "Hell yeah, dog."

"One more thing. It can't happen until tomorrow. Okay?"

"I'm straight."

I left the jail and cabbed it back home. In my room I did more coke, ate some codeine, and stared at the eighty-thousand dollar life insurance policy I'd taken out on Lyle Tibbits, which I'd bought posing as his brother, using fake identification. It would become effective tonight at midnight.

Eighty grand would buy a lot of pain relief. It might even be enough to help me forget.

I drank until I couldn't feel Earl anymore, and then I drank some more.

When Monday rolled around I cashed my policy and met Jack at Joe's Pool Hall and whipped her butt with my new thousand dollar Balabushka custom-made pool cue.

School Daze

Jack Daniels fans are usually polarized when it comes to Harry McGlade. Some love him. Some hate him. Personally, I love the guy. Harry let's me be goofy, which is something I really enjoy writing, but normally have to tone it down because it takes away from the storyline. But in a Harry McGlade short story, the storyline takes a back seat to the goofiness, and I try to see how many jokes I can cram into the least amount of space. This one sold to the anthology Uncage Me edited by Jennifer Jordan.

"Cute kid," I said.

The kid looked like a large pink watermelon with buck teeth and bug eyes. If I hadn't already known it was a girl, I couldn't have guessed from the picture. What was that medical name for children with a overdeveloped heads? Balloonheadism? Bigheaditis? Melonoma? Freak?

"She takes after her mother."

Yeeech. My fertile mind produced an image of a naked Mrs. Potatohead, unhooking her bra. I shook away the thought and handed the picture back to the proud Papa.

"Where is Mom, by the way?"

Mr. Morribund leaned close enough for me to smell his lunch—tunafish on rye with a side order of whiskey. He was a thin guy with big eyes who wore an off-the-rack suit with a gold Save The Dolphins tie tack.

"Emily doesn't know I'm here, Mr. McGlade. She's at home with little Rosemary. Since we received the news she's been... upset."

"I sympathize. Getting into the right pre-school can mean the difference between summa cum laude at Harvard and offering mouth sex in back alley Dumspters for crack money. I should know. I've seen it."

"You've seen mouth sex in back alley Dumpsters?"

I nodded my head in what I hoped what looked like a sad way. "It isn't pretty, Mr. Morribund. Not to look at, or to smell. But I don't understand how you expect me to get little Rotisserie—"

"It's Rosemary."

"—little Rosemary into this school if they already turned down your application. Are you looking for strong-arm work?"

"No, nothing like that."

I frowned. I liked strong-arm work. It was one of the perks of being a private eye. That and breaking and entering.

"What then? Breaking and entering? Some stealing, maybe?"

I liked stealing.

Morribund swallowed, his Adam's apple wiggling in his thin neck. If he were any skinnier he wouldn't have a profile.

"The Salieri Academy is the premier pre-school in the nation, Mr. McGlade. They have a waiting list of thousands, and to even have a chance at attending you have to fill out the application five years before your child is conceived."

"That's a long time to wait for nookie." But then, if I were married to Mrs. Potatohead, I wouldn't mind the wait.

"It's the reason we took so long to have Rosemary. We paid the application fee, and were all but assured entrance. But three days after Rosemary was born, our application was denied."

"Did they give a reason?" Other than the fact that your kid looks like an albino warthog who has been snacking on an air compressor?

"No. The application says they reserve the right to deny admittance at their discretion, and still keep the fee."

"How much was the fee?"

"Ten thousand dollars."

Ouch. You could rent a lot of naughty videos for that kind of money. And you'd need to, because those things get boring after the third or fourth viewing.

"So what's the deal? You want me to shake the guy down for the money."

He shook his head. "Nothing of the sort. I'm not a violent man."

"Spell it out, Mr. Morribund. What exactly do you want me to do? Burn down the school?"

I liked arson.

"Goodness, no. The Salieri School is run by a man named Michael Sousse."

"And you want me to kidnap his pet dog and take pictures of me throwing it off a tall building, using my zoom lens to capture its final barks of terror as it takes the express lane to Pancakeville? Because that's where I draw the line, Mr. Morribund. I may be a thug, a thief, and an arsonist, but I won't harm any innocent animals unless there's a bonus involved."

Morribund raised an eyebrow. "You'd do that to a dog? The Internet said you love animals."

"I do love animals. Grilled, fried, and broiled. Or stuffed with cheese. I'd eat any animal if it had enough cheese on top. It wouldn't even have to be dead first."

"Oh."

Morribund made a face, and I could tell he was thinking through things.

I glanced again at his Save the Dolphins tie tack and realized I might have been a little hasty with my meat-lovers rant.

"I had a dog once," I said.

"Really?"

"Never tried to eat him. Not once."

I mimed crossing my heart. Morribund stared at me. When he spoke again, his voice was lower, softer.

"Headmaster Sousse, he's a terrible man. A hunter. Gets his jollies shooting poor little innocent animals. His office is strewn with so-called hunting trophies. It's disgusting."

"Sounds awful," I said, stifling a yawn.

"Mr. McGlade," he leaned in closer, giving me more tuna and bourbon. "I want you to find out something about Sousse. Something that I could use to convince him to accept our application."

I scratched my unshaven chin. Or maybe it was my unshaved chin. I get those words confused.

"I understand. You want me to dig up some dirt. Something you can use to blackmail Sousse and get Rheumatism—"

"Rosemary."

"—into his school. Well, you're in luck, Mr. Morribund, because I'm very good at this kind of thing. And even if I don't find anything incriminating in his past, I can make stuff up."

"What do you mean?"

"I can take pictures of him in the shower, and then Photoshop in the Vienna Boy's Choir washing his back. Or I can make it look like he's pooping on the floor of the White House. Or being intimate with a camel. Or eating a nun. Or..."

"I don't want the sordid details, Mr. McGlade. I simply want some kind of leverage. How much will something like that cost?"

I leaned back in my chair and put my hands behind my head, showing off my shoulder holster beneath my jacket. I always let them see the gun before I discussed my fees. It dissuaded haggling.

"I get four hundred a day. Three days minimum, in advance. Plus expenses. I may need to bring in a computer expert to do the Photoshop stuff. He's really good."

I took a pic out of my desk drawer and tossed it to him. Morribund flinched. I smiled at his reaction.

"Looks real, doesn't it?"

"This is fake?"

"Not a single baby harp seal was harmed."

"Really?"

"Well actually, they were all clubbed to death and skinned. But the laughing guy in the parka wasn't really there. We Photoshopped him into the scene. That's the beauty and magic of jpeg manipulation. Look at this one." I threw another photo onto his lap. "Check out that bloody discharge. And those pustules. Don't they look real? It's like they're going to burst all over your hands."

Morribund frowned. "I've seen enough."

"Want to see one with my head on Brad Pitt's body with Ron Jeremy's junk?"

"I really don't."

"How about one of a raccoon driving a motorcycle? He's wearing sunglasses and flipping the bird."

Morribund stood up.

"I'm sure you'll come up with something satisfactory. When can you get started?"

I fished an appointment book out of my top drawer. It was from 1996, and only contained doodles of naked butts. I pretended to scrutinize it.

"You're in luck," I said, pulling out a pen. I drew another butt. A big one, that took up the entire third week of September. "I can start as soon as your check clears."

"I don't trust checks."

"Credit card?"

"I dislike the high interest rates. How about cash?"

"Cash works for me."

After he handed it over I got his phone number, he found his own way to the door, and I did the Money Dance around my office, making happy noises and shaking my booty.

Things had been slow around the agency lately, due to my lack of renewing my Yellow Pages ad. I didn't get many referrals, because I charged too much and wasn't good at my job. Luckily, Morribund had found me through my Internet site. The same computer geek who did my Photoshop work was also the webmaster of my homepage. Google "Chicago cheating spouse sex pictures" and I was the fourth listing. If you Google "naked rhino make-over" I was number two. I still didn't understand the whole keyword thing. That's probably why Morribund thought I was an animal lover.

A quick check of my watch told me I wasn't wearing one, so I looked at the display on my cell phone. Almost two in the afternoon. Time to get started.

I booted up the computer to search for the Salieri School and Christopher Sousse. But instead, I wound up on YouTube, and watched videos of a monkey in a funny hat, a fat woman falling down the stairs, and a Charlie Brown cartoon that someone dubbed over with the voice track to Goodfellas.

After wasting almost an hour, I went to MySpace and read all of my messages from all of my friends, all of whom seemed to work in the paid escort industry.

After that, I checked my eBay bids, my Hotmail account, and added a new entry to my blog about the high cost of parking in the city.

After that, porn.

Finally, I located the Salieri School's website, found their phone number, and dialed.

"Salieri Academy for Exceptionally Gifted Four-Year-Olds, where children are our future and should be heavily invested in, this is Miss Janice, may I help you?"

Miss Janice had a voice like a hot oil massage, deep and sensual and full of petroleum.

"My name is McGlade. Harrison Harold McGlade. I'd like to enroll my son Stimey into your school."

"I'm sorry sir, there's a minimum five year waiting period to get accepted into the Salieri academy. How old is your son now?"

"He's seven."

"We only accept four-year-olds."

"He's got the mind of a four-year-old. Retard. Mom dropped him down an escalator, he fell for forty minutes. Very sad. All someone had to do was hit the off switch."

"I don't understand."

"Why? You a retard too?"

"Mr. McGlade..."

"I'm willing to pay money, Miss Janice. Big money. I'll triple your enrollment fee."

"I'm sorry."

"Okay, I'll double it."

"I don't think that..."

"Look, honey, is Mikey there? He assured me I'd be treated better than this."

"You know Mr. Sousse?"

"Yeah. We played water polo together in college. I saved his horse from drowning."

"Perhaps I should put you through to him."

"Don't bother. I'll be there in an hour with a suitcase full of cash. I won't bring Stimey, because he's with his tutor tonight, learning how to chew. Keep the light on for me."

I hung up, feeling smug. I hadn't shared this with Morribung, but this case really hit home for me. Years ago, when I was a toddler, I'd been forced to drop out of pre-school because I kept biting and hitting the other children. The unfairness of it, being discriminated against because I was a bully, still haunted me to this day.

I hit the computer again and prowled the Internet for dirt on Sousse. Nothing jumped out at me, other than a minor news article a few weeks back about one of his teachers being dismissed for reasons unknown. According to the story, Sousse was deeply embarrassed by the incident and refused to comment.

Then I surfed for Morribund and his wife and kid, and found zilch.

Then I surfed for naked pictures of Catherine Zeta Jones until it was time for me to keep my appointment.

But first, I needed to gear up.

I wound my spy tie around my neck, careful with the wires. Concealed in the tie clip was a digital camera, a unidirectional microphone, and a 20 gigabyte mp3 player loaded with bootleg Tori Amos concerts. It weighed about two pounds, and hurt my back to wear. But it would be my best chance at clandestinely snapping a few photos of Mr. Sousse during our meeting—photos I could later retouch so it looked like he was molesting a pile of dirty laundry.

People would pay a lot of money to keep their dirty laundry out of the news.

Forty minutes later I was pulling into a handicapped parking spot in front of the Salieri Academy on Irving Park Road. Last year, I'd bought a handicapped parking sticker from a one-legged man in line at the DMV. It only cost me ten dollars. He had demanded five hundred, but I simply grabbed the sticker and strolled away at a leisurely pace. Guy shouldn't be driving with only one leg anyway.

The Academy was a large, ivy-covered brick building, four stories high, in the middle of a residential area. As I was reaching for the front door it began to open. A woman exited, holding the hand of a small boy. She was smartly dressed in skirt and blazer, high heels, long brown hair, maybe in her mid-thirties. The boy looked like a honey-baked ham stuffed into a school uniform, right down to the bright pink face and greasy complexion. When God was dishing out the ugly, this kid got seconds.

I played it smooth. "Wouldn't let you in, huh?"

"Excuse me?"

I pointed my chin at the child.

"Wilbur, here. All he's missing is the curly tail. The Academy won't take fatties, right?"

The boy squinted up at me.

"Mother, is this stupid man insinuating that I have piggish attributes?"

I made a face. "Who are you calling stupid? And what does insinuating mean?"

"Just ignore him, Jasper. We can't be bothered by plebeians."

"Hey lady, I'm 100% American."

"You're 100% ignoramus."

"What do dinosaurs have to do with this?"

She ushered the little porker past me—no doubt off to build a house of straw—and I slipped through the doorway and into the lobby. There were busts of dead white guys on marble pedestals all around the room, and the artwork adorning the walls was so ugly it had to be expensive. I crossed the carpeted floor to the welcoming desk, set on a riser so the secretary looked down on everyone. This particular secretary was smoking hot, with big sensuous lips and a top drawer pulled all the way out. Also, large breasts.

"May I help you, Sir?"

Her voice was sultry, but her smile hinted that help was the last thing she wanted to give me. I got that look a lot, from people who thought they were superior somehow due to their looks, education, wealth, or upbringing. It never failed to unimpress me.

"I called earlier, Miss Janice. I'm here to see Mikey."

Her smile dropped a fraction. "I informed Mr. Sousse that you were coming, and he regrets to inform you that—"

"Cork up that gas leak, sweetheart. I'm really a private detective. I'd like a chance to talk with Mr. Sousse about some embarrassing facts I've uncovered about one of your teachers here," I said, referring to that incident I'd Googled. "Of course, if he doesn't want to talk with me, he can hear about it on the ten o'clock news. But I doubt it will do much for enrollment, especially after that last unfortunate episode."

Miss Janice played it coy. "Whom on our staff are you referring to?"

"Are you Mr. Sousse? I can avert my eyes if you want to lift your skirt and check."

She blushed, then picked up the phone. I gave her a placating smile similar to the one she greeted me with.

"Do you have ID?" she asked, still holding the receiver.

I flashed my PI license. She did some whispering, then hung up.

"Mr. Sousse will see you now."

"How lucky for me."

She stared. I stared back.

"You gonna tell me where his office is, or should I just wander around, yelling his name?"

She frowned. "Room 315. The elevator is down the hall, on the left."

I hated to leave with an attractive woman annoyed with me, so I decided to disarm her with wit.

"You know, my father was an elevator operator. His career had a lot of ups and downs."

Miss Janice kept frowning.

"He hated how people used to push his buttons," I said.

No response at all.

"Then, one day, he got the shaft."

She crossed her arms. "That's not funny."

"You're telling me. He fell six floors to his death."

Her frown deepened.

"Tell me, do they have heat on your planet?" I asked.

"Mr. Sousse is expecting you."

I nodded, my work here done. Then it was into the elevator and up to the third floor.

Sousse's office was decorated in 1960's Norman Bates, with low lighting that threw shadows on the stuffed owls and bear heads and antlers hanging on the walls. Sousse, a stern-looking man with glasses and a bald head, sat behind a desk the size of a small car shaped like a desk, and he was sneering at me when I entered.

"Miss Janice said you're a private investigator." His nostrils flared. "I don't care for that profession."

"Don't take it literally. I'm not here to investigate your privates. I just need to ask you a few questions."

A stuffed duck—of all things—was propped on his desktop, making it impossible for me to get a clear shot of his face with my cleverly concealed camera tie. I moved a few steps to the left.

"Which of my staff are you inquiring about?"

"That's confidential."

"If you can't tell me who we're discussing, why is it you wanted to see me?"

"That's confidential too."

I shifted right, touched the tie bar, heard the shutter click. But the lighting was pretty low.

"I don't understand how I'm supposed to—"

"Does this office have better lights?" I interrupted. "I'm having trouble seeing you. I'm getting older, and got cadillacs in my eyes."

"Cadillacs?"

I squinted. "Who said that?"

"Do you mean cataracts?"

"I don't like your tone," I said, intentionally pointing at a moose head.

Sousse sighed, all drama queen, and switched on the overhead track lighting.

Click click went my little camera.

"Did you hear something?" he asked.

I snapped a few more pics, getting him with his mouth open. My tech geek should be able to Photoshop that into something particularly rude.

"Does your tie have a camera in it?" he asked.

I reflexively covered up the tie and hit the button for the mp3 player. Tori Amos began to sing about her mother being a cornflake girl in that whiney, petulant way that made her a superstar. I fussed with the controls, and only succeeded in turning up the volume.

Sousse folded his arms.

"I think this interview is over."

"Fine," I said, loud to be heard over Tori. "But you'll be hearing from me and Morribund again."

"Who?"

"Don't play coy. People like you disgust me, Mr. Sousse. Sure, I'm a carnivore. But I don't get my jollies hunting down ducks and mooses and deers and squirrels." I pointed to a squirrel hanging on the wall, dressed up in a little cowboy outfit. "What kind of maniac hunts squirrels?"

"I'm not a hunter, you idiot. I abhor hunting. I'm a taxidermist."

"Well, then I'm sure the IRS would love to hear about your little operation. You better hope you have a good accountant and that your taxidermist is in perfect order."

I spun on my heels and got out of there.

Mission accomplished. I should have felt happy, but something was nagging at me. Several somethings, in fact.

On my way through the lobby, I stopped by Miss Janice's desk again.

"When Sousse fired that teacher a few weeks ago, what was the reason?"

"That's none of your business, Mr. McGlade."

"Some sex thing?"

"Certainly not!"

"Inappropriate behavior?"

"I won't say another word."

"Fine. If you want me to pick you up later and take you to dinner, stay silent."

"I'd rather be burned alive."

"We can do that after we've eaten."

"No. I think you're annoying and repulsive."

"How about a few drinks? The more you drink, the less repulsive I get."

She folded her arms and her voice went from sultry to frosty. "Employees of the Salieri Academy don't drink, Mr. McGlade."

"I understand. How about we take a handful of pills and smoke a bowl?"

"I'm calling security."

"No need. I'm outtie. Catch you later, sweetheart."

I winked, then headed back to my office. When I arrived, I spend a good half hour on the Internet, digging deeper into the Salieri story, using a reverse phone directory to track a number, and looking up the words insinuating, plebian, ignoramous, and taxidermist. Then I gave Morribund a call and told him I had something for him.

An hour later he showed up, looking expectant to the point of jubilation. Jubilation is another word I looked up.

"Did you get the pictures, Mr. McGlade?"

"I got them."

"You're fast."

"I know. Ask my last girlfriend."

We stared at each other for a few seconds.

"So, are you going to give them to me?"

"No, Mr. Morribund. I'm not."

He leaned in closer, the whiskey coming off him like cologne. "Why? You want more money?"

"I'll take all the money you give me, but I'm not going to give you the photos."

"Why not?"

I smiled. It was time for the big revealing expositional moment.

"There are a lot of things I hate, Mr. Morribund. Like public toilets. And the Red Sox. And massage girls who make you pay extra for happy endings. But the thing I hate the most is being lied to by a client."

"Me? Lie to you? What are you talking about?"

"You don't want to get your daughter into the Salieri Academy. You don't even have a daughter."

His eyes narrowed.

"You're insane. Why would you think such a thing?"

"When I went to the Academy, I ran into some kid in a Salieri uniform, and he was uglier than a hatful of dingle-berries with hair on them. If he got in, then the school had no restrictions according to looks. Isn't that right, Mr. Morribund? Or should I use your real name... Nathan Tribble?"

He sighed, knowing he was beaten. "How did you figure it out?"

"You didn't pay me with a check or credit card, because you didn't have any in the name you gave me. But you did give me your real phone number, and I looked it up in the Internet. I also found out you once worked at the Salieri Academy. Fired a few weeks ago. For drinking, I assume."

"It never affected my job! I was the best instructor that stupid school ever had!"

I didn't care about debating him, because I wasn't done with my brilliant explanation yet.

"You came to me because you found me on the Internet and thought I liked dogs. That's why you wore that Save the Dolphins tie tack. You said Sousse was a hunter, to make me dislike him so I'd go along with your blackmail scheme."

"Enough. We've established I was lying."

But I still had more exposing to expose, so I went on.

"Sousse isn't a hunter, Tribble. He's a taxidermist. And you're no animal lover either. You can't be pro-dolphin and also eat tuna. Tuna fisherman catch and kill dolphins all the time. But your breath smelled of tuna during our last meeting."

"Why are you telling me things I already know?"

"Because that's what I do, Tribble. I figure out puzzles by putting together all the little pieces until they all fit together and form a full picture, made of the little puzzle pieces I've fit together. Or something."

"You're a low-life, McGlade. All you do is take dirty pictures of people. Or you make up dirty pictures when there are none to take."

"I may be a low-life. And a thief. And a voyeur. And an arsonist. And a leg-breaker. But I'm not a liar. You're the liar, Tribble. And you made a big mistake. You lied to me."

Tribble snorted. "So? Big deal. I got fired, and I wanted to take revenge. I figured you wouldn't do it if I asked, so I made up the story about the daughter, and added the pro-animal garbage to get you hooked. What does it matter? Just give me the damn pictures and you can go play Agatha Christie by yourself in the shower."

I stood up.

"Get out of my office, Tribble. I'm going to make two calls. The first, to

Sousse, to tell him what you've got planned. I bet he can make sure you'll never get a teaching job in this town again. The second call will be to a buddy of mine at the Chicago Police Department. She'll love to learn about your little blackmail scheme."

Tribble looked like I just peed in his oatmeal.

"What about the money I gave you?"

"No give-backsies."

He balled his fists, made a face, then stormed out of my office.

I grinned. It had been a productive day. I'd made a cool twelve hundred bucks for only a few hours of work, and that was only the beginning of the money train.

I got on the phone to my tech geek, and told him I was forwarding a photo I needed him to doctor. I think Sousse would look perfect Photshopped into a KKK rally, wearing a Nazi armband and goose-stepping.

Sure, I wasn't a liar. But I was a sucker for a good blackmail scheme.

Not bad for a pre-school drop-out.

Overproof

My friend Libby Fischer Hellmann edited an anthology called Chicago Blues, published by Bleak House in 2007. I wrote a Jack story for her, based on a premise I thought of while stuck in traffic downtown. Why do cars get gridlocked? Here's one possible answer...

The man sat in the center of the southbound lane on Michigan Avenue, opposite Water Tower Place, sat cross-legged and seemingly oblivious to the mile of backed-up traffic, holding a gun that he pointed at his own head.

I'd been shopping at Macy's, and purchased a Gucci wallet as a birthday gift for my boyfriend, Latham. When I walked out onto Michigan I was hit by the cacophony of several hundred honking horns and the unmistakable shrill of a police whistle. I hung my star around my neck and pushed through the crowd that had gathered on the sidewalk. Chicago's Magnificent Mile was always packed during the summer, but the people were usually moving in one direction or the other. These folks were standing still, watching something.

Then I saw what they were watching.

I assumed the traffic cop blowing the whistle had called it in—he had a radio on his belt. He'd stopped cars in both directions, and had enforced a twenty meter perimeter around the guy with the gun.

I took my .38 Colt out of my purse and walked over, holding up my badge with my other hand. The cop was black, older, the strain of the situation heavy on his face.

"Lt. Jack Daniels, Homicide." I had to yell above the car horns. "What's the ETA on the negotiator?"

"Half hour, at least. Can't get here because of the jam."

He made a gesture with his white gloved hand, indicating the gridlock surrounding us.

"You talk to this guy?"

"Asked him his name, if he wanted anything. Told me to leave him alone. Don't have to tell me twice."

I nodded. The man with the gun was watching us. He was white, pudgy, mid-forties, clean shaven and wearing a blue suit and a red tie. He looked calm but focused. No tears. No shaking. As if it was perfectly normal to sit in the middle of the street with a pistol at your own temple.

I kept my Colt trained on the perp and took another step toward him. If he flinched, I'd shoot him. The shrinks had a term for it: suicide by cop. People who didn't have the guts to kill themselves, so they forced the police to. I didn't want to be the one to do it. Hell, it was the absolute last thing I wanted to do. I could picture the hearing, being told the shooting was justified, and I knew that being in the right wouldn't help me sleep any better if I had to murder this poor bastard.

"What's your name?" I asked.

"Paul."

The gun he had was small, looked like a .380. Something higher caliber would likely blow through both sides of his skull and into the crowd. This bullet probably wasn't powerful enough. But it would do a fine job of killing him. Or me, if he decided he wanted some company in the afterlife.

"My name is Jack. Can you put the gun down, Paul?"

"No."

"Please?"

"No."

That was about the extent of my hostage negotiating skills. I dared a step closer, coming within three feet of him, close enough to smell his sweat.

"What's so bad that you have to do this?"

Paul stared at me without answering. I revised my earlier thought about him looking calm. He actually looked numb. I glanced at his left hand, saw the wedding ring.

"Problems with the wife?" I asked.

His Adam's apple bobbled up and down as he swallowed. "My wife died last year."

"I'm sorry."

"Don't be. You married?"

"Divorced. What was your wife's name, Paul?"

"Doris."

"What do you think Doris would say if she saw you like this?"

Paul's face pinched into a sad smile. My Colt Detective Special weighed twenty-two ounces, and my arm was getting tired holding it up. I brought my left hand under my right to brace it, my palm on the butt of the weapon.

"Do you think you'll get married again?" he asked.

I thought about Latham. "It will happen, sooner or later."

"You have someone, I'm guessing."

"Yes."

"Does he like it that you're a cop?"

I considered the question before answering. "He likes the whole package."

Paul abruptly inhaled. A snort? I couldn't tell. I did a very quick left to right sweep with my eyes. The crowd was growing, and inching closer—one traffic cop couldn't keep everyone back by himself. The media had also arrived. Took them long enough, considering four networks had offices within a few blocks.

"Waiting for things to happen, that's a mistake." Paul closed his eyes for a second, then opened them again. "If you want things to happen, you have to make them happen. Because you never know how long things are going to last."

He didn't seem depressed. More like irritated. I took a slow breath, smelling the cumulative exhaust of a thousand cars and buses, wishing the damn negotiator would arrive.

"Do you live in the area, Paul?"

He sniffled, sounding congested. "Suburbs."

"Do you work downtown?"

"Used to. Until about half an hour ago."

"Do you want to talk about it?"

"No."

"Can you give me more than that?"

He squinted at me. "Why do you care?"

"It's my job, Paul."

"It's your job to protect people."

"Yes. And you're a person."

"You want to protect me from myself."

"Yes."

"You also want to protect these people around us."

"Yes."

"How far away are they, do you think? Fifteen feet? Twenty?"

A strange question, and I didn't like it. "I don't know. Why?"

Paul made a show of looking around.

"Lot of people here. Big responsibility, protecting them all."

He shifted, and my finger automatically tensed on the trigger. Paul said something, but it was lost in the honking.

"Can you repeat that, Paul?"

"Maybe life isn't worth protecting."

"Sure it is."

"There are bad people in the world. They do bad things. Should they be protected too?"

"Everyone should be protected."

Paul squinted at me. "Have you ever shot anyone, Jack?"

Another question I didn't like.

"When I was forced to, yes. Please don't force me, Paul."

"Have you ever killed anyone?"

"No."

"Have you ever wanted to?"

"No."

Paul made a face like I was lying. "Why not? Do you believe in God? In heaven? Are you one of those crazy right-to-lifers who believe all life is sacred? Do you protest the death penalty?"

"I believe blood is hard to get off of your hands, even if it's justified."

He shifted again, and his jacket came open. There was a spot of something on his shirt. Something red. Both my arms were feeling the strain of holding up my weapon, and a spike of fear-induced adrenalin caused a tremor in my hands.

"What's that on your shirt, Paul? Is that blood?"

He didn't bother to look. "Probably."

I kept my voice steady. "Did you go to work today, Paul?"

"Yes."

"Did you bring your gun to work?"

No answer. I glanced at the spot of blood again, and noticed that his stomach didn't look right. I'd first thought Paul was overweight. Now it looked like he had something bulky on under his shirt.

"Did you hurt anyone at work today, Paul?"

"That's the past, Jack. You can't protect them. What's done is done."

I was liking this situation less and less. That spot of blood drew my eyes like a beacon. I wondered if he was wearing a bullet proof vest under his business suit, or something worse.

"I don't want to go to jail," he said.

"What did you do, Paul?"

"They shouldn't have fired me."

"Who? Where do you work?"

"Since Doris died, I haven't been bringing my 'A Game.' That's understandable, isn't it?"

I raised my voice. "How did you get blood on your shirt, Paul?"

Paul glared at me, but his eyes were out of focus.

"When you shot those people, did they scream?" he asked.

I wasn't sure what he was after, so I stayed silent.

He grinned. "Doesn't it make you feel good when they scream?"

Now I got it. This guy wasn't just suicidal—he was homicidal as well. I took a step backward.

"Don't leave, Jack. I want you to see this. You should see this. I'm moving very slow, okay?"

He put his hand into his pocket. I cocked the hammer back on my Colt. Paul fished out something small and silver, and I was a hair's breadth away from shooting him.

"This is a detonator. I've got some explosives strapped to my chest. If you take another step away, if you yell, I'll blow both of us up. And the bomb is strong enough to kill a lot of people in the crowd. It's also wired to my heartbeat. I die, it goes off."

I didn't know if I believed him or not. Explosives weren't easy to get, or to make. And rigging up a detonator—especially one that was hooked into your pulse—that was really hard, even if you could find the plans on the Internet. But Paul's eyes had just enough hint of psychosis in them that I stayed put.

"Do you doubt me, Jack? I see some doubt. I work at LarsiTech, out of the Prudential Building. We sell medical equipment. That's where I got the ECG electrode pads. It's also where I got the radioactive isotopes."

My breath caught in my throat, and my gun became impossibly heavy. Paul must have noticed my reaction, because he smiled.

"The isotopes won't cause a nuclear explosion, Jack. The detonator is too small. But they will spread radioactivity for a pretty good distance. You've heard of dirty bombs, right? People won't die right away. They'll get sick. Hair will fall out. And teeth. Skin will slough off. Blindness. Leukemia. Nasty business. I figure I've got enough strapped to my waist to contaminate the whole block."

All I could ask was, "Why?"

"Because I'm a bad person, Jack. Remember? Bad people do bad things."

"Would Doris...approve...of this?"

"Doris didn't approve of anything. She judged. Judged every little thing I did. I half expected to be haunted by her ghost after I shot her, telling me how I could have done a better job."

I didn't have any saliva left in my mouth, so my voice came out raspy.

"What happened today at LarsiTech?"

"A lot of people got what was coming to them. Bad people, Jack. Maybe they weren't all bad. I didn't know some of them well enough. But we all have bad in us. I'm sure they deserved it. Just like this crowd of people."

He looked beyond me.

"Like that woman there, pointing at me. Looks nice enough. Probably has a family. I'm sure she's done some bad things. Maybe she hits her kids. Or she stuck her mom in a nursing home. Or cheats on her taxes. We all have bad in us."

His Helter Skelter eyes swung back to me.

"What have you done that's bad, Jack?"

A cop's job was to take control of the situation, and somehow I'd lost that control.

"You're not thinking clearly, Paul. You're depressed. You need to put down the detonator and the gun."

"You have five seconds to tell me something bad you've done, or I press the button."

"I'll shoot you, Paul."

"And then a lot of people will die, Jack. Five..."

"This isn't a game, Paul."

"Four..."

"Don't make me do this."

"Three..."

Was he bluffing? Did I have any options? My .38 pointed at his shoulder. If I shot him, it might get him to drop the detonator. Or it might kill him and then his bomb would explode. Or it might just piss him off and get him to turn his gun on me.

"Two..."

It came out in a spurt. "I cheated on my boyfriend with my ex husband."

The corners of Paul's eyes crinkled up.

"Does your boyfriend know, Jack?"

"Yes."

"He found out, or you told him?"

I recalled the pained expression on Latham's face. "I told him."

"He forgave you?"

"Yes."

Paul chewed his lower lip, looking like a child caught with his hand in the cookie jar.

"Did it feel good to hurt him, Jack?"

"No."

Paul seemed to drink this in.

"You must have known it would hurt him, but you did it anyway. So some part of you must not have minded hurting him."

"I didn't want to hurt him. I just cared more about my needs than his."

"You were being selfish."

"Yes."

"You were being bad."

The word stuck like a chicken bone in my throat. "Yes."

His thumb caressed the detonator, and he licked his lips.

"What's the difference between that and what I'm doing right now?"

The gun weighed a hundred pounds, and my arms were really starting to shake.

"I broke a man's heart. You're planning on killing a bunch of people. That's worse."

Paul raised an eyebrow. "So I'm a worse person than you?"

I hesitated, then said, "Yes."

"Do you want to shoot me?"

"No."

"But I'm bad. I deserve it."

"Bad things can be forgiven, Paul."

"Do you think your boyfriend would forgive me if I killed you?"

I pictured Latham. His forgiveness was the best gift I'd ever gotten. It proved that love had no conditions. That mistakes weren't deal breakers.

I wanted to live to see Latham again.

Regain control, Jack. Demand proof.

"Show me the bomb," I said to Paul. My tone was hard, professional. I wasn't going to neutralize the situation by talking. Paul was too far gone. When dealing with bullies, you have to push back or you won't gain their respect.

"No," he said.

Louder, "Show me the bomb!"

At the word bomb a collective wail coursed through the crowd, and they began to stampede backward.

He began to shake, and his eyes became mean little slits. "What did I say about yelling, Jack?"

Paul's finger danced over the detonator button.

"You're bluffing." I chanced a look around. The perimeter was widening.

"I'll prove I'm not bluffing by blowing up the whole—"

I got even closer, thrusting my chin at him, steadying my gun.

"I'm done with this, Paul. Drop the gun and the detonator, or I'm going to shoot you."

"If you shoot me, you'll die."

"I'm not going to believe that unless you show me the goddamn bomb."

Time stretched out, slowed. After an impossibly long second he lowered his eyes, reaching down for his buttons.

I was hoping he was bluffing, praying he was bluffing, and then his shirt opened and I saw the red sticks of dynamite.

Son of a bitch. He wasn't bluffing.

I couldn't let him press that detonator. So I fired.

Thousands of hours on the shooting range meant the move was automatic, mechanical. His wrist exploded in blood and bone, and before the scream escaped his lips I put one more in the opposite shoulder. He dropped both his gun and the detonator. I kicked them away, hoping I hadn't killed him, hoping he'd be alive until help came.

I stared at his chest, saw two electrode pads hooked up to his heart. His waist was surrounded by explosives, and in the center was a black box with a radiation symbol on it.

Paul coughed, then slumped onto his back. His wrist spurted, and his shoulder poured blood onto the pavement like a faucet. Each bullet had severed an artery. He was doomed.

I shrugged off my jacket, pressed it to the shoulder wound, and yelled, "Bomb! Get out of here!" to the few dozen idiots still gawking. Then I grabbed Paul's chin and made him look at me.

"How do I disarm this, Paul?"

His voice was soft, hoarse. "...you...you killed me..."

"Paul! Answer me! How can I shut off the bomb!"

His eyelids fluttered. My blazer had already soaked through with blood. "...how..."

"Yes, Paul. Tell me how."

"...how does..."

"Please, Paul. Stay with me."

His eyes locked on mine.

"...how does it feel to finally kill someone?"

Then his head tilted to the side and his mouth hung open.

I felt for the pulse in his neck. Barely there. He didn't have long.

I checked the crowd again. The traffic cop had fled, and the drivers of the surrounding cars had abandoned them. No paramedics rushed over, lugging life-saving equipment. No bomb squad technicians rushed over, to cut the wires and save the day. It was only me, and Paul. Soon it would be only me, and a few seconds later I'd be gone too.

Should I run, give myself a chance to live? How much contamination would this dirty bomb spread? Would I die anyway, along with hundreds or thousands of others? I didn't know anything about radiation. How far could it travel? Could it go through windows and buildings? How much death could it cause?

Running became moot. Paul's chest quivered, and then was still.

I knew even less about the inner working of the human body than I did about radiation. If I started CPR, would that trick the bomb into thinking Paul's heart was still beating?

I didn't have time to ponder it. Without thinking I tore off the electrodes and stuck them up under my shirt, under my bra, fixing them to my chest, hoping to find my heartbeat and stop the detonation.

I held my breath.

Nothing exploded.

I looked around again, saw no help. And none could get to me, with the traffic jam. I needed to move, to get to the next intersection, to find a place where the bomb squad could get to me.

But first I called Dispatch.

"This is Lieutenant Jack Daniels, from the 26th District. I'm on the corner of Michigan and Pearson. I need the bomb squad. A dirty bomb is hooked up to my heartbeat. I also need someone to check out a company downtown called LarsiTech, a medical supply company in the Prudential Building. There may have been some homicides there."

I gave the Dispatch officer my cell number, then grabbed Paul's wrist and began to drag him to the curb. It wasn't easy. My grip was slippery with blood, and the asphalt was rough and pulled at his clothes. I would tug, make sure the electrodes were still attached, take a step, and repeat.

Halfway there my cell rang.

"This is Dispatch. The bomb squad is on the way, ETA eight minutes. Are you sure on the company name, Lieutenant?"

"He said it several times."

"There's no listing for LarsiTech in the Prudential Building. I spelled it several different ways."

"Then where is LarsiTech?"

"No place I could find. Chicago had three medical supply companies, and I called them all. They didn't report any problems. The phone book has no LarsiTech. Information has no listing in Illinois, or the whole nation."

I looked down at Paul, saw the wires had ripped out of the black box. And that the black box had a local cable company's name written on the side.

And that the radiation symbol was actually a sticker that was peeling off.

And that the dynamite was actually road flares with their tops cut off.

Suicide by cop.

I sat down in the southbound lane on Michigan Avenue, sat down and stared at my hands, at the blood caked under the fingernails, and wondered if I'd ever be able to get them clean.

Bereavement

In 2005 I decided that I knew so many thriller authors I should edit an anthology. It developed into a collection of hitman stories called These Guns For Hire. I'm hugely proud of that antho, which was published in 2006 by Bleak House. I also discovered that the easiest way to get published is to stick one of your own stories in the anthology that you're editing.

"Why should you care? Guys like you got no scruples."

If I had any scruples, I would have fed this asshole his teeth. Or at least walked away.

But he was right.

"Half up front," I said. "Half at the scene."

He looked at me like flowers had suddenly sprouted out of my bald head, Elmer Fudd-style.

"At the scene?"

I'd been through this before, with others. Everyone seemed to want their spouse dead these days. Contract murder was the new black.

I leaned back, pushing away the red plastic basket with the half-eaten hot dog. We were the only customers in Jimmy's Red Hots, the food being the obvious reason we dined alone. The shit on a bun they served was a felony.. If my stomach wasn't clenched tight with codeine withdrawal spasms, I might have complained.

"You want her dead," I said, fighting to keep my voice steady. "The cops always go after the husband."

He didn't seem to mind the local cuisine, and jammed the remainder of his dog into his mouth, hoarding it in his right cheek as he spoke.

"I was thinking she's home alone, someone breaks in to rob the place, gets surprised and kills her."

"And why weren't you home?"

"I was out with friends."

He was a big guy. Over six feet, neck as thick as his head so he looked like a redwood with a face carved into it. Calloused knuckles and a deep tan spoke of a blue collar trade, maybe construction. Probably considered killing the little lady himself, many times. A hands-on type. He seemed disappointed having to hire out.

Found me through the usual channels. Knew someone who knew someone. Fact was, the sicker I got, the less I cared about covering my tracks. Blind drops and background checks and private referrals were things of the past. So many people knew what I did I might as well be walking around Chicago wearing a sandwich board that said, "Phineas Troutt–He Kills People For Money."

"Cops will know you hired someone," I told him. "They'll look at your sheet."

He squinted, mean dropping over him like a veil.

"How do you know about that?"

The hot dog smell was still getting to me, so I picked up my basket and set it on the garbage behind out table.

"Let me guess," I said. "Battery."

He shrugged. "Domestic bullshit. Little bitch gets lippy sometimes."

"Don't they all."

I felt the hot dog coming back up, forced it to stay put. A sickening, flu-like heat washed over me.

"You okay, buddy?"

Sweat stung my eyes, and I noticed my hands were shaking. Another cramp hit, making me flinch.

"What are you, some kinda addict?"

"Cancer," I said.

He didn't appear moved by my response.

"Can you still do this shit?"

"Yeah."

"How long you got?"

Months? Weeks? The cancer had metastasized from my pancreas, questing for more of me to conquer. At this stage, treatment was bullshit. Only thing that helped was cocaine, tequila, and codeine. Being broke meant a lot of pain, plus withdrawal, which was almost as bad.

I had to get some money. Fast.

"Long enough," I told him.

"You look like a little girl could kick your ass."

I gave him my best tough-guy glare, then reached for the half-empty glass bottle of ketchup. Maintaining eye contact, I squeezed the bottle hard in my trembling hands. In one quick motion, I jerked my wrist to the side, breaking the top three inches of the bottle cleanly off.

"Jesus," he said.

I dropped the piece on the table and he stared at it, mouth hanging open like a fish. I shoved my other hand into my pocket, because I cut my palm pretty deep. Happens sometimes. Glass isn't exactly predictable.

"You leave the door open," I told him. "I come in around 2am. I break your wife's neck. Then I break your nose."

He went from awed to pissed. "Fuck you, buddy."

"Cops won't suspect you if you're hurt. I'll also leave some of my blood on the scene."

I watched it bounce around behind his Neanderthal brow ridge. Waited for him to fill in all the blanks. Make the connections. Take it to the next level.

His thoughts were so obvious I could practically see them form pictures over his head.

"Yeah." He nodded, slowly at first, then faster. "That DNA shit. Prove someone else was there. And you don't care if you leave any, cause you're a dead man anyway."

I shrugged like it was no big deal. Like I'd fully accepted my fate.

"When do we do this?"

"When can you have the money ready?"

"Anytime."

"How about tonight?"

The dull film over his eyes evaporated, revealing a much younger man. One who had dreams and hopes and unlimited possibilities.

"Tonight is great. Tonight is perfect. I can't believe I'm finally gonna be rid of the bitch."

"Till death do you part. Which brings me to the original question. Why don't you just divorce her?"

He grinned, showing years of bad oral hygiene.

"Bitch ain't keeping half my paycheck for life."

Ain't marriage grand?

He gave me his address, we agreed upon a time, and then I followed him outside, put on a baseball cap and some sunglasses, escorted him down a busy Chinatown sidewalk to the bank, and rammed a knife in his back the second after he punched his PIN into the enclosed ATM.

I managed to puncture his lung before piercing his heart, and he couldn't draw a breath, couldn't scream. I put my bleeding hand under his armpit so he didn't fall over, and again he gave me that look, the one of utter disbelief.

"Don't be surprised," I told him, pressing his CHECKING ACCOUNT button. "You were planning on killing me tonight, after I did your wife. You didn't want to pay me the other half."

I pressed WITHDRAW CASH and punched in a number a few times higher than our agreed upon figure.

He tried to say something, but bloody spit came out.

"Plus, a large ATM withdrawal a few hours before your wife gets killed? How stupid do you think the cops are?"

His knees gave out, and I couldn't hold him much longer. My injured palm was bleeding freely, soaking into his shirt. But leaving DNA was the least of my problems. This was a busy bank, and someone would be walking by any second.

I yanked out the knife, having to put my knee against his back to do so because of the suction; gravity knives don't have blood grooves. Then I wiped the blade on his shirt, and jammed it and the cash into my jacket pocket.

He collapsed onto the machine, and somehow managed to croak, "Please."

"No sympathy here," I told him, pushing open the security door. "Guys like me got no scruples."

Pot Shot

A lot of my readers like Herb, but for some reason I don't enjoy using him in shorts as much as Jack, Harry, and Phin. This is a rare exception. I originally wrote this as a chapbook, to give away at writing conferences. It deals with Herb's retirement, a topic later covered in greater detail in my novel Dirty Martini.

"How did you know pot roast is my favorite?"

Detective First Class Herb Benedict stepped into the kitchen, following the aroma. He gave his wife Bernice a peck on the cheek and made a show of sniffing deeply, then sighing.

"I've been making pot roast every Friday night for the past twenty-two years, and you say that every time you come home."

Herb grinned. "What happens next?"

"You pinch me on the bottom, change into your pajamas, and we eat in the family room while watching HBO."

"Sounds pretty good so far." He gently tugged Bernice away from the stove and placed his hands on her bottom, squeezing. "Then what?"

Bernice gave Herb's ample behind a pinch of its own.

"After HBO we go upstairs, and I force you to make love to me."

Herb sighed. "A tough job, but I have to repay you for the pot roast."

He leaned down, his head tilted to kiss her, just as the bullet plinked through the bay window. It hit the simmering pot with the sound of a gong, showering gravy skyward.

Herb reacted instinctively. His left hand grabbed Bernice and pulled her down to the linoleum while his right yanked the Sig Sauer from his hip holster and trained it on the window.

Silence, for several frantic heartbeats.

"Herb..."

"Shh."

From the street came the roar of an engine and screaming tires. They quickly blended into Chicago traffic. Herb wanted to go have a look, but a burning sensation in his hip stopped him. He reached down with his free hand, feeling dampness.

"Herb! You're been shot!"

He brought the fingers to his mouth.

"No—it's juice from the pot roast. Leaked down the stove."

Motioning for his wife to stay down, Herb crawled over to the window and peered out. The neighborhood was quiet.

He turned his attention to the stove top. The stainless steel pot had a small hole in the side, pulsing gravy like a wound.

Herb wondered which was worse; his Friday night plans ruined, or the fact that someone just tried to kill him.

He looked into the pot and decided it was the former.

"Dammit. The bastards killed my pot roast."

He tore himself away from the grue and dialed 911, asking that they send the CSU over. And for the CSU to bring a pizza.

#

Officer Dan Rogers leaned over the pot, his face somber.

"I'm sorry, Detective Benedict. There's nothing we can do to save the victim."

Herb frowned around a limp slice of sausage and pepperoni. Over two dozen gourmet pizza places dotted Herb's neighborhood, and the Crime Scene Unit had gone to a chain-store. The greasy cardboard box the pie came in probably had more flavor.

"You might think you're amusing, but that's an eighteen dollar roast."

"I can tell. Look at how tender it is. It's practically falling off the bone. And the aroma is heavenly. It's a damn shame."

Officer Hajek snapped a picture. "Shouldn't let it go to waste. When you're done, can I take it home for the dog?"

Herb watched Roberts attack the roast with gloved hands and wanted to cry at the injustice of it all. Another slice of pizza found its way into Herb's mouth, but it offered no comfort.

"And...gotcha, baby!"

Rogers held up his prize with a pair of forceps. The slug was roughly half an inch long, shaped like a mushroom and dripping gravy.

It looked good enough to eat.

"I think it's a 22LR. Must have been a high velocity cartridge. Punched a hole through the window without shattering it."

Herb and Rogers exchanged a knowing look, but didn't speak aloud because Bernice was nearby. Your typical gang member didn't bring a rifle on a drive-by shooting. Twenty-two caliber long range high speeds were favored by hunters.

And assassins.

Herb's mind backtracked over his career, of all the men he'd put away who held a grudge. After thirty-plus years on the force, there were too many to remember. He'd have to wade through old case files, cross-reference with recent parolees...

"Herb?"

"Hmm? Yes, Bernice?"

His wife's face appeared ready to crack. Herb had never seen her so fragile before.

"I...I called the glazier. They're open twenty-four-hours, so they're sending someone right away to fix the window, but they might not be here until late, and I don't know if–"

Herb took her in his arms, rubbed her back.

"It's okay, honey."

"It's not okay."

"You don't have to worry. Look how big a target I am, and they still missed."

"Maybe we should put an APB out for a blind man," Hajek offered.

Bernice pulled away, forcefully.

"This isn't a joke, Herb. You don't know what it's like, being a cop's wife. Every morning, when I kiss you before you go to work, I don't know if..."

The tears came. Herb reached for her, but Bernice shoved away his hands and hurried out of the kitchen.

Herb rubbed his eyes. No pot roast, no HBO, and certainly no nookie tonight. The evening's forecast; lousy pizza and waiting around for the glass man.

Being a cop sure had its perks.

#

The alarm went off, startling Herb awake.

Bernice's side of the bed remained untouched. She'd stayed in the guest room all night.

He found her in the kitchen, frying eggs. The stainless steel pot with the hole in it rested on top of their wicker garbage can, too large to fit inside.

"Smells good. Denver omelet?"

Bernice didn't answer.

"The glass guy said that homeowner's insurance should cover the cost. If you have time later today, can you give our agent a call? The bill is by the phone."

Bernice remained silent, but began to furiously stir the eggs. They went from omelet to scrambled.

"There will be a squad car outside all day. Let me give you their number in case..."

"In case of what?" Bernice's red eyes accused him. "In case someone tries to kill me? No one's after me, Herb. I don't have any enemies. I'm a housewife."

Herb wanted to get up and hold her, but knew she wouldn't allow it.

"I'll also have an escort, all day. It's standard procedure."

"I don't care about procedure."

"There's nothing more I can do, Bernice."

"Yes there is. You can retire."

Herb let the pain show on his face.

"I've got six more years until full pension."

"Forget the full pension. We've got our savings. We've got our investments. We can make it work."

"Bernice..."

"This isn't about money, and you know it. You'll never leave the Force. Not until they kick you out or..."

Bernice's eyes locked on the holey pot.

Herb had no reply. He skipped breakfast, showered, shaved, and began to dress. Normally, Bernice laid out an ironed shirt for him.

Not today.

"I'll be at the Center all day."

Her voice startled Herb. She stood in the bedroom doorway, arms folded.

"I'd prefer if—"

"If I stay home? You go on with your life, and I have to hide in the house?"

Herb sighed.

"It's my job, Bernice."

"I see. Volunteering doesn't count as a job because I'm not getting paid."

"I didn't say that."

Bernice walked away. Herb took a shirt from the hanger and put it on, wrinkles and all. He instructed the team outside to follow Bernice wherever she went, and then waited for his escorts to arrive to take him to work.

#

"It could be a thousand different people."

Herb's partner, Lt. Jacqueline Daniels, looked up over the stack of printouts. Jack wore her brown hair up today, revealing gray roots. Her hands cradled a stained coffee mug.

"You only have yourself to blame, Herb. If you were a lousy cop, this pile would be a lot smaller."

Herb blinked at the case files, a career's worth, propped on the desk. Though the amount was substantial, it didn't seem big enough. He opened another Twinkie and eased it in, wishing it was a Denver Omelet.

"I always wanted to be a cop. Even as a kid. I blame Dragnet. Joe Friday was my hero. I used to talk like him all the time. Drove my parents crazy."

"You've got some Twinkie filling in your mustache, Mr. Friday."

Herb wiped at his face. "Maybe I should transfer to Property Crimes.

They never get death threats."

"You just pushed it over two inches."

Herb used his sleeve.

"What do you think, Jack?"

"Better, but now some of it is up your nose. Want to use my hand mirror?"

"I meant about the transfer."

Jack set aside the report she'd been reading. "Seriously?"

"I'm a fin away from retirement. These are supposed to be my golden years. I should be golfing and taking cruises."

"You hate golf. And the ocean."

"I also hate getting shot at."

Herb picked up a case file from a few years ago, gave it a token glance, and tossed it in the maybe pile. He could feel Jack staring at him, so he met her gaze.

"You think I'm crazy, don't you? You think after two weeks at Property Crimes I'll be going out of my mind with boredom."

Jack smiled, sadly.

"Actually, I think Property Crimes will be very lucky to get you."

Herb let her reply sink in. The more he thought it over, the more confident he felt. This was right.

"I'm going to tell Bernice."

"Good idea. But before you do, wipe the sugar out of your nose."

#

The Burketold Center was a dirty, crumbling building many years older than the senior citizens it catered to. Funded by tax dollars, the Center served as a game room/social area/singles mixer for the area's ten-plus nursing homes. Buses came several times a day, dropping off seniors for bingo, swing dancing, and craft classes.

The Center provided these services free of charge, the only condition being attendees had to be over sixty years old.

Herb walked through the automatic doors and took everything in.

To the left, four elderly men sat around a table as rickety as they were, noisily playing cards. In the pot, along with a pile of chips, were a set of dentures.

To the left, a solitary old woman twisted the knobs on a foosball table. She mumbled to herself, or perhaps to an imaginary opponent.

A TV blared in the corner, broadcasting the Food Network to three sleeping ladies. To the right, an ancient man with pants hiked up to his chest repeatedly kicked a Coke machine. Herb approached him.

"Did the machine take your money, sir?"

The old man squinted at Herb with yellow eyes.

"No, it did not take my money. But if you kick it in the right spot, it spits out free sodas. I've gotten six Mountain Dews so far today."

Herb left the guy to his larceny. In just a few short years, Herb would be turning sixty. Then he, too, would be able to join the fun for free. The thought didn't comfort him.

He located the front desk and found a cheerful-looking man holding down the fort. The man wore a loose fitting sweater with a stag's head stitched into the pattern, and his smile was so wide it looked to crack his face. Herb placed him in his early fifties.

"May I help you?"

"I'm looking for Bernice Benedict."

"Oh. And you are...?"

"Her husband, Herb."

Smiling Guy hesitated, then extended a hand.

"Pleased to meet you, Herb. Bernice has told me a lot about you. I'm Phil Grabowski."

Herb took the hand and found it plump and moist. He vaguely recalled Bernice mentioning the name Phil before.

"Hi, Phil. Great work you're doing here."

"Thanks. We try to do our part. It's a real heartbreaker reaching the autumn years and finding there's no one to share them with."

Phil chuckled, but it sounded painfully forced. Perhaps being around geriatrics all the time wrecked havoc on one's social skills.

"Is Bernice around?"

"She's calling bingo in room 1B, through that door and down the hall."

"Thanks." Herb nodded a good-bye and began to turn away.

"Bernice...she mentioned what happened last night. Terrible thing."

Herb's first reaction was annoyance. Bernice shouldn't have been relating police matters. But shame quickly overcame irritation.

Of course Bernice would mention it to her friends at work. As she should. What other outlet did she have?

Herb could feel himself flush. Bernice had worked at the Center for seven years, and he'd never visited once. This man, Phil, was obviously a close friend of hers, and he didn't know a thing about him.

Herb wondered how much harm he'd done to his marriage by putting his job first.

He also wondered if it was too late to make it up to her.

"Yeah, well, that won't be happening anymore."

Phil offered another face-splitting smile. "Really?"

It went against Herb's private nature to share his intentions with a stranger, but he thought it was a step in the right direction.

"I'm transferring to a different division." He almost bit his tongue. "I'm also reducing my hours."

"Why, that's wonderful. Bernice will be thrilled. She's...she's quite the trophy, you know."

"Nice to meet you, Phil."

Phil grinned wildly. Herb headed off in search of 1B, his wife's voice guiding him.

"G-15. That's G-15. You've got a G-15 on your card there, Mrs. Havensatch. Right under the G, dear. There it is."

Herb paused in the doorway, watching her. Love, pride, and responsibility all balled-up together to form a big lump in his throat. He rapped his knuckle on the frame and walked in.

"Bernice?"

"Herb?" His wife appeared surprised, but the anger from this morning had gone from her face. "What are you doing here? Is everything okay?"

"Look, honey, can we talk for a second?"

"I'm in the middle of bingo."

Herb felt a dozen pairs of eyes on him. He rubbed the back of his neck.

"I'm transferring to Property Crimes. And reducing my hours."

Bernice blinked.

"You're kidding."

"I'm not."

"When are you going to do this?"

"I already talked to Jack. Tomorrow morning, first thing."

Herb had expected a dozen different reactions form his wife, but crying wasn't one of them. She took several quick steps to him, and folded herself into his arms.

"Oh, Herb. I've wanted this for so long."

"So you're happy?"

"Yes."

"Bingo!"

A geriatric in the front row held her card above her head and cackled madly.

"I'll be with you in just a moment, Mrs. Steinmetz."

Herb stroked her hair. All of his indecision melted away. He'd made the right choice. Her friend Phil was right. Bernice was a real trophy.

Trophy. The word snagged in his mind. People won trophies in sports, but they also shot trophies. Like that ten point buck on Phil's sweater.

"Bernice—your friend Phil. Is he a hunt..."

The bullet caught Herb in the meaty part of his upper shoulder, spinning him around. Before hitting the floor, he glimpsed Phil, clutching a rifle in the doorway.

Screams filled the room, Bernice's among them. Herb tugged at his hip holster, freeing his Sig. His left arm went numb from his finger tips to his armpit, but he could feel the spreading warmth of gushing blood, and he knew the wound was bad.

"Drop the gun, Herb!"

Phil had the .22 pointed at Herb's head. Herb hadn't brought his gun around yet. Maybe, if he rolled to the side...

Too late. Bernice stepped in his line of fire.

"Phil! Stop it!"

"I'm doing it for you, Bernice! He's no good for you!"

Herb chanced a look at his shoulder wound. Worse than he thought. If he didn't stop the bleeding soon, he wouldn't make it.

"I love him, Phil."

"Love him? He's never home, and when he is, you said it's just the same, boring routine!"

"I like the same, boring routine. And I like my husband. Stop acting crazy and put down the gun."

Bernice took a step towards him, her hands up in supplication.

"Bernice..." Herb's voice radiated strength. "He won't shoot you. Walk out and call the police."

"Shut up!"

Bernice turned and looked at Herb. He nodded at his wife, willing her to move.

"I'll kill her! I'll kill both of you!"

Bernice stepped to the side. Phil's gun followed her.

Herb's gun followed Phil.

Detective First Class Herb Benedict fired four shots, three to the chest and one to the head.

All of them hit home.

Phil dropped, hard. Bernice rushed to her husband.

"Herb! Herb, I'm so sorry!"

Herb's eyes fluttered twice, and then closed.

"Bingo!" Mrs. Steinmetz yelled.

#

The food redefined horrible, but Herb ate everything. Even the steamed squash. Assuming it was steamed squash.

"I can't wait to get out of here and eat some real food."

Bernice stroked his arm, below the IV.

"We need to talk, Herb."

Herb didn't like the tone of her voice. She sounded so sad. He shook his head, trying to clear the codeine cloud, trying to concentrate.

"Bernice, honey, I'll make it up to you. I know I haven't been there. I know I've been spending too much time at work. Give me a chance, and I'll change."

Bernice smiled.

"That's what I want to talk to you about." Bernice took a deep breath. "I don't want you to transfer to Property Crimes."

Herb did a damn good impression of confused.

"But I thought..."

"When you told me you wanted to transfer, it was a dream come true for me. But then, with Phil..."

Herb reached out with his good hand, held hers.

"You're a good cop, Herb Benedict. It would be selfish of me to keep you from that."

"That's okay. You're allowed to be selfish."

Bernice's eyes glassed over.

"You know, every day when you go to work, I worry about you. But seeing you in action..."

Herb smiled.

"Was I dashing?"

"You were magnificent. You saved more than me and you. Phil had...problems."

"No kidding."

After his death, a search of Phil Grabowski's apartment uncovered a large cache of weapons and eighteen notebooks full of handwritten, paranoid ranting. Herb was only one name on a long list of targets.

"I can't deprive you of your job, Herb. And I can't deprive Chicago of you. You've got six years left to do good for this city. I want you to use those years well."

Herb pulled Bernice close and held her tight, despite the twenty-odd stitches in his shoulder.

"You know, the doctor says I'll be out of here by next Friday."

Bernice touched his cheek.

"Just in time for pot roast."

"Pot roast is my favorite, you know."

"I think you've mentioned that before."

"But this Friday, why don't we go out to eat instead? Someplace nice, romantic."

Bernice's eyes lit up. She looked like a teenager again.

"I'd like that."

"And then afterwards, maybe some nookie."

"That sounds perfect, but you know what?"

"What?"

Bernice grinned, and it was positively wicked.

"We don't have to wait until Friday for that."

She closed the door to the room and turned out the light.

Last Request

Phin has been in four of the six Jack Daniels books so far, Whiskey Sour, Rusty Nail, Fuzzy Nave, and Cherry Bomb. In those books, Jack tempers some of Phin's darker moments. Not so in this story. This is also my favorite first line of anything I've written.

I picked up a transsexual hooker named Thor, all six feet of her, at the off ramp to Eau Claire, Wisconsin, as I was driving up north to kill a man.

She had on thigh-high black vinyl boots, red fishnet stockings, a pink mini skirt, a neon green spandex tube top, and a huge blonde wig that reminded me of an octopus. I could have spotted her from clear across the county.

"You looking for action?" she said after introducing herself.

"I'm always looking for action."

"Tonight's your lucky night, handsome. I'm getting out of this biz. You give me a ride, you can have whatever you want for free."

I opened the door, rolled up the window, and got back on the road.

Thor spent five miles trying to pay for her ride, but the painkillers had rendered me numb and useless in that area, and eventually she gave up and reclined her seat back, settling instead for conversation.

"So where are you headed?" she asked. She sounded like she'd been sucking helium. Hormone therapy, I guessed. I couldn't tell if her breasts were real under the tube top, but her pink micro mini revealed legs that were nice no matter which sex she was.

"Rice Lake."

I yawned, and shifted in my seat. It was past one in the morning, but the oppressive July heat stuck around even when the sun didn't. I had the air conditioning in the Ford Ranger cranked up, but it didn't help much.

"Why are you going to Rice Lake?" she asked.

I searched around for the drink holder, picked up the coffee I'd bought back in the Dells, and forced down the remaining cold dregs, sucking every last molecule of caffeine from the grit that caught in my teeth.

"Business."

She touched my arm, hairless like the rest of me.

"You don't look like a businessman."

The road stretched out ahead of us, an endless black snake. Mile after mile of nothing to look at. I should have gotten a vehicle with a manual transmission, given my hand something to do.

"My briefcase and power ties are in the back seat."

Thor didn't bother to look. Which was a good thing.

"What sort of business are you in?"

I considered it. "Customer relations."

"From Chicago," Thor said.

She noticed the plates before climbing in. Observant girl. I wondered, obliquely, how far she'd take this line of questioning.

"Don't act much like a businessman, either."

"How do businessmen act?" I said.

"They're all after one thing."

"And what's that?"

"Me."

She tried to purr, and wound up sounding like Mickey Mouse. Personally, I didn't find her attractive. I had no idea if she was pre-op, post-op, or a work in progress, but Thor and I weren't going to happen, ever.

I didn't tell her this. I might be a killer, but I'm not mean.

"Where are you headed?" I asked.

She sighed, scratching her neck, posture changing from demure seductress to one of the guys.

"Anywhere. Nowhere. I don't have a clue. This was a spur of the moment thing. One of my girlfriends just called, said my former pimp was coming after me."

"How former?"

"I left him yesterday. He was a selfish bastard."

She was quiet for a while. I fumbled to crank the air higher, forgetting where the knob was. It was already up all the way. I glanced over at Thor, watched her shoulders quiver in time with her sobs.

"You love him," I said.

She sniffled, lifted up her chin.

"He didn't care about me. He just cared that I took his shit."

This got my attention.

"You holding?" I asked. Codeine didn't do as good a job as coke or heroin.

"No. Never so much as smoked a joint, if you can believe it."

I would have raised an eyebrow, but they hadn't grown back yet. Maybe I'd be dead before they did.

"It's true, handsome. Every perverted little thing I've ever done I've done stone cold sober. Lots of men think girls like me are all messed up in the head. I'm not. I have zero identity issues, and my self esteem is fine, thank you."

"I've never met a hooker with any self esteem," I said.

"And I've never met a car thief on chemotherapy."

I glanced at her again. Waited for the explanation.

"You couldn't find the climate control," Thor said. "And you're so stoned on something you never bothered to adjust the seat or the mirrors. Vicodin?"

I nodded, yawned.

"You okay to drive?"

"I managed to pick you up without running you over."

Thor clicked open a silver-sequined clutch purse and produced a compact. She fussed with her make-up as she spoke, dabbing at her tears with a foundation sponge.

"So why did you pick me up?" she asked. "You're not the type who's into transgender."

"You're smart. Figure it out."

She studied me, staring for almost a full minute. I shifted in my seat. Being scrutinized was a lot of work.

"You stole the car in Chicago, so you've been on the road for about six hours. You're zonked out on painkillers, probably sick from chemotherapy, but you're still driving at two in the morning. I'd say you just robbed a bank, but you don't seem jumpy or paranoid like you're running from something. That means you're running to something. How am I doing so far?"

"If I had any gold stars, you'd get one."

She stared a bit longer, then asked.

"What's your name?"

"Phineas Troutt. People call me Phin."

"Sort of a strange name."

"This from a girl named Thor."

"My father loved comic books. Wanted a tough, macho, manly son, thought the name would make me strong."

I glanced at her. "It did."

Thor smiled. A real smile, not a hooker smile.

"Are you going to Rice Lake to commit some sort of crime, Phin?"

"That isn't the question. The question is why I picked you up."

"Fair enough. If I still believed in knights in shining armor, I'd say you picked me up because you felt bad for me and wanted to help. But I think your reason was purely selfish."

"And that reason is?"

"You were falling asleep behind the wheel, and needed something to keep you awake."

I smiled, and it morphed into a yawn.

"That's a damn good guess."

"But is it true?"

"I'm definitely enjoying the company."

She kept watching me, but it was more comfortable this time.

"So who are you going to kill in Rice Lake, Phin?"

I stayed quiet.

"No whore ever gets into a car without checking the back seat," Thor said. "A forty dollar trick can turn into a gang rape freebie, a girl's not careful."

I wondered what she meant, then remembered what was lying on the back seat. What I hadn't bothered to put away. "You saw the gun."

"People normally keep those things hidden. You should try to be inconspicuous."

"I'm not big on inconspicuous."

"That box of baby wipes. Are you a proud papa, or are they for something else?"

"Sometimes things get messy." Which was an understatement. "So if you saw the gun, why did you get in?"

Thor laughed, throaty and seductive. She could shrug the whore act on and off like it was a pair of shoes.

"The streets are dangerous, Phin. A working girl has to carry more protection than condoms."

She reached into the top of her knee high black vinyl boot, showed me the butt of a revolver.

"Mine's bigger," I said.

"Mine's closer."

I nodded. The road stretched onward, no end in sight.

"So how much do you charge, for your services?" Thor asked.

"Depends."

"On what?"

"The job. How much I need the money."

"Does it matter who the person is?"

"No."

"Don't you think that's cold?"

"Everyone has to die sometime," I said. "Some of us sooner than others."

Another stretch of silence. Another stretch of road.

"I've got eight hundred bucks," Thor said. "Is that enough?"

"For your pimp. The selfish bastard."

"He is. I earned this money. Earned every cent. But in this area, every whore, from the trailer girls to the high class escorts, has to pay Jordan a cut."

"And you didn't pay."

"He knows how important my transformation is. One more operation, and I'm all woman. Holding out was the only way I could make it."

"I thought you loved him."

"Just like he says, love and business are two separate things."

Her breathing sped up. Over the hum of the engine, I thought I heard her heart beating. Or maybe it was mine.

"Why don't you kill him yourself, with your little boot revolver." I said.

"Jordan has the cops in his pocket. They'd catch me."

"Unless you had an alibi when it happened."

Thor nodded. "Exactly. You drop me off at a diner. I spend three hours with a cup of coffee. We both get something we need."

I considered it. Eight hundred was twice as much as I was making on this job. Years ago, if someone told me that one day I'd drive twelve hours both ways to kill a man for a lousy four hundred bucks, I would have laughed it off.

Things change.

The pinch in my side, growing bit by bit as the minutes passed, would eventually blossom into a raw explosion of pain. I was down to my last three Vicodin, and only had twenty-eight cents left to my name. I needed more pills, along with a bottle of tequila and a few grams of coke.

Codeine for the physical. Cocaine and booze for the mental. Dying isn't easy.

"So what do you say?" Thor asked.

"What kind of man is Jordan?"

"You said it doesn't matter. Does it?"

"No."

I waited. The car ate more road. The gas gage hovered over the E.

"He's a jerk. A charming jerk, but one just the same. I thought I loved him, once. Maybe I did. Or maybe I just loved to have a good looking man pay attention to me, make me feel special."

"Murder will pretty much ruin any chance of you two getting back together."

"I'll try to carry on," she said, reapplying her lipstick.

Gas station, next exit. I made up my mind. A starving dog doesn't question why his belly is empty. His only thought is filling it.

"I'll do it," I said.

"Really?"

"Yes."

Thor smiled big, then gave me a hug.

"Thanks, Phin. You're my knight in shining armor after all."

"I'll need the money up front," I said. "You got it on you?"

"Yeah. Take this exit. There's a Denny's. You can drop me off there."

I took the exit.

We pulled into the parking lot. It was close to empty, but I killed the lights and rolled behind the restaurant near the Dumpsters, so no one would see us together. When I hit the breaks, Thor stayed where she was.

"Second thoughts?" I asked.

"How do I know you won't take my money and run?"

"All I have left is my word," I said.

She considered it, then fished a roll of bills from her purse. When she was counting, I put my hand on her leg.

Thor smiled at me.

"I didn't think you were into me," she said. "Finish the job, and then I'll throw in a little bonus for you."

"I just need to finish my other job first," I told her.

"I understand."

My hand moved down her knee, found the revolver, and tugged it out.

With the windows closed I doubt anyone heard the gunshots, even though they were loud enough to make my ears ring.

I took the cash, hit the button to recline Thor's seat until she was out of sight, and rolled down her window. I hated to let the heat in, but the glass was conspicuously spattered with her blood, and I didn't need to make any more mistakes. Then I pulled out of the parking lot and got back on the highway, heading south.

Jordan had told me, over the phone, that I'd find Thor working the Eau Claire off ramp. He said to dump the body somewhere up the road, then meet him in the morning. The few hours wait were so he could establish an alibi.

A few miles up the road I pulled over, yanked Thor out of the car, and got behind the wheel again before another car passed. Then I grabbed the box of baby wipes in the back seat. As I drove I cleaned up my hands, then the passenger side of the vehicle. There wasn't too much of a mess. Small gun, small holes. I was lucky Thor got in the car at all, after spying the gun I'd sloppily left in plain sight. Stupid move on my part.

Hers, too.

When I reached Eau Claire I headed to where I thought Jordan would be. He'd be angry to see me so soon, but that wouldn't last very long. Just until I shot him in the head.

I had nothing against Jordan. I had nothing against Thor, either. But a deal is a deal, and as I told the lady, all I had left was my word.

The Necro File

A word of warning. If this isn't the most offensive thing I've ever written, it comes close. I began this as an experiment, to try and write an anti-story. Stories normally have rules that need to be followed in order for them to work. I kept all of these rules in mind while writing this, and threw each of them out the window. It was a lot of fun, and other people feel the same way. The brave folks at Dark Arts books published it in their anthology Like A Chinese Tattoo, edited by Bill Breedlove. Readers beware—this one doesn't pull any punches. It's Harry McGlade Uncensored.

Chapter 1

"It's my husband, Mr. McGlade. He thinks he can raise the dead."

The woman sitting in front of my desk was named Norma Cauldridge. She had the figure of a Barlett pear and so many freckles that she was more beige than Caucasian. She also came equipped with a severe overbite, a lazy eye, and a mole on her cheek. Not a Cindy Crawford type of mole, either. This one looked like she glued the end of a hotdog to her face. A hairy hotdog.

Plus, she smelled like sweaty feet.

Any man married to her would certainly have to raise the dead every time she wanted sex. But I didn't become a private investigator to meet femme fatales. Well, actually I did. But mostly I did it for the money. And hers was green just like anyone else's.

I took a can of Lysol aerosol deodorizer from my desk and gave the air a spritz. Now it smelled like sweaty feet and pine trees. With a hint of lavender.

"I get four hundred a day, plus expenses," I told her.

I put away the air freshener and tried to sneak a look behind her large round Charlie Brownish head. When she walked into my office a minute ago, I'd been watching the National Cheerleading Finals on cable. The TV was still on, but I had muted the sound to be polite.

"I didn't tell you what I want you to do yet."

She was a whiner too. Nasally and high-pitched. It's like God took a dare to make the most unattractive woman possible.

"You want me to take pictures of him acting crazy, so you can use them in the divorce."

On television a group of nubile young twenty-somethings did synchronized cartwheels and landed in splits. I love cable.

"How did you know?" Norma asked.

I glanced at Norma. The only splits she ever did were banana.

"It's my job to know, ma'am. I'll need your address, his place of work, and the first three days' pay in advance."

Norma's face pinched.

"I still love him, Mr. McGlade. But he's not the same man I married. He's...obsessed."

Her shoulders slumped, and the tears came. I nudged over the box of Kleenex I kept on the desk for when I surfed certain internet sites.

"It's not your fault, Mrs. Drawbridge."

"Cauldridge."

"A man is talking, sweetie. Don't interrupt."

"Sorry."

"The fact is, Nora, some men aren't meant to marry. They feel trapped, tied down, so they seek out different venues."

She sniffled. "Necromancy?"

"I've seen all sorts of perversions in my business. One day he's a good husband. The next day, he's a card-carrying necrosexual. Happens all the time."

More tears. I made a mental note to look up "necromancy" in the dictionary. Then I made another mental note to buy a dictionary. Then I made a third mental note to buy a pencil, because I always forgot my mental notes. Then I watched the cheerleaders do high kicks.

When Norma finally calmed down, she asked, "Do you take Visa?"

I nodded, wondering if I could buy used cheerleading floormats on eBay. Preferably ones with stains.

Chapter 2

Ebay didn't have any.

Instead I bid on a set of used pom-pons and a coach's whistle. I also bid on some old Doobie Brothers records. That led to placing a bid on a record player, since mine was busted. Then I bid on a carton of copier toner, because it was so cheap, and then I had to bid on a copier because I didn't have one. But after thinking about it a bit, I realized I didn't really need a copier, and those Doobie Brothers albums were probably available on CD for less than the cost of a record player.

I tried to cancel my bids, but those eBay jerks wouldn't let me. The jerks.

I buried my anger in online pornography. Three minutes later, I headed out the door, slightly winded and ready to get some work done.

Chapter 3

This chapter is even shorter than the last one.

Chapter 4

George Drawbridge worked as a teller for Oak Tree Bank. At a branch office. It was only three o'clock, and his wife told me he normally stayed until five, so I had plenty of time to grab a few beers first. Chicago is famous for its stuffed crust pizza, and I indulged in a small pie at a nearby joint and entertained myself by asking everyone who worked there if they made a lot of dough.

An hour later, after they asked me to leave, I sat on the sidewalk across the street from the bank, hiding in plain sight by pretending I was homeless. This involved untucking my shirt and pockets, messing up my hair, and holding up a sign that said *"I'm homeless"* written on the back of the pizza box.

Other possibilities had been, *"Will do your taxes for food"* and *"I'm just plain lazy"* and my favorite *"this is a piece of cardboard."* But I went with brevity because I still didn't have a pencil and had to write it in sauce.

I sat there for a little over and hour before George Drawbridge appeared.

He looked like the picture his wife gave me, which wasn't a surprise because it was a picture of him. Balding, thin, pinkish complexion, with a nose so big it probably caused back problems. After exiting the bank he immediately went right, moving like he was in a huge hurry. I almost lost him, because it took over a minute to pick up the eighty-nine cents people had thrown onto the sidewalk next to me. But I managed to catch up just as he boarded a northbound bus to Wrigleyville.

Unfortunately, the only seat left on the bus was next to George. So that's where I parked my butt, because I sure as hell wasn't going to stand if I didn't have to.

I gave him a small nod as I sat down.

"I'm not following you," I told him.

George didn't answer. He didn't even look at me. His eyes were distant, out there. And up close I noticed his rosy skin tone wasn't natural—he was sunburned. Only on the left side of his face too, like Richard Dreyfuss in that Spielberg movie about aliens. The one where he got sunburned on only the left side of his face. I think it was *Star Wars*.

Unlike his wife, George didn't smell like sweaty feet. He smelled more like ham. Honey baked ham. So much so that I wondered if he had any ham on him. I've been known to stuff my pockets with ham whenever I visited an all-you-can-eat buffet. After all, ham is pricey.

I restrained myself from asking if he indeed had any pocket ham, but couldn't help humming the Elton John song *"Rocketman"* and changing the lyrics in my head.

"Pocket ham... And I think I'm gonna eat a long, long time..."

I didn't know the rest of the song, so I kept think-singing that line over and over. After a few stops George stood up and left the bus. I followed him, keeping my distance so I didn't make him nervous. But after walking for a block I realized I could stand on the guy's shoulders and piss on his head and he still wouldn't notice me. George Drawbridge was seriously preoccupied.

We went into an Ace Hardware Store, and George bought twenty feet of nylon clothesline He also bought something called a magnetron. I knew that there was something I needed to buy, but I couldn't remember what it was, and I hadn't written it down because I needed to buy a pencil. So I got one of those super large cans of mega energy drink. It contained three times the recommended daily allowance of taurine, whatever the hell taurine was.

After the hardware store it was back to the bus stop. We were the only two people there. George didn't pay any attention to me, but I was worried all of this close contact might get him a little suspicious. So I made sure I stood behind him, where he couldn't see me. Then I popped open my mega can and took a sip.

The flavor on the can said "Super Berry Mix." The berries must have been mixed with battery acid and diarrhea juice, but with a slightly worse taste. It burned my nose drinking it, to the point where I may have lost some nostril hair. Plus it was a shade of blue only found in nature as part of neon beer signs. I could barely choke down the last forty-six ounces.

The bus came. Again, the only seat available was next to George. I took it, and pulled my shirt up over my mouth and nose to disguise myself.

"Goddamn germs on public transportation," I said, loud enough for most of the bus to hear. This provided a clever reason for my conspicuous face-hiding behavior. I said it seven more times, just to be sure.

We took the bus to Jefferson Park, a northwest side neighborhood named after that famous politico, Thomas Park. George exited on Foster. I followed, tailing him up Pulaski and into the Montrose Cemetery, my mind racing like a race car on a race track, driven by a race car driver, named Race.

I never liked cemeteries. Not because I'm afraid of ghosts, even though when I was a child all the kids used to tease me because they thought I was. They would dress up like ghosts and try to scare me by visiting my house at night and threatening to hang us all because my family didn't go to church. They usually left after burning a cross on our lawn. Damn ghosts.

No, I hated graveyards for much more realistic reasons. When a person died they shouldn't be kept around, like leftovers. People had a freshness date. Death meant *discard*, not preserve in a box. What ghoul thought that one up? Fifty thousand years ago, did some caveman plant Grandma in the ground hoping to grow a Grandma Tree? What fruit did *that* bear? Saggy wrinkly breasts that hung to the ground and smelled like Ben Gay and pee-pee? And what's with neckties? Why are men forced to wear a strip of cloth around their necks good for absolutely nothing except getting caught in things like doors and soup?

As my computer-like mind pondered these imponderables, George cleverly gave me the slip by walking someplace I could no longer see him. That left me with three options.

1. Wait at the entrance for him to come out.

2. Search for him.

3. Drain the lizard. Those eighty ounces of Super Berry Taurine had expanded my bladder to the size of a morbidly obese child, named Race.

I opted for number 3, and chose *Mary Agnes Morrison, Loving Wife and Mother*, to sprinkle. Maybe the taurine would liven up her eternity.

I soaked her pretty good, and had enough left over for the rest of the Morrison family, including the *Loving Husband and Father*, the *Beloved Uncle*, and the *Slutty Skank Daughter*.

I made that last tombstone up, but it would sure be cool if it was real, wouldn't it? And wouldn't it be cool if someone made a flying car? One that gave you head while you drove? I'd buy one.

I shook twice, corralled the one-eyed stallion, and began to look for George. An autumn breeze cooled the sweat on my face, neck, ears, hair, armpits, back, legs, and hands, which made me aware that I was sweating. I put a hand to my heart and discovered it was beating faster than Joe Pesci in a Scorsese flick. Because he beats people in those flicks. Beats them fast.

Why was I so edgy? Had my subconscious tapped into some sort of collective, primal fear? Did my distant ancestors, with their reptile brains and their bronze weapons made of stone, leave some sort of genetic marker in my DNA that made me sensitive to lurking danger?

I did a 360, looking for pointy-headed ghosts with gas cans. All I saw were tombstones, stretching on for as far as I could see. Hundreds. Thousands. Maybe even billions.

"Easy, McGlade. Nothing to be afraid of. It's not like you desecrated their graves or anything."

Noise, to my left. I had my Magnum in my hand so fast that it probably looked like it magically appeared there to anyone watching, even though I didn't think anyone was watching.

Anyone *alive.*

My eyes drifted up an old, scary-looking tree, which had branches that looked like scary branch-shaped fingers, but with six fingers instead of the usual five, which made it even scarier. The sun was going down behind the tree, silhouetting some sort of nest-shaped mass on an extended limb that I guessed was a nest.

"Chirp," went the nest.

My first shot blew the nest in half, and two more severed the branch from the tree.

"Dammit, McGlade. Stay cool. You just assassinated a bird."

Which saddened me greatly. Magnum rounds were a buck-fifty each. Plus, I didn't have any extras on me. I needed to stay cool.

"Chirp," went the nest.

BLAM! BLAM!

By heroic effort I didn't shoot the nest a sixth time, instead walking briskly in the opposite direction. I was in a state that might be called "hyper-awareness," which was a lot like being the lone antelope at the watering hole. I could feel the stares of flying insects, and hear the grass growing. It was freaking me out a little bit, so I began to run, tripping over something on the ground, skidding face-first against a tombstone. A damp tombstone.

Mary Agnes Morrison.

I scurried away, palms and knees wet, and saw the bright red object that caused me to fall.

The empty can of Super Berry Mix energy drink.

So my paranoia wasn't really paranoia after all. It was just an unhealthy amount of caffeine in my veins. Which would have been kind of funny if I wasn't soaked with my own piss. Along with the taurine, the drink apparently contained a full day's supply of irony.

I stood up and shook out my pants legs.

"Get a grip, McGlade. And stop talking to yourself. You always know what you're going to say anyway."

I took three or ten deep breaths, holstered my weapon, and then set out looking for George.

I had no idea that in just two minutes I was going to die.

Chapter 5

I didn't actually die. I'm lying to make the story more exciting, because this part is sort of slow.

It starts to pick up in Chapter 8. Trust me, it's worth the wait. There's sodomy.

Chapter 6

It was a fruitless search, but that didn't matter—I wasn't looking for fruit. After a few minutes, I'd found him. He'd given me the slip by cleverly disguising himself as a group of three bawling women. Closer inspection, and some grab ass, revealed they really were women after all. I did my "pretend to be blind and deaf" act and stumbled away before any of them called the police or their lawyers.

Luckily, I caught sight of an undisguised George heading into the mausoleum. I never liked mausoleums. Burying the dead was bad enough. Putting them in the walls was just begging for mice to move in. And not the kind of mice who wear red pants and open up amusement parks. I'm talking about dirty, vicious, baby-face-eating mice, the size of rats.

Actually, I'm talking about rats.

Speaking of non-sequiturs, I really needed to take another leak. The mausoleum was decent-sized, with a few hundred vaults stacked four high. Well lit, temperature controlled, silk plants next to marble benches every twenty feet. It was the kind of place that would have a bathroom, I thought, while pissing on one of the silk plants. The pot it was in wasn't any realer than the plant, because all of my piss leaked out the bottom. I stepped over the puddle and commenced the search.

One of the techniques they teach you in private eye school is how to conduct a search, I bet. I have no idea, because I didn't go to private eye school. I wasn't even sure that private eye school actually existed. But it did in my fantasies. All the teachers were naked women, and wrong answers were punished with spankings. And the water fountains were actually beer fountains. If they had a school like that, I'd go for sure.

George wasn't down the first aisle. He wasn't down the second aisle either. Or the first aisle, which I checked again because I got confused.

"You do this?"

I spun around, wondering who spoke. It was some little old caretaker guy, clutching a mop. He pointed at the puddle on the floor.

"It was that other guy," I said, thinking fast. "You see him anywhere?"

"I only seen you, buddy. Did you go to the bathroom on my floor? There's a bathroom right there behind you. What kind of man does a thing like this?"

"That's what happens when you don't go to college."

"You piss on the floor?"

"You get a job cleaning up piss on the floor."

I left the guy to his menial labor and peeked down the second aisle again. Still no George. That led me down the third aisle, and I caught a glimpse of George crawling into a hole in the wall.

Closer inspection revealed it wasn't a hole. It was a vault. He'd crawled into someone's open tomb. I didn't even want to think why he'd do that, but my mind thought of it anyway, and then started thinking of it in enough detail that made me nauseous, yet oddly disgusted. Maybe a necromancer was someone who got his freak on with corpses. It was certainly a cheap date—only a few bucks for Lysol and Vaseline—and unless your game was really weak you'd pretty much always score. Still, I liked my women partially awake, and aware enough to be able to fight me off and tell me no. Because *no* means try harder.

I crouched down, peering into the blackness, and saw nothing but the aforementioned blackness. I fished out my keys, which had a mini flashlight attached to the ring, and illuminated the situation.

This wasn't a grave after all. In the hole was a slide, like you'd find in a children's playground, if the playground was in a mausoleum, and the children were all dead. Probably wouldn't be a lot of kids begging to go to a park like that. Not the dead ones, anyway.

I gritted my teeth. There was only one way to find out where this slide went.

"Hey, old caretaker guy!" I yelled. "Where does this slide go?"

"Go to hell!"

"I told you, it wasn't me. I had asparagus on my pizza. Does it smell like asparagus?"

"Go to hell!"

I rubbed my chin. Maybe old caretaker guy was trying to tell me that this slide went straight to hell. I didn't really believe him. First of all, I didn't see any flames, and there wasn't any smoke or brimstone or screams of the damned. Second, hell doesn't really exist. It's a fairy tale taught by parents to make their kids behave. Like Santa Claus. And the death penalty.

Still, going down a pitch black slide in a mausoleum wasn't on my list of things to do before I died. My list was mostly centered around Angelina Jolie.

"This *does* smell like asparagus, you bastard!"

A glanced over my shoulder. Old caretaker guy was hobbling toward me, his drippy asparagus mop raised back like a baseball bat—a stinky, wet baseball bat that you wouldn't want to use in a baseball game, because you wouldn't get any hits, and because it was soaked with urine and stinked.

I decided, then and there, I wasn't going to play ball with old caretaker guy. Which left me no choice. I took a deep breath and dove face-first down the slide.

Chapter 7

When I was ten years old, my strange uncle who lived in the country took me into his barn and showed me a strange game called *milk the cow*. The game involved a strong grip, and used a combination of squeezing and stroking until the milk came. I remember it was weird, and hurt my arm, but kind of fun nonetheless.

Afterward, we fed the cow some hay and used the fresh milk to make pancakes. When we finished breakfast, we watched a little television. It was a portable, with a tiny ten-inch screen.

Many years later, my strange uncle got arrested, for tax evasion. So I have no idea why I'm bringing any of this up.

The slide was a straight-shot down, no twists or curve. The dive jostled my grip and my key light winked out, shrouding me in darkness, like a shroud. I had no idea how fast I was going or how far I traveled. Time lost all meaning, but time really didn't matter much anyway since I'd bought a TiVo. Minutes blurred into weeks, which blurred into seconds, which blurred into more seconds. When I finally reached the bottom, I tucked and rolled and athletically sprang to my butt, one hand somewhere near my holster, the other cupped around my boys to protect them, not to fondle them, even though that's what it might have looked like.

I listened, my highly attuned sense of hearing sensing a whimpering sound very near, which I will die before admitting came from me, even though it did.

I'd landed on my keys. Hard.

When I stood, they remained stuck in me, hanging from my inner left cheek like I'd been stabbed by some ass-stabbing key maniac. I bit my lower lip, reached back, and tugged them out, which made the whimpering sound get louder. It hurt so bad I didn't even find it amusing that I now had a second hole in my ass, and perhaps could even perform carnival tricks, like pooping the letter X. That's a carnival I'd pay extra to see.

I found the key light and flashed the beam around, reorienting my orientation. I was in some sort of secret lower level beneath the mausoleum. Dirt walls, with wooden beams holding up the ceiling, coal mine style. To my left, a large wooden crate with the cryptic words TAKE ONE painted on the side. I refused. Why did I need a large wooden crate?

Noise, from behind. I spun around, reaching for my gun, and a dark shape tumbled off the slide, ramming into me and causing my keys to go flying, blanketing me in a blanket of darkness.

The ensuing struggle was viscous and deadly, but my years of mastering Drunken Jeet Kune Do Fu from watching old Chinese karate movies paid off. Just as I was about to deliver the Mad Crazy Hamster Fist killing blow, my attacker got some sort of weapon between us and smacked me in the face. The blow staggered me, and I reached up and felt the extensive damage, my whole head bathed in warm, sticky liquid that smelled a lot like asparagus.

Then a light blinded me. A real flashlight, not the dinky one I had on my keys. I squinted against the glare, and saw him. Old caretaker guy. A light in one hand. His mop in the other.

I spat, then spat again. My mouth had been open when he hit me.

"I'm a private detective. My name is McGlade. I'm on a case."

"Does your case involve pissing on my floor?"

I spat again. I could taste the asparagus. And the piss. It tasted like I always guessed piss would taste like. Pissy.

"Listen, buddy, you're violating federal marshal law by interfering with my investigation. Climb back up the slide and go call 911. Tell them there's a 10-69 in progress, with, uh, malice aforethought and misdemeanor prejudicial something, rampart."

My knowledge of cop lingo didn't galvanize him into action.

"Climb up the slide? How?"

"Hands and knees, old man."

"I'll get all dirty."

"You're a janitor."

"I'm a caretaker."

"You clean up in a cemetery. Dirt shouldn't bother you."

The flashlight moved off of my face and swept the area.

"What is this place? Some sort of secret lower level under the mausoleum?"

I spat again. "No duh."

"Look, there's a crate."

Old caretaker guy waddled over to the wooden TAKE ONE box, opened the top, and pulled out a brown robe.

"I guess we're supposed to take the robes."

"Obviously."

I walked over, grabbing a robe for myself. It was made out of felt, and had a large hood. A monk's robe. Or rather, a store-bought Halloween monk's costume.

Old caretaker guy put his on, and as he was tugging it over his head I gave him a Crazy Hamster Elbow to the chin. He went down, hopefully in need of some facial reconstructive surgery. I scooped up his flashlight, located my keys, and limped down the tunnel.

I followed the path a few dozen yards into the darkness, ducking overhead beams when they appeared overhead, keeping an eye peeled for rats, and giant spiders, and that guy I was supposed to be following, I think his name was Fred or George or something common and only one syllable. Maybe Tom. Yeah, Tom.

No, it was Fred.

The air down here was cool and heavy and smelled like asparagus piss, but for the most part it was clean. That meant ventilation, either in the form of an exit, or an air osmosis recirculator, and I'm pretty sure that osmosis thing didn't exist because I just made it up.

The tunnel ended at a large metal door, the kind with a slot at eye-level that opened up so some moron could ask you for a password. Which is exactly what happened. The slot opened, and a pair of eyes stared out at me, and whoever belonged to those eyes asked for a password.

"Tom sent me," I said.

"That's not the password."

"Tom didn't say there was a password."

"Tom who?"

"Tom," I improvised, "from Accounting."

"How is Tom?"

"Good. Just got over a cold, still kind of congested."

"It's great you know Tom, but I'm not supposed to let you in without a password."

I was tempted to give him a Three Stooges eye poke through the slot.

"Look," I reasoned, "why else would I be down here?"

"I have no idea. Maybe you got lost."

"I'm wearing the robe." I did a little sashay to emphasize the fact.

"Maybe you're a cop."

"I'm not a cop."

"How do I know that?"

"Because I don't have a badge. You want to frisk me to check?"

"No. You smell like pee-pee."

I set my jaw. "Doesn't anyone ever forget the password?"

The eyes shrugged. "Sure. Happens all the time."

"So what happens then?"

"I ask them for the back-up password."

I drew my Magnum, jammed it in the slot.

"Is the back-up password *open the fucking door or I'll blow your head off?*"

"Yep that's the password."

He opened the door. I considered smacking password boy in the head, and it seemed like a good idea, so I gave him a little love tap with the butt of my pistol. When he fell over, I gave him another little love tap in the stomach, with my foot. This made my ass hurt even more, so I kicked him again, which hurt even more, so I kicked him again for causing me pain, and again, and again until the pain got so bad I had to stop, but I didn't, I kicked him once more.

Then I wandered through a short hallway and into a large open area, roughly the size of a woman's basketball court, which is the same size as a men's basketball court, but a woman's court has bouncing boobs. I noticed little details like that. Unfortunately, this room didn't have bouncing boobs. It had a dozen-plus boneheads in robes, all carrying flashlights, standing around and chanting something monkish.

I wormed my way into the group and considered the camera in my pocket. Mrs. Drawbridge had hired me to take pictures of her husband acting nutty. This qualified, but it was too dark to make out any details, and a flash might cause attention. Plus, these jamokes all had their hoods on, making positive ID pretty impossible.

I scanned the room, seeing if I could find Tom. I spotted him through my clever detective technique of looking around, and noticed his bag from the hardware store, still clenched in his hand. Maybe I could get up close, shove the camera in his face, get a quick snapshot, then run away.

"Attention, everyone!"

The chanting stopped. One of the wannabe monks had his hands up over his head, his knuckles brushing the dirt ceiling. Everyone stared at him.

"Let us form the sacred pentagon, and pray to Anubis, god of the dead, to bless the ceremony this evening. All hail, Anubis!"

"All hail, Anubis!" the monks chanted in reply.

Then we all arranged ourselves in a five-sided square around something in the center of the room. As I probably should have guessed—but didn't because I was too busy rubbing my painful throbbing ass—in the center of the room was a coffin.

The head monk shouted, "Who shall be the first to partake in the carnal pleasures of beyond the grave?"

I looked around, wondering what idiot would be stupid enough to bone a corpse, then found myself shoved into the center of the circle.

"My friend will go!"

I spun around, aiming the flashlight. It was old caretaker guy, a big grin creasing his face.

"This first has been chosen!" head monk bellowed. Two other monks— big ones—grabbed my arms and escorted me to the coffin.

"Guys, I'm new here. I'd sort of prefer to wait until next time before violating any dead people."

I tried to pull away, but these monks had supernatural strength. The weight of the situation began to weigh on me. Sex with a cadaver wasn't on the list of things I wanted to do before I died, unless the cadaver was Angelina Jolie.

Then I stopped struggling, because I realized this had to be some kind of joke. Like a hazing prank, and when the coffin opened a stripper would pop out and blow me. That made a lot more sense than a society of necrophiliacs meeting secretly under one of Chicago's largest cemeteries. Right?

I smiled, hoping the stripper had big tits, not even protesting when I was depantsed by one of the hulky monk guys. They also took my gun. I figured that was okay—I only needed one type of gun to handle a hot stripper. You know what I mean.

My penis. I'm talking about my penis.

"Okay." I clapped my hands together. "Let's do this."

Another monk opened the coffin, and I stared in grinning expectation at a naked dead man.

"That's a guy," I said.

Head monk came in close and whispered. "Couldn't find girl this time. It doesn't matter. Death is death. It's all a turn-on. You're here to get laid, right?"

I eyed the body. A chubby bald white guy, late fifties. The Y cut across his chest indicated he was autopsied. Death was probably a heart attack, based on the size of his gut.

"I'm actually not really feeling it right now," I said.

"We can flip him over, if that helps."

"I don't think it will help."

"How fresh is it?" someone in the crowd yelled.

"Planted eight days ago," head monk answered.

The crowd cheered.

"I got sloppy seconds!"

"I got thirds!"

"I want to go last, when he's so full he's leaking out of his nose!"

I tried to step away, but the inhumanly muscular monks held me firm.

"I'm really not horny right now," I insisted. "In fact, I may never be horny again."

"My friend is shy!" That damn old caretaker guy again. "He doesn't like to pitch! He prefers catching!"

"No problem. Fetch the bicycle pump!"

Someone brought over a bike pump, complete with needle tip. The head monk fussed around with the poor dead guy's junk, then pushed the needle into the pee hole at the shriveled tip. I had an anti-erection, my dick actually retreating into my body as I watched.

He began to pump. And, incredibly, the corpse's johnson responded by filling out in length and width, until it stuck up like a tent pole. The monk kept pumping, and then the scrotum inflated. First apple-sized. Then grapefruit. Then soccer ball. I winced, waiting for the *POP*, but he quit before it got to medicine ball proportions. Which is a good thing, because balls that big would be bad medicine indeed.

"This is wrong on so many levels," I said.

Someone stuck a tube of KY into my hand, the head monk said, "Have fun," and then I was tossed onto the corpse, the coffin lid slamming closed above me with devastating finality.

Chapter 8

I lied. There isn't any sodomy in this chapter. Instead, there was a good minute of mindless screaming panic, followed by a minute of mindless yelling terror, and another two minutes of unmanly begging.

"We're not opening up until you finish," head monk spoke through the coffin lid.

"I'm finished." I hoped I sounded sincere. "It was fantastic. Best dead sex I ever had."

He wasn't buying. "The only way you're getting out of there is by embracing your necrophilia. That's why you came, isn't it? That's why we're all here. To make our fantasies come true. To taste the forbidden."

"I tasted it. It's like rotten meat, and disappointingly unresponsive."

"We can stay here all night if we have to."

I collected my thoughts, the sum total of which were *Get me the fuck out of here.* Then I calmed down a little. Then I started screaming again. Then calm. Then more screaming. Then even more screaming.

Finally, I took a deep breath, and really started screaming.

Being hysterical is pretty exhausting, so I took a time-out and tried to rationalize what to do next, other than scream.

Unfortunately, clearing my head made me even more aware of my current situation, and how disgustingly horrible it was. I was trapped in a coffin, lying on top of a naked dead guy with nuts the size of a basketball. A curly-haired basketball with a bratwurst glued onto the top. It pressed against my pelvis in a way that could only be described as awful.

My upper half wasn't any happier, with my face inches away from a dead man's. He didn't really smell like rotting meat. Not exactly. It was more like meat that was about to go bad, but dunked in formaldehyde first. His flesh was waxy, sort of stiff, and cold in a way that only dead people get. I moved my hands up across his nude, hairy chest, fighting the urge to vomit, and then pressed my elbows into his gut to force some distance between us.

It was a mistake. His autopsy meant his ribs had been cut away, and no ribs meant no internal support. My elbows ripped through the stitches and my arms disappeared into his still-moist body cavity.

I felt things. Horrible things. Squishy things. To prevent the organs from leaking, the clever embalmer had placed them in plastic bags, like some sort of lunch snacks from hell. I thanked the darkness that it was dark and I couldn't see anything, because I had no light. But I screamed anyway.

When the screaming finally stopped, I screamed a little more, and then realized the only way I was going to get out of here is to do what women have been probably doing with me ever since I'd been sexually active.

I'd have to fake it.

Unfortunately, the only way to fake a sexual movement is to perform a sexual movement. So I locked my knees on either side of his hips, his giant scrotum tucked beneath my legs like a fleshy bicycle seat, and began the humping motion. I also began to cry.

The coffin went with the rhythm, back and forth and back and forth, and it was a high end model which meant springs in the cushion which meant this felt even more like the real thing. Even though I couldn't see I squeezed my eyes shut and invented gods in my imagination so I could pray to them to make this end. I tried to think back on happy times, but too many of my happy times involved sex and that didn't help me block out the unhappy fact that I was fake dry-humping a corpse. I tried thinking about happy times when I was a kid, and unwillingly focused on the time I was six years old and my mother bought me a Hoppity Horse for my birthday, and how I used to love bouncing up and down the neighborhood and, oh goddamn it...

I threw up in my mouth. Energy drink and pizza mixed with stomach acid. I swallowed it because adding puke to this situation was possibly the only thing that could make it worse.

Scratch that last thought. My pelvic gyrations had loosened up some trapped air in the nether regions of the cadaver, prompting extreme flatulence. He ripped one so loud it sounded like a trumpet. But is sure as hell didn't smell like one. You think you know stink? Dead guy farts are number one on the stinkmeter. It was so bad, I'm sure if I could see I would have seen green gas.

"Do it! Give it to him!"

I wasn't sure who the head monk was cheering on, me or the dead guy. But I knew in order to properly fake it, I had to add some vocals to the rhythm.

"Oh, daddy!" I moaned, trying not to breathe. "Oh, yes, daddy!"

Someone slapped on the top of the coffin, urging me on. There was more corpse farting, more crying, more humping, and finally I couldn't handle this anymore without a complete nervous breakdown and I cried out

"Oh, god!" and then went still.

Eventually, miraculously, the coffin lid opened. I made it. I was alive. Amazingly, wonderfully alive. Now I needed to find my gun and eat a bullet.

The strongarm monks pulled me out of the coffin, my arms slupping from the dead man's chest cavity, glistening with guck.

"Congrats!" head monk said, giving me an *attaboy* slap on the back. "You really rocked his dead world!"

I wiped my hands on his fake robe.

The rest of the perverts queued up for their shot at playing Megaball, and I managed to stumble into my pants. I even got my gun back. I cocked the hammer and stared deep into the blessed release promised by the inside of the barrel, and then remembered I only had one bullet left, and if anyone should die, it was old caretaker guy.

I looked around for the bike pump, flitting with the idea of filling his nads up with air before sending him to hell. Or maybe I would just pump him up and let him live. Live out the remainder of his pathetic life with unusually large testicles. The humiliation he'd suffer. The stares. The laughter. Plus, it would be impossible to find pants.

Regrettably, the bike pump was nowhere to be found. Neither was old caretaker guy. And I'd apparently won the loser trifecta, because Bill, the man I'd been hired to follow, was also MIA.

Some pinhead hopped into the coffin with Frankengroin, and I picked up the flashlight and made my way to the exit before the groaning began. I needed some fresh air. I also needed a hatchet and some steel wool, so I could access and scour the last half an hour from my brain.

Conveniently, the exit was a large door marked EXIT, which opened up to some concrete steps. I took them up, and they ended in a maintenance closet, which opened up into the mausoleum. It was an easier—and faster— entrance than the nightmare slide, but lacked the dramatic effect.

I pulled out my gun, did a quick search for old caretaker guy, scared the hell out of some grieving old man, mourning his dead wife or some similar maudlin bullshit, and then made my way through the cemetery, across the street, and into the first place that sold liquor.

Three shots and two beers later, I called the police.

Chapter 9

The cop I called was a somewhat tasty little morsel named Lieutenant Jackie "Jack" Daniels. So-so face, great legs, nice rack, especially for an older broad. I knew her back in the day, when we were partners in blue, and she continued to have a crush on me almost two decades later.

"I don't owe you shit, McGlade. And if you bother me again I'm going to send some uniforms over to trash your apartment and beat you with phone books for so long you'll have area codes embedded in your skin."

"Pay attention, Jackie. I'm offering you a prime bust here. As we speak, there's a group of perverts running a train on a dead guy with gonads the size of a Thanksgiving turkey."

"Let me guess. Is it a *Butterball*?"

"They have to be stopped. Would you want some loonies digging you up and poking your cooter after you've been laid to eternal rest?"

"Sex with a corpse, disgusting as it is, isn't a crime, Harry. Didn't you read *Bloody Mary* by JA Konrath? There was a character in there, did the same thing."

"I listened to part of the audiobook. The author thinks he's funny, but he's not."

"It's a he? I thought a woman wrote those books."

I tried to make my voice sound soothing, a tough trick because I had screamed myself raw.

"Jackie, partner, be a good cop and send a team over to the cemetery. You'll get brownie points from the Captain, a little TV spotlight, and the satisfaction knowing that you got a bunch of lunatic perverts off the street."

"What do I charge them with, McGlade? Public indecency? You want me to waste manpower on a minor misdemeanor?"

"Aggravated sexual assault. Trust me. It was aggravating."

"Who's going to press charges? The cadaver? You want to bring a corpse to trial? The cross examination would be riveting, I bet."

I clenched my fist. "Dammit, Jackie! I was violated in ways you can't even begin to understand. I'll never be the same. My sex life might very well be ruined, and I won't be able to ever watch basketball on TV again. And I love basketball. If you don't arrest these assholes I'm going to go on a killing spree and when they bring me in I'll tell them you could have stopped it just by doing your job."

She sighed big, but I knew I'd won. "Cut the melodrama, McGlade. I'll send a few uniforms over to check it out."

"If you arrest a creepy old caretaker guy, call me. I'm going to impale him on his mop and make him clean all the floors in Union Station."

"I got extra tickets to the Bulls game tomorrow. Want them?"

"You can really be a mean bitch sometimes, Jackie."

I hung up, ordered another tequila, drank it, ordered another, drank it, then called a taxi to take me back to my condo to really start drinking.

Chapter 10

My plan had been to drink so much I didn't dream. And when I peeled my eyes open, I thought it worked. I couldn't remember a single nocturnal image, let alone any nightmares.

Then I realized I was lying naked on the kitchen floor, straddling a head of lettuce.

"Oh hell no."

Like any freaked-out person, I needed answers. So I searched Google, using the terms "post dramatic stress disorder sex with corpses and giant testicles" which linked me to a bunch of unhelpful porn sites. I dutifully surfed them anyway, but there were no answers there.

Then I went to eBay, and I was still the top bidder on everything. Lousy eBastards. I decided I just wouldn't pay if I won, but then I'd get negative feedback, and negative feedback was permanent. I'm proud of my 99.4% positive score. My only bad mark came from some jerk who didn't read the whole product description, only the header. I sold him a mint Babe Ruth baseball card for $260. The card had some tears and a few bends, but I'd stapled some mint leaves to it. Which I mentioned, in two point font, at the bottom of the listing. Some guys can't take a joke.

Next I checked my email, where I discovered I'd won the Irish lottery, inherited eighty million dollars from an unknown relative, and was asked to shuffle funds into my bank account from the President of Rwanda. They all got my standard response: enthusiastic replies with an attachment supposedly containing my routing number. The attachment really contained an email bomb, which once opened would bombard their computers with tens of thousands of naked pictures of actress Bea Arthur. I called it the Maude Virus.

I had a bit of a hangover, my ass still hurt from where I'd fallen on my keys, and I was hungry. But the only food I had in the condo was that head of lettuce, which I wasn't going to eat even if I were starving to death, so I changed into a slightly less dirty suit and hit the corner convenience store for an overpriced cup of joe, a dose of Advil, and a prepackaged cheese Danish.

It was a gorgeous Chicago day, the sun shining, the lakeshore breeze blowing, the pigeons singing their lovely song. I leaned against the storefront window and called my client.

"Hello?"

"Is this Maxine Drawbridge?"

"It's Norma Cauldridge."

I rubbed my nose. "Hi, Maxine. It's Harry McGlade. I need more money."

"Did you find something out, Mr. McGlade?"

"I did. And it's ugly. Real ugly. Plus, I was gravely injured during my surveillance." I smiled at my unintentional pun, which was actually intentional. "I'm not going near him again without more cash."

"I've already paid you twelve hundred dollars."

My nose still itched, so I scratched it. On the inside.

"I want double that. Think of it as an investment. When the lawyers see the dirt I've got on old Roy, you'll take the freak for every dime he has."

I removed my finger, noted something gray and waxy stuck to the end. I'd been picking my nose for years, and this was the strangest booger I'd ever seen.

"Who's Roy?"

"Whatever the hell his name is."

I took a closer look. Sniffed. It smelled familiar.

"Do you have pictures?"

"I will. Send the money to my PayPal account. My email is... oh god..."

The odor was rotten meat and formaldehyde. Somehow, while I was in the coffin, I'd gotten a hunk of dead flesh up my nose. Dead flesh covered in boogers. And a nose hair.

I leaned over and puked up the coffee, Danish, and Advil. Eighteen bucks and change, shot to hell.

"Mr. McGlade? Are you there?"

I wiped a toe through the puke, looking for the Advil. They were probably still good. Instead, I saw something that made me want to quit eating forever.

Part of a human ear.

I got closer, sure it had to be some coincidentally-shaped chunk of chewed Danish.

No, it was an ear. The upper, cartilagey part. I often nibbled women's ears when we were fooling around. I must have got caught up in the role-playing and bitten off a hunk.

"Mr. McGlade?"

"Scratch that. I want triple."

"That's outrageous."

"Lady, I went to third base with a dead guy last night, all because of your husband. Pay me, or find some other schmuck to do your dirty work."

"You did what with a dead guy?"

"Don't believe me? You want to talk to him?"

I held my cell phone over the ear. Then I realized I was acting a bit hysterical. Maybe I was still asleep, and this was just a dream.

I felt my backside, wondering if the pain in my ass was truly from sitting on my keys, or from something that was *still up there...*

I stuck my hand inside my pants, reaching down the plumber's crack...

It's a dream, it has to be a dream...

A pigeon waddled over, pecked up the ear, and ran off. My fingers crept closer...

"Mr. McGlade?"

A dream, all a dream, just a harmless dream...

And then I touched the severed end of something that shouldn't be there. Something that felt like a Pepperidge Farm County Style Breakfast Sausage Link.

"Please!" I cried out. "If there's any decency left in this cruel world, let this be a dream!"

Chapter 11

It was a dream. I woke up in bed next to an empty bottle of tequila. Blessedly, there was no head of lettuce between my legs. And the puddle of puke on my pillow didn't contain anything resembling human flesh. I did a nose check and an ass check, and they were both free and clear.

So much for drinking away the nightmares.

I rolled out of bed, padded to the can, showered, dressed in a slightly less dirty suit than yesterday, and visited the local convenience store for a coffee, Danish, and some Advil. That should have been my tip off I'd been dreaming—paying eighteen bucks for those three items. I forked over the real-life money—twenty-six bucks—then called Mrs. Drawbridge and demanded quadruple my rate. She reluctantly agreed, and mentioned her husband was in bed, still asleep. I decided to stakeout her house and tail him. And this time, I'd be taking some sophisticated equipment.

I returned to the condo and entered my Crime Lab. It was actually an extra bedroom that I converted into a crime lab by stocking it with spy stuff and writing *Crime Lab* on the door. The modern private detective had to stay current with modern gadgetry, so I bought all of the latest high-tech stuff. Phone tappers. Listening devices. Infra red things. A remote control tank with a miniature video camera hooked up to the turret. Cell phone jammers. A set of brass knuckles with a microchip inside that played Pat Benatar when I socked somebody. All the essentials.

I popped the SanDisk memory card out of the tank and plugged it into my computer, to check the footage I'd recorded during my practice run. The video was a little choppy, but more than acceptable.

The first scene was of a dog in Grant Park, urinating.

Cut to the same dog, pooping.

Cut to another dog, pooping.

Cut to the first dog, eating the second dog's poop.

Cut to a third dog, trying to hump the first dog, who was still munching on the poop.

Cut to the poop, which didn't look like it warranted being eaten.

Cut to some gangbanger punk, running off with my tank.

Cut to me explaining to the cop why I fired my gun in a populated area, and then me getting arrested.

With some editing, and the right soundtrack, the footage could be the backbone of a really good documentary about urban crime, and the amusing social lives of dogs.

I opened up a fresh SanDisk card, put that in the tank, and loaded everything into in a gym bag, along with a digital camera that could shoot night-vision, a Bionic Ear listening cannon, and a little wind-up nun that shot sparks out of her eyes. Thusly equipped, I high-tailed it over to the long term garage, jumped in my stakeout car—an inconspicuous green Chevy El Camino with yellow racing stripes on the hood—and drove to Jim Drawbridge's house.

The key to any successful stakeout is three-fold: Food, tunes, and a pot to piss in. The food should consist of chips and snack cakes. Sugar and carbohydrates jack up the insulin level, which leads to a heighten sense of awareness, probably. The music should be high energy, like heavy metal, but don't include the power ballads. The piss pot can be an old milk jug or thermos. Try to avoid cellophane potato chip bags, as I've learned from experience they tend to leak.

Since I never knew when I'd have to go on a stakeout, I kept my car stocked with everything I needed. But once I found a suitable vantage point—on the street directly in front of Jim's house—I realized I was less stocked than I should have been. I was way low on sugary snacks, but had a surplus of urine in an old apple juice bottle. Unless it was, perhaps, actually apple juice. A quick sniff would tell me.

It was urine. And I needed to stop eating asparagus.

I took a moment to muse about the gratuitous amount of bodily fluids that seem to have come up in this case, and cracked open the door and dumped the piss onto the street, where it made a foamy little river down the curb and to the sewer drain.

Then I cranked up the Led Zeppelin, licked the crust out of some old Twinkie wrappers, and waited for Jim to show up.

After half an hour, the coffee needed to be set free, so I filled up half the apple juice bottle. The secret to zero splatter is aiming for the inside edge, and then squeezing dry rather than shaking.

After an hour, Mrs. Drawbridge came out of the house and knocked on my window.

"George left before you got here."

"Do you have any snacks?"

"No."

I noticed she had some orange powder in the corner of her unattractive mouth.

"You have cheese curls," I said.

"No I don't."

"Bring me the cheese curls."

She folded her arms. "I don't have any."

"You have Cheetos dust on your lips."

"I was eating carrots."

"Were they powdered carrots?"

"Maybe."

"Bring me the goddamn Cheetos, or I'm off the case."

She frowned and waddled off. I called after her, "And anything Hostess or Dolly Madison!"

I air guitared in perfect synchronization with Jimmy Page until the ugly wife returned with my treats. The Cheetos bag only had a few left in the bottom, and Mrs. Drawbridge's cheeks were puffed out chipmunk-style. She also brought me half a raspberry Zinger.

"You ate them," I said, stating the obvious.

She shook her head. "Mmphmtmummuffff."

"Don't lie. You did. You're still chewing."

"Ummurrfumamamm."

"Are too."

She swallowed, and I watched the large lump slide down her throat.

"I think my husband went to his parent's house," she said after smacking her lips.

"What am I supposed to do with half a Zinger? It's like the size of my thumb."

"I said I think my husband went to his parent's house."

"Who?"

"My husband. After his parents died, he refused to sell it. I'm not allowed to go over there. He's got all kinds of locks and security devices. I think he may be hiding something."

I scarfed down the rest of the cheese curls, then washed them down with the remaining half a Zinger. It wasn't even half. Maybe a third, at best.

"I'm the detective, lady. I'll decide if he's hiding anything. Gimme the address."

She gave it to me. It was in the neighborhood of Streeterville, less than a mile away.

"I'll call you in exactly two hours. If you don't hear from me, I want you to call Lt. Jacqueline Daniels in District 26 and tell her where I am. Tell her it's an emergency. Did you get that?"

"Yeah. Is that apple juice?"

I glanced at my pee bottle.

"Yeah. But it's warm."

"I have ice in the house."

"Help yourself."

She took the piss, and I started the car and drove off. Little did I know I was about to face the darkest moment of my entire career. A moment so dark, that had I known it was coming, I would have done something else instead, like see a movie, or go to the zoo and bang on the windows in the monkey house. But I didn't know what was going to happen, because I couldn't predict the future, because if I could I would have predicted the lottery numbers and been super-rich and never would have needed the money that caused me to go to that house in Streeterville, which was the darkest moment of my entire career. So that's where I went. Unbeknownst to me.

In hindsight, I really shouldn't have gone.

Chapter 12

aka The Darkest Moment Of My Career

So I had no idea I was heading into the darkest moment of my career, but I went anyway.

Before going there, however, I stopped for red hots at Fat Louie's Red Hots on Clark and got a dog with the works. It was terrible, and I have really low standards. In my humble opinion, hot dogs shouldn't have veins. Or anything resembling a foreskin. I could barely choke the third one down.

Uncomfortably sated, I pressed onward to Phil's parent's house. The house was unassuming enough. Split-level, single family, red brick exterior. There was an oak tree out front, and a chainlink fence partitioning off the tiny backyard. I parked on the street, then took out my remote control surveillance tank. After double-checking the batteries, servos, memory card, remote sensor, camera focus, tread alignment, and wireless frequency, I gingerly set the tank down in the street and a taxi ran it over.

Damn taxi jerks. I decided to charge it to Mrs. Drawbridge's bill.

My next course of action was to figure out my next course of action. I played a little more air guitar, broke an air string, put on a new one and spent a minute air tuning it, and then decided on my approach.

I could put on my ghillie suit—a mesh shirt and pants with real and fake grass and shubbery sewn into it that I ordered from PsychoSniper.com—and then slowly belly-crawl across the lawn, traverse the fence using a carbide steel bolt cutter, inch my way into the backyard, creep up the porch in slow increments stopping often to pretend to be a potted plant, trick his surveillance system by recording a loop from his outdoor camera and feeding the playback into the main line, drill into his door frame using a cordless screwdriver to disable the burglary alarm sensor, pick the pick-proof Schlage deadbolt, and sneak inside his house using my Invisible Voyeur NightVision Goggles, which I bought at CautiousStalker.org.

Or I could knock on the front door and ask what's up.

"What's up?" I asked when the front door opened.

Since I'd seen him yesterday, Ken had gone from half a sunburned face to a full sunburned face. The smell coming from his house was real bacon, which sure beat the smell of fake bacon, which my mother used to make out of soy and library paste and brown Crayons.

"Who are you?"

"Housing inspector." I flashed him my PI badge, too fast for him to read it. "I'm here to check for gas leaks. Are you leaking any gases?"

"No. Can I see that badge again?"

"I smell something. Are you cooking in there?"

"No, I'm not."

"Is it bacon?" I smacked my lips. "I love bacon. I read somewhere that you could shave with bacon. Rub it on your face raw, and it lubricates better than shaving cream. Have you ever heard of that?"

"No."

"I tried it once. Closest shave I ever had. But I got an E. Coli infection and they had to remove eight yards of my large intestine. Can I come in?"

"No. Hey, you look kind of familiar."

I flashed an *aw shucks* grin. "I get that a lot. I've made a few videos. You might know my screen name, *Sir Dix-A-Lot.*"

"I don't think that's it."

"Ever see *Snow White and the Seven Blowjobs?*"

"No."

"*Robin Hood, Prince of Anal?*"

"I don't think so."

"*The Empire Strikes Scat?*"

"Maybe you should come in. I may have some gases for you to check on."

I nodded, stepping into his humble abode. It was no surprise he let me in. Fast talking is one of my special skills. That and being able to swallow pills. If I had a super power, it would be the ability to swallow a whole handful of pills at once. Big pills too. None of that baby aspirin crap for babies. I secretly hoped that one day I'd get cancer, and the doctor would prescribe me a lot of pills, and he'd tell me to space them out throughout the day because there were so many, but I'd tell him no need to and grab the whole handful and swallow them up right there while he watched, amazed.

That's what I was thinking about when Phil hit me in the head with the hammer.

Chapter 13

I awoke from a terrible dream that I was trapped in a coffin with an inhumanly large-testicled man, to the terrible reality of being tied to a chair in some freak's basement.

Said freak was standing over me, staring.

"You're awake," he said.

"No I'm not."

I shook my head, which caused a spike of pain. My left eye stung, and I looked down my nose and saw some dried blood on my cheek. The freak still held the hammer. He waved it in front of my face in a way I'm sure he thought was menacing, which actually was pretty menacing.

"Yes you are! And I know what you want! That whore hired you!"

"Which whore? I know a lot of whores."

He poked me in the chest with the hammer. "She hired you to spy on me! To find out what secrets I had hidden in my parent's house! Well, now you'll be privy to those secrets, Mr. Private Eye! Because I'm going to show them to you!"

I checked my bonds, noted he had used the same clothesline he'd purchased at the hardware store. The knots were tight, expert. My legs were bound as well, tied to the steel chair legs of the steel chair, which was made of steel. The basement was unfurnished, concrete floor, I-beams and joists exposed in the ceiling, menacing curtains sectioning off the area we were in.

"Got any aspirin?" I asked. "Some asshole hit me with a hammer."

"Silence!"

"And can you please stop shouting? I'm right here. It's not like I'm in another part of the house and you're calling me for dinner."

The freak chuckled, the nostrils on his large nose flaring out.

"Oh, funny you should mention dinner. Because the main course..." He cackled.

"Yeah?" I asked.

"The main course..." More cackling.

"What's the main course, Emeril?"

"The... main course... is..." Hysterical laughter now.

I interrupted him. "I got it. The main course is me. You're going to eat me. Scary. What a scary guy you are."

"Not me, Mr. McGlade. You're going to be a snack," cackle cackle, "for my... zombie wife!"

I waited for the giggles to die down before I said, "Dude, your wife isn't a zombie."

"Yes she is."

"She's not even dead. I just saw her like an hour ago."

"Not that hag. I mean my first wife. The love of my life, tragically taken from me after only one year of marriage."

"So what about that ugly chick back at your house?"

"Her? I married her for the money."

I smiled. "Thank god. I thought you were totally nuts there for a minute."

"No kidding. She's a real heifer, isn't she?"

"I said in the first chapter that it was like God took a dare to make the most unattractive woman possible."

"Yes, that's Norma."

"Who?"

"My second wife! But now it's time for you to meet my first wife! And to feed her! Do you know what a necromancer is, Mr. McGlade?"

I shrugged. Not an easy task when tied up. "I meant to look it up."

"It's someone who has the power to raise the dead. Since Roberta died..."

"Who?"

"My first wife."

"This is a lot of names to keep straight. Can you write them down on a sticky pad for me?"

He didn't take the bait. I'd hoped he would have gone off in search of a sticky pad, which would have given my time to scoot my chair over to the menacing curtains hanging from the ceiling and hide behind them. He'd never think to look for me there, and would probably go watch TV or something.

But he was too smart to be tricked.

"Since Roberta died, I've been searching for a way to bring her back. Now, through a combination of magic and science—something I call sci-magic—I have finally gained mastery over death! Behold, Mr. McGlade, the living dead!"

He cast aside the menacing curtain. Hanging from the ceiling was a dead body.

"Is that her?" I asked.

"That, indeed, is Roberta, my Zombie Wife!"

He spread out his hands, as if waiting for applause. Even if I wasn't tied up, I wouldn't have applauded.

"That's not a zombie," I said. "That's a dead chick hanging on a rope."

"Really, Mr. McGlade? Really?"

"Yeah. Really."

"Well, watch this then." He turned to face the corpse. "Roberta, my love, come to me!"

Phil grabbed an overhead rope, and Roberta swung forward using a system of weights and pulleys. He made her wave at me.

"You're butt nuts," I said.

"She lives, Mr. McGlade! And she thirsts for your flesh! For nothing else can quell the hunger of the living dead! Isn't that right, Roberta?"

He tugged another rope, and she nodded. Actually, it was more of a sideways flop then a nod.

"Look, buddy, this has all been tremendously entertaining, but what do you say we untie me, I go to the cops, and you get put in a nice room with soft rubber walls so you don't hurt yourself?"

"I'm not crazy! Roberta is one of the walking dead!"

"More like the swaying dead."

He got in my face. "Admit she's undead!"

"No."

"But she moves! See!"

He made her do a little dance.

"You're making her move using pulleys and ropes, like some strange sad puppet."

He raised the hammer, aiming for the same spot where he hit me before.

"Say she's a zombie!"

"She a zombie," I said quickly. "You're a genius who has conquered death. I'm in awe of your brilliance."

He stared at me hard, and then spun and yanked the dead chick closer. I realized she was naked, and her boobs were missing. I always notice little things like that. Her skin had become dark brown and wrinkly, like a giant raisin. Whack job had also cut some blue eyes from a magazine or poster, and stapled them over her eye sockets. Her teeth were bared, the corners of her mouth turned up. Twist ties, to make it look like she was smiling.

It was kind of endearing, in a raving psychotic way.

"Roberta does seem sort of tired today." He caressed what was left of her cheek. "Perhaps she needs another treatment. I shall fetch the Rejuvenation Ray!"

He scuttled insanely off, and I wondered what time it was, and if his butt ugly whore of a second wife had remembered to call Lieutenant Jackie when I failed to check in. Then I remembered I'd given her a bottle full of piss and told her it was apple juice, so I probably couldn't count on that particular horse to come in.

Like it had happened so many times before, the burden of saving my own skin rested on my own skin. I needed to figure out some sort of ingenious plan to escape. If I could only do that, then I'd be free.

Freak boy returned, pushing a wheeled wine cart stacked with electronic equipment. He shoved it in front of his living undead zombie wife who was really just a putrefying corpse.

"Behold the Rejuvenation Ray, Mr. McGlade!"

"How do you know my name, anyway?"

"Your wallet."

"I had eight bucks in there. It better still be in there."

"I didn't take your money."

"And a Blockbuster Video card. They charge you five bucks if you lose that."

"Silence! Through magnetron technology, I have harnessed the life-giving properties of ordinary microwaves, coaxing the spirit back into the body!"

"That's a big microwave?"

"Behold!"

He hit a switch, and the stack of electronics hummed and whirred, throwing off an huge amount of heat. Most of it was directed at Roberta, the undead living zombie wife. Some of it came my way, and it hurt like a bad sunburn.

Then the smell hit me. Honey baked ham and bacon strips. I watched through squinty eyes as Roberta sizzled and popped and exuded a scent that was downright mouth-watering.

Now it all made sense. Phil's sunburn. Why he smelled like ham. Why his first wife's skin was so brown and wrinkly. Why his second wife smelled like sweaty feet.

Actually, this didn't explain why his second wife smelled like sweaty feet. But I guessed that to be a hygiene thing.

Blofeld finally turned off the microwave stack, then embraced his hanging wife. The embrace became a kiss. The kiss became a nibble. The nibble became a corn-on-the-cob chow-down, and I realized what had happened to the zombie's breasts.

"And now!" He wiped the grease off his mouth with his sleeve. "Now it is time for Roberta to feast!"

Fred reached under the cart, pulled out a meat cleaver. Didn't see too many meat cleavers, outside of a butcher shop.

"What shall we start with, Roberta? The leg? Yes, I agree. The leg looks delicious. Do you prefer the left on or the right one, dear? Yes, the left one."

He raised the cleaver. There are few things more terrifying than being tied to a chair about to be hacked up by a lunatic so he could feed the pieces to his dead wife who he thinks is actually a zombie and is hanging from the ceiling using an admittedly clever series of weights and pulleys.

"Stop!" I yelled.

Incredibly, he stopped.

"What?"

"Your parents!" I said, speaking quickly. "What would your parents think?"

"Why don't we... ask them!"

He stepped over to the menacing curtain, and with a flourish drew it back. Mom and Dad were hanging there, roped together so it looked like Dad was giving it to Mom, doggy-style.

"Oops!" Fred said, tugging on ropes and making his parents bump uglies. "Daddy! Why are you hurting Mommy?"

He pulled the cord again and again, Dad's hips rising and falling. A shrink would have a field day with this guy. Field days were fun. I liked dodge ball best.

"Say that again, Daddy? You're wrestling? What wrestling move is that?"

It looked, to my untrained eye, like a sodomyplex. I tore my eyes away and pointed at something with my chin. "What's that hanging next to them?"

"Fluffy. My cat."

"And those tiny things?"

"My goldfish, BA and Hannibal. Fluffy loves to chase them around. Don't you, Fluffy?"

More manic pulling of ropes, and the three dead animals knocked into each other. While he was preoccupied, I called out in my best falsetto, "Honey, it's Roberta!"

John turned his attention back to Roberta the zombie living bacon wife.

"Dearest? Did you say something?"

"I said," I said, "We should let Mr. McGlade go. I'm not hungry right now."

Nut job was buying it. He wrapped his arms around her, nuzzling against her tasty ribs.

"But you need to eat, honey. You're getting thinner and thinner."

"Tack a couple of tomatoes to my chest. I'll look a lot better."

Bert began to laugh. A chilling laugh that chilled me. He spun, pointing the cleaver at my nose.

"You idiot! Do you think I'm that stupid?"

"Yes."

"What good husband doesn't know the sound of my wife's own voice?"

"You, I was hoping."

"Enough of this tomfoolery! This ends now!"

He launched himself at me, screaming and drooling insanely, his probably very sharp cleaver raised for the killing blow.

Then Lieutenant Jackie Daniels shot him in the head.

Chapter 14

"You're an idiot, McGlade," Jackie said, using the cleaver to cut away the ropes.

Carl was dead on the floor. He was finally with his wife. Because she was dead on the floor too. Jack had made me sit there until the Crime Scene Unit arrived, taking pictures and gathering evidence. They cut the bodies down before they freed me.

"So how did you know I was here?" I asked.

Jack wore a short skirt and heels that probably cost a fortune but still looked kind of slutty, just how I liked them.

"Norma Cauldridge," she said.

"Who?"

"George Cauldridge's wife."

"Who?"

"She called me, wanted me to arrest you for trying to poison her. I asked where you were, and she said probably here. After we nabbed those necrophiliacs at the cemetery last night, I needed to find you anyway to get your statement. Lucky I heard your girlish screams which gave me probable cause to bust in here without a warrant."

I wasn't listening, because it sounded like a boring infodump.

"Can I give you my statement tomorrow?" I asked. "I gotta take a monster dump. I had some hot dogs earlier that are going to look better coming out than going in."

Jackie leaned in close. I braced myself for the kiss. It didn't come.

"Did you give Norma a bottle full of your urine and tell her it was apple juice?"

"Maybe. Did she drink any?"

"She said the second glass went down rough. She's going to sue you, McGlade."

"She can take a number. Seriously. I've got one of those number things. I swiped it from the deli." I grinned. "You can come over later, and watch me cut the cheese. You know you want to."

"I'd rather gouge out my own eyes with forks."

"Don't be coy. This could be a way to pay back what you owe me."

She cocked her hips, hot and sexy. "Excuse me? I just saved your ass, McGlade."

"Are you kidding? This is front page news. You'll probably get a promotion. There's no need to thank me. It's all part of the service I perform."

"I really think I hate you."

"Really, Jackie?" I raised an eyebrow. "Really?"

She nodded. "Yeah, really. Be in my office tomorrow morning for your statement. And try to stay of trouble until then."

I stood up, stretched, and gave her one of my famous Harry McGlade smiles.

"I'll try. But trouble is my business." I winked. "And business is good."

Truck Stop

This is co-written by my alter-ego, Jack Kilborn, author of Afraid, Trapped, and Endurance. Jack also wrote SERIAL with Blake Crouch. This is a prequel to SERIAL, featuring the character of Donaldson. It also features Taylor, from Afraid. And expanded version of this story is in SERIAL UNCUT.

"He who is unjust, let him be unjust still; he who is filthy, let him be filthy still; he who is righteous, let him be righteous still..." —REVELATION

Chapter One

Taylor liked toes.

He wasn't a pervert. At least, not *that* kind of pervert. Taylor didn't derive sexual gratification from feet. Women had other parts much better suited for that type of activity. But he was a sucker for a tiny foot in open-toed high heels, especially when the toenails were painted.

Painted toes were yummy.

The truck stop whore wore sandals, the cork wedge heels so high her toes were bent. She had small feet—they looked like a size five—and her nails matched her red mini skirt. Taylor spotted her through the windshield as she walked over to his Peterbilt, wiggling her hips and wobbling a bit. Taylor guessed she was drunk or stoned. Perhaps both.

He climbed out of his cab. When his cowboy boots touched the pavement he reached his hands up over his head and stretched, his vertebrae cracking. The night air was hot and sticky with humidity, and he could smell his own sweat.

The whore blew smoke from the corner of her mouth. "Hiya, stranger. My name's Candi. With an I."

"I'm Taylor. With a T."

He smiled. She giggled, then hiccupped.

Even in the dim parking lot light, Candi with an I was nothing to look at. Mid-thirties. Cellulite. Twenty pounds too heavy for her skirt and halter top. She wore sloppy make-up, her lipstick smeared, making Taylor wonder how many truckers she'd already blown on this midnight shift.

But she did have very cute toes. She dropped her cigarette and crushed it into the pavement, and Taylor licked his lower lip.

"Been on the road a long time, Taylor?"

"Twelve hours in from Cinci. My ass is flatter than roadkill armadillo."

She eyed his rig. He was hauling four bulldozers on his flatbed trailer. They were heavy, and his mileage hadn't been good, making this run much less profitable than it should have been.

But Taylor didn't become a trucker to get rich. He did it for other reasons.

"You feeling lonely, Taylor? You looking for a little company?"

Taylor knew he could use a little company right now. He could also use a meal, a hot shower, and eight hours of sleep.

It was just a question of which need he'd cater to first.

He looked around the truck stop lot. Pretty full for late night in Bumblefuck, Wisconsin. Over a dozen rigs and just as many cars. The 24 hour gas station had a line for the pumps, and *Murray's Eats*, the all-night diner, appeared full.

On either side of the cloverleaf there were a few other restaurants and gas stations, but *Murray's* was always busy because they boasted more than food and diesel. Besides the no-hassle companionship the management and local authorities tolerated, *Murray's* had a full-size truck wash, a mechanic on duty, and free showers.

After twelve hours of caffeine sweating in this muggy Midwestern August, Taylor needed some quality time with a bar of soap just as badly as he needed quality time with a parking lot hooker.

But it didn't make sense to shower first, when he was only going to get messy again.

"How much?" he asked.

"That depends on—"

"Half and half," he cut her off, not needing to hear the daily menu specials.

"Twenty-five bucks."

She didn't look worth twenty-five bucks, but he wasn't planning on paying her anyway, so he agreed.

"Great, sugar. I just need to make a quick stop at the little girls' room and I'll be right back."

She spun on her wedges to leave, but Taylor caught her thin wrist. He knew she wasn't going to the washroom. She was going to her pimp to give him the four Ps: Price, preferences, plate number, parking location. Taylor didn't see any single men hanging around; only other whores, and none of them were paying attention. Her pimp was probably in the restaurant, unaware of this particular transaction, and Taylor wanted to keep it that way.

"I'm sorta anxious to get right to it, Candi." He smiled wide. Women loved his smile. He'd been told, many times, that he was good-looking enough to model. "If you leave me now, I might just find some other pretty girl to spend my money on."

Candi smiled back. "Well, we wouldn't want that. But I'm short on protection right now, honey."

"I've got rubbers in the cab." Taylor switched to his brooding, hurt-puppy dog look. "I need it bad, right now, Candi. So bad I'll throw in another ten spot. That's thirty-five bucks for something we both know will only take a few minutes."

Taylor watched Candi work it out in her head. This john was hot to trot, offering more than the going rate, and he'd probably be really quick. Plus, he was cute. She could probably do him fast, and pocket the whole fee without having to share it with her pimp.

"You got yourself a date, sugar."

Taylor took another quick look around the lot, made sure no one was watching, and hustled Candi into his cab, climbing up behind her and locking the door.

The truck's windows were lightly tinted—making it difficult for anyone on the street to see inside. Not that Candi bothered to notice, or care. As soon as Taylor faced her she was pawing at his fly.

"The bedroom is upstairs." Taylor pointed to the stepladder in the rear of the extended cab, leading to his overhead sleeping compartment.

"Is there enough room up there? Some of those spaces are tight."

"Plenty. I customized it myself. It's to die for."

Taylor smiled, knowing he was being coy, knowing it didn't matter at this point. His heart rate was up, his palms itchy, and he had that excited/sick feeling that junkies got right before they jabbed the needle in. If Candi suddenly had a change of heart, there wasn't anything she could do about it. She was past the point of no return.

But Candi didn't resist. She went up first, pushing the trap door on the cab's ceiling, climbing into the darkness above. Taylor hit the light switch on his dashboard and followed her.

"What is this? Padding?"

She was on her hands and knees, running her palm across the floor of the sleeper, testing its springiness with her fingers.

"Judo mats. Extra thick. Very easy to clean up."

"You got mats on the walls too?" She got on her knees and reached overhead, touching the spongy material on the arced ceiling, her exposed belly jiggling.

"Those are baffles. Keeps the sound out." He smiled, closing the trap door behind him. "And in."

The lighting was subdued, just a simple overhead fixture next to the smoke alarm. The soundproofing was black foam, the mats a deep beige, and there was no furniture in the enclosure except for an inflatable rubber mattress and a medium-sized metal trunk.

"This is kind of kinky. Are you kinky, Taylor?"

"You might say that."

Taylor crawled over to the trunk at the far end of the enclosure. After dialing the combination lock, he opened the lid. Then he moved his Tupperware container aside and took out a fresh roll of paper towels, a disposable paper nose and mouth mask, and an aerosol spray can. He ripped off three paper towels, then slipped the mask on over his face, adjusting the rubber band so it didn't catch in his hair.

"What is that, sugar?" Candi asked. Her flirty, playful demeanor was slipping a bit.

"Starter fluid. You squirt it into your carburetor, it helps the engine turn over. Its main ingredient is diethyl ether."

He held the paper towels at arm's length, then sprayed them until they were soaked.

"What the fuck are you doing?" Candi looked panicked now. And she had good reason to be.

"This will knock you out so I can tie you up. You're not the prettiest flower in the bouquet, Candi with an I. But you have the cutest little toes."

He grinned again. But this wasn't one of his attractive grins. The whore shrunk away from him.

"Don't hurt me, man! Please! I got kids!"

"They must be so proud."

Taylor approached her, on his knees, savoring her fear. She tried to crawl to the right and get around him, get to the trap door. But that was closed and now concealed by matting, and Taylor knew she had no idea where it was.

He watched her realize escape wasn't an option, and then she dug into her little purse for a weapon or a cell phone or a bribe or something else that she thought might help but wouldn't. Taylor hit her square in the nose, then tossed the purse aside. A small canister of pepper spray spilled out, along with a cell phone, make-up, Tic-Tacs, and several condoms.

"You lied to me," Taylor said, slapping her again. "You've got rubbers."

"Please…"

"You lying little slut. Were you going to pepper spray me?"

"No… I…"

"Liar." Another slap. "I think you need to be taught a lesson. And I don't think you'll like it. But I will."

Candi's hands covered her bleeding nose and she moaned something that sounded like, "Please… My kids…"

"Does your pimp offer life insurance?"

She whimpered.

"No? That's a shame. Well, I'm sure he'll take care of your children for you. He'll probably have them turning tricks by next week."

Taylor knocked her hands away and pressed the cold, wet paper towels to her face. Not hard enough to cut off air, but hard enough that she had to breathe through them. Even though he wore a paper face mask, some of the pungent, bitter odor got into Taylor's nostrils, making his hairs curl.

It took the ether less than a minute to do its job on the whore. When she finally went limp, Taylor placed the damp towels in a plastic zip-top bag. Then he took several bungee cords out of the trunk and bound Candi's hands and arms to her torso. Unlike rope, the elastic bands didn't require knots, and were reusable. Taylor wrapped them around Candi tight enough for her to lose circulation, but that didn't matter.

Candi wouldn't be needing circulation for very much longer.

While the majority of his murder kit was readily available at any truck stop, his last piece of equipment was specially made.

It looked like a large board with two four-inch wide holes cut in the middle. Taylor flipped the catch on the side and it opened up on hinges, like one of those old-fashion jail stocks that prisoners stuck their heads and hands into. Except this one was made for something else.

Taylor grabbed Candi's left foot and gingerly removed her wedge. Then he placed her ankle in the half-circle cut into the wood. He repeated the action with her right foot, and closed the stock.

Now Candi's bare feet protruded through the boards, effectively trapped.

He locked the catch with a padlock, and then set the stock in between the floor mats, where it fit snuggly into a brace, secured by two more padlocks.

Play time.

Taylor lay on his stomach, taking Candi's right foot in his hands. He cupped her heel, running a finger up along her sole, bringing his lips up to her toes.

He licked them once, tasting sweat, grime, smelling a slight foot odor and a faint residue of nail polish. His pulse went up even higher, and time seemed to slow down.

Her little toe came off surprisingly easy, no harder than nibbling the cartilage top off a fried chicken leg.

Taylor watched the blood seep out as he chewed on the severed digit—a blood and gristle-flavored piece of gum—and then swallowed.

This little piggy went to market.

He opened up his mouth to accommodate the second little piggy, the one who stayed home, when he realized something was missing.

Where was the screaming? Where was the begging? Where was the thrashing around in agony?

He crawled around the stock, alongside Candi's head. Ether was a pain in the ass to get the dose right, and he'd lost more than one girl by giving her too big a whiff. Luckily, Candi was still breathing. But she was too deeply sedated to let some playful toe-munching wake her up.

Taylor frowned. Like sex, murder was best with two active participants. He gathered up the whore's belongings, then rolled away from her, over to the trap door.

He'd get a bite to eat, maybe enjoy one of *Murray's* famous free showers. Hopefully, when he got back, *Sleeping Homely* would be awake.

Taylor used one of the ether-soaked paper towels to wipe the blood off his chin and fingers, stuffed them back into the bag, then headed for the diner.

Chapter Two

"Where are you?"

"I have no idea." My cell was tucked between my shoulder and my ear as I drove. "I think I'm still in Wisconsin. Wouldn't there be some kind of sign if I entered another state?"

"Don't you have the map I gave you?" Latham asked. "The directions?"

"Yeah. But they aren't helping."

"Are you looking at the map right now?"

"Yes."

The map might have done me some good if I'd been able to see what was on it. But the highway was dark, and the interior light in my 1989 Nova had burned out last month.

"You can't see it, can you?"

"Define *see*."

I heard my fiancée sigh. "I just bought you a replacement bulb for that overhead lamp. I saw you put it in your purse. It's still in your purse, isn't it?"

"Maybe."

"And you can't replace the bulb now, because it's too dark."

"That's a good deduction. You should become a cop."

"One cop in this relationship is enough. Why didn't you take my GPS when I insisted?"

"Because I didn't want you to get lost."

A billboard was coming up on my right. MURRAY'S - NEXT EXIT. That was nice to know, but I had no idea what *Murray's* was, or how far the exit was. Not a very effective advertisement.

"*My* interior light works, Jackie. I could have used Mapquest."

"Mapquest lies. And don't call me Jackie. You know I hate it when people call me Jackie."

"And I hate it when you say you'd be here three hours ago, and you're still not here. You could have left at a reasonable hour, Jack."

He had a point. This was my first real vacation—and by that I mean one that involved actually travelling somewhere—in a few years. Latham had rented a cabin on Rice Lake, and he had driven there yesterday from Chicago to meet the rental owners and get the keys. I was supposed to go with him, and we'd been planning this for weeks, but the murder trial I'd been testifying at had gone longer than expected, and since I was the arresting officer I needed to be there. As much as I loved Latham, and as much as I needed some time away from work, my duty to put criminals away ranked slightly higher.

"Your *told-you-so* tone isn't going to get you laid later," I said. "Just help me figure out where I am."

Another sigh. I shrugged it off. My long-suffering boyfriend had suffered a lot worse than this in order to be with me. I figured he had to be incredibly desperate, or a closet masochist. Either way, he was a cutie, and I loved him.

"Do you see the mile markers alongside the road?"

I didn't see any such thing. The highway was dark, and I hadn't noticed any signs, off-ramps, exits, or mile markers since I'd left Illinois. But I hadn't exactly been paying much attention, either. I was pretty damn tired, and had been zoning out to AM radio for the last hour. FM didn't work. Sometimes I wish someone would shoot my car, put it out of my misery.

"No. There's nothing out here, Latham. Except *Murray's*."

"What's *Murray's*?"

"I have no idea. I just saw the sign. Could be a gas station. Could be a waterpark."

"I don't remember passing anything called *Murray's*. Did the sign have the exit number?"

"No."

"Are you sure?"

I made a face. "The defense attorney never asked me if I was sure. The defense attorney took me at my word."

"He should have also made you take my GPS. You see those posts alongside the road with the reflectors on them?"

"Yeah."

"Keep watching them."

"Why should—" The next reflector had a number on top. "Oh. Okay, I'm at mile marker 231."

"I don't have Internet access here at the cabin. I'll call you back when I find out where you are. You're okay, right? Not going to fall asleep while driving?"

I yawned. "I'm fine, hon. Just a little hungry."

"Stop for something if it will keep you awake."

"Sure. I'll just pull over and grab the nearest cow."

"If you do, bring me a tenderloin."

"Really? Is your appetite back?" Latham was still recovering from a bad case of food poisoning.

"It's getting there."

"Aren't you tired? You should rest, honey."

"I'm fine."

"Are you sure?"

"I'm sure. I'll call soon with your location."

My human GPS unit hung up. I yawned again, and gave my head a little shake.

On the plus side, my testimony had gone well, and all signs pointed to a conviction.

On the minus side, I'd been driving for six straight hours, and I was hungry, tired, and needed to pee. I also needed gas, according to my gauge.

Maybe Murray could take care of all my needs. Assuming I could find Murray's before falling asleep, running out of fuel, starving to death, and wetting my pants.

The road stretched onward into the never-ending darkness. I hadn't seen another car in a while. Even though this was a major highway (as far as I knew), traffic was pretty light. Who would have thought that Northern Wisconsin at two in the morning on a Wednesday night was so deserted?

I heard my cell phone ring. My hero, to the rescue.

"You're not on I-94," he said. "You're on 39."

"You sound annoyed."

"You went the wrong way when the Interstate split."

"Which means?"

"You drove three hours out of the way."

Shit.

I yawned. "So where do I go to get to you?"

"You need some sleep, Jack. You can get here in the morning."

"Three hours is nothing. I can be there in time for an early breakfast."

"You sound exhausted."

"I'll be fine. Lemme just close my eyes for a second."

"That's not even funny."

I smiled. The poor sap really did care about me.

"I love you, Latham."

"I love you, too. That's why I want you to find a room somewhere and get some rest."

"Just tell me how to get to you. I don't want to sleep alone in some cheap hotel with threadbare sheets and a mattress with questionable stains. I want to sleep next to you in that cabin with the big stone fireplace. But first I want to rip off those cute boxer-briefs you wear and… hello? Latham?"

I squinted at my cell. No signal.

Welcome to Wisconsin.

I yawned again. Another billboard appeared.

MURRAY'S FAMOUS TRUCK STOP. FOOD. DIESEL. LODGING. TRUCK WASH. SHOWERS. MECHANIC ON DUTY. TEN MILES.

Ten miles? I could make ten miles. And maybe some food and coffee would wake me up.

I pressed the accelerator, taking the Nova up to eighty.

Murray's here I come.

Chapter Three

Taylor paused at the diner entrance, taking everything in. The restaurant was busy, the tables all full. He spotted three waitresses, plus two cooks in the kitchen. Seated were various truckers, two with hooker companions. Taylor knew the owners encouraged it, and wondered what kind of cut they got.

He saw what must have been Candi's pimp, holding court at a corner table. Rattleskin cowboy boots, a gold belt buckle in the shape of Wisconsin, fake bling on his baseball cap. He was having a serious discussion with one of his whores. The rest of the tables were occupied by truckers. Taylor didn't see any cops; a pimp in plain sight meant they were being paid off.

The place smelled terrific, like bacon gravy and apple pie. Taylor's stomach grumbled. He located the emergency exit in the northeast corner, and knew there was also a back door that led into the kitchen; Taylor had walked the perimeter of the building before entering.

With no tables available, he approached the counter and took a seat there, between the storefront window and a pudgy, older guy nursing a cup of coffee. It was a good spot. He could see his rig, and also see anyone approaching it or him.

Taylor hadn't been to Murray's in over a year, but the printed card sticking in the laminated menu said their specialty was meatloaf.

"Meatloaf is good," the old guy leaned over and said.

"I didn't ask for your opinion."

"You were looking at the card. Thought I'd be helpful."

He examined the man, a grandfatherly type with thinning gray hair and red cheeks. Taylor wasn't in the best of moods—one toe was barely an appetizer for him—and he was ready to tell Grandpa off. But starting a scene meant being remembered, and that wasn't wise.

"Thank you," Taylor managed.

"You're welcome."

A waitress came by, wearing ugly scuffed-up gym shoes. Taylor ordered coffee and the meatloaf. The coffee was strong, bitter. Taylor added two sugars.

"Showers are good here too," his fat companion said.

Taylor gave him another look.

Is this guy trying to pick me up?

The man sipped his coffee and didn't meet Taylor's stare.

"Look, buddy. I just want to eat in peace. No offense. I've been on the road for a long time."

"No offense taken," the fat man said. He finished his coffee, then signaled the waitress for a refill. "Just telling you the showers are good. Be sure to get some quarters. They've got a machine, sells soap. Useful for washing off blood."

All of Taylor's senses went on high alert, and he felt himself flush. This guy didn't look like a cop—Taylor could usually spot cops. He wore baggy jeans, a plaid shirt, a Timex. On the counter next to his empty cup was a baseball cap without any logo. A few days' worth of beard graced his double chin.

No, he wasn't law. And he wasn't cruising him, either.

So what the hell does he want?

"What do you mean?" Taylor asked, keeping his tone neutral.

"Drop of blood on your shirt. Another spot on your collar. Some under your fingernails as well. You wiped them with ether, but it didn't completely dissolve. Did you know that ether was first used as a surgical anesthetic back in 1842? Before that, taking a knife to a person meant screaming and thrashing around." The man held a beefy hand to his mouth and belched. "'Course, some people might like the *screaming and thrashing around* part."

Taylor bunched his fists, then forced himself to relax. Had this guy seen him somehow? Did he know about Candi in the sleeper?

No. He couldn't have. Tinted windows on his cab. No windows at all in the sleeping compartment.

He took a casual glance around, trying to spot anyone else watching. No one seemed to be paying either of them any attention.

Taylor dropped his hand, slowly reaching for the folding knife clipped to his belt. He considered sliding it between this guy's ribs right there and getting the hell out. But first Taylor needed to know what Grandpa knew. Maybe he could lead him to the bathroom, get him into a stall…

Taylor froze. His knife was missing.

"Take it easy, my friend," said the old, fat man. "I'll give you your knife back when we're through."

Taylor wasn't sure what to say, but he believed everyone had an angle. This guy knew more than he should have. But what was he going to do with his information?

"Who are you?" Taylor asked.

"Name's Donaldson. And you probably meant to ask *What are you?* You've probably figured out I'm not a cop, not a Fed. Thanks, Donna." He nodded at the waitress as she refilled his coffee. "Actually, I'm just a fellow traveler. Enjoying the country. The sites. The *people*." Donaldson winked at him. "Same as you are."

"Same as me, huh?"

Donaldson nodded. "A bit older and wiser, perhaps. At least wise enough to not use that awful ether anymore. Where do you even get that these days? I thought ether and chloroform were controlled substances."

"Starter fluid," Taylor said. This conversation was getting surreal.

"Clever."

"So what is it exactly you do, Donaldson?"

"For work? Or do you mean with the people I encounter? I'm a courier, that's my job. I travel all around, delivering things to people who need them faster than overnight. As for the other—well, that's sort of personal, don't you think? We just met, and you want me to reveal intimate details of my antisocial activities? Shouldn't we work up to that?"

So far, Donaldson had been the embodiment of calm. He didn't seem threatening in the least. They might have been talking about the weather.

"And you spotted me because of the blood and the ether smell?"

"Initially. But the give-away was the look in your eyes."

"And what sort of look do my eyes have, Donaldson?"

"This one." Donaldson turned and looked at Taylor. "The eyes of a predator. No pity. No remorse. No humanity."

Taylor stared hard, then grinned. "I don't see anything but regular old eyes."

Donaldson held the intense gaze a moment longer, then chuckled. "Okay. You caught me. The eyes don't tell anything. But I caught you casing the place before you walked in. Looking for cops, for trouble, for exits. A man that careful should have noticed some spots of blood on his shirt."

"Maybe I cut myself shaving."

"And the ether smell?"

"Maybe the rig was giving me some trouble, so I cleaned out the carburetor."

"No grease or oil under your nails. Just dried blood."

Taylor leaned in close, speaking just above a whisper.

"Give me one good reason I shouldn't kill you, Donaldson."

"Other than the fact I have your knife? Because you should consider this a golden opportunity, my friend. You and I, we're solitary creatures. We don't ever talk about our secret lives. We never share stories of our exploits with anyone. I've been doing this for over thirty years, and I've never met another person like us. A few wannabes. More than a few crazies. But never another hunter. Like we are. Don't you think this is a unique chance?"

The meatloaf came, steaming hot. But Taylor wasn't hungry anymore. He was intrigued. If Donaldson was what he claimed to be, the fat man was one hundred percent correct. Taylor had never talked about his lifestyle with anyone, other than his victims. And then, it was only to terrify them even more.

Sometimes, Taylor had fantasies of getting caught. Not because he harbored any guilt, and not because he wanted to be locked up. But because it would be nice, just once, to be open and honest about his habits with the whole world. To let a fellow human being know how clever he'd been all these years. Maybe have some shrink interview him and write a bestselling book.

How interesting it would be to talk shop with someone as exceptional as he was.

"So you want to swap stories? Trade tactics? Is that it, Donaldson?"

"I can think of duller ways to kill some time at a truck stop."

Taylor cut the meatloaf with his fork, shoved some into his mouth. It was good.

"Fine. You go first. You said you don't like ether. So how do you make your—" Taylor reached for the right words "—*guests* compliant."

"Blunt force trauma."

"Using what?"

"Trade secret."

"And what if you're too... *aggressive*... with your use of blunt force?"

"An unfortunate side-effect. Just happened to me, in fact. Just picked up a tasty little morsel, but her lights went out before I could have any fun with her."

"Picked up? Hitcher?"

Donaldson sipped more coffee and grinned. "Didn't you know about the dangers of hitchhiking, son? Lots of psychos out there."

Taylor shoved more meatloaf into his mouth, and followed it up with some mashed potatoes. "Hitchers might be missed."

"So could truck stop snatch."

Taylor paused in mid-bite.

"Your fly is open. And I saw how you were measuring the resident pimp." Donaldson raised an eyebrow. "Have you relieved him of one of his steady sources of income?"

Now it was Taylor's turn to grin. "Not yet. She'll be dessert when I'm done with this meatloaf."

"And once you're finished with her?"

Taylor zipped up his fly. "I like rivers. Water takes care of any trace evidence, and it's tough for the law to pinpoint the location where they were dumped in. You?"

"Gas and a match. First a nice spritz with bleach. Bleach destroys DNA, you know."

"I do. Got a few bottles in the truck."

Taylor still couldn't assess what sort of threat Donaldson posed. But he had to admit, this was fun.

"So, here's the ten-thousand dollar question," Donaldson asked. "How many are you up to?"

Taylor wiped some gravy off his mouth with a paper napkin. "So that's where we stand? Whipping out our dicks and seeing whose is bigger?"

"I've been at this a very long time." Donaldson belched again. "Probably since before you were born. I've read about others like us; I love those true crime audiobooks. They help pass the time on long trips. I collect regular books, too. Movies. Newspaper articles. If you've done the same research I have, then you know none of our American peers can prove more than forty-eight. That's the key. *Prove.* Some boast high numbers, but there isn't proof to back it up."

"So are you asking me how many I've done, or how many I can prove?"

"Both."

Taylor shrugged. "I lost count after forty-eight. Once I had one in every state, it became less about quantity and more about quality."

"You're lying," Donaldson said. "You're too young for that many."

"One in every state, old man."

"Can you prove it?"

"I kept driver's licenses, those that had them. Probably don't have more than twenty, though. Not many whores carry ID."

"No pictures? Trophies? Souvenirs?"

Taylor wasn't going to share something that personal with a stranger. He pretended to sneer. "Taking a trophy is like asking to get caught. I don't plan on getting caught."

"True. But it is nice to relive the moment. Traveling is lonely, and memories unfortunately fade. If it wasn't so dangerous, I'd love to videotape a few."

That would be nice, Taylor thought, finishing the last bit of meatloaf. *But my trophy box will have to suffice.*

"So how many are you up to, Grandpa?"

"A hundred twenty-seven."

Taylor snorted. "Bullshit."

"I agree with you about the danger of keeping souvenirs, but I have Polaroids from a lot of my early ones."

"Dangerous to carry those around with you."

"I've got them well hidden." Donaldson stared at him, his eyes twinkling. "Would you be interested in seeing them?"

"What do you mean? One of those *I'll show you mine if you show me yours* deals?"

"No. Well, not exactly. I'm not interested in seeing your driver's license collection. But I would be interested in paying a little visit to your current guest."

Taylor frowned. "I'm not big on sharing. Or sloppy seconds."

Donaldson slowly spread out his hands. "I understand. It's just that… you know how it is, when you get all worked up, and then they quit on you."

Taylor nodded. Having a victim die too soon felt like having something precious stolen from him.

"You don't seem like the shy type," Donaldson continued. "I thought, perhaps, you wouldn't mind doing your thing when someone else was there to watch."

Taylor smiled. "Aren't you the dirty old man."

Donaldson smiled back. "A dirty old man who doesn't have the same distaste of sloppy seconds as you apparently have. I see no problem in going second. As long as there's something left for me to enjoy myself with."

"I leave all the major parts intact."

"Then perhaps we can come to some sort of arrangement."

"Perhaps we can."

Donaldson's smile suddenly slipped off his face. He'd noticed the same thing Taylor had.

A cop had walked into the restaurant.

Woman, forties, well built, a gold star clipped to her hip. But even without the badge, she had that swagger, had that *look*, that Taylor had spent a lifetime learning to spot.

"Here comes trouble," Donaldson said.

And, as luck would have it, trouble sat down right next to them.

Chapter Four

After filling my gas tank and emptying my bladder, I went in search of food.

The diner was surprisingly full this late at night. Truckers mostly. And though I hadn't worked Vice in well over a decade, I was pretty sure the only women in the place were earning their living illegally.

Not that I judged, or even cared. One of the reasons I switched from Vice to Homicide was because I had no problems with what consenting adults did to themselves or each other. I'd done a few drugs in my day, and as a woman I felt I should be able to do whatever I wanted with my body. So the scene in the diner was nothing more to me than local color. I just wanted some coffee and a hot meal, which I believed would wake me up enough to get me through the rest of my road trip and into the very patient arms of my fiancée.

I expected at least one or two catcalls or wolf whistles when I entered, but didn't hear any. Sort of disappointing. I was wearing what I wore to court, a brown Ann Klein pantsuit, clingy in all the right places, and a pair of three inch Kate Spade strappy sandals. The shoes were perhaps a bit frivolous, but the jury couldn't see my feet when I took the stand. I left for Wisconsin directly from court, and wore the shoes because Latham loved them. I had even painted my toenails to celebrate our vacation.

Maybe the current diners were too preoccupied with the hired help to know another woman had entered the place. Or maybe it was me. Latham said I gave off a "cop vibe" that people could sense, but he assured me I was still sexy. Still, a Wisconsin truck stop at two in the morning filled with lonely, single men, and I didn't even get a lecherous glance. Maybe I needed to work-out more.

Then I realized I still had my badge clipped to my belt. Duh.

I quickly scoped out the joint, finding the emergency exit, counting the number of patrons and employees, identifying potential trouble. An absurdly dressed man in expensive boots and a diamond studded John Deere cap stared hard at me. He gave me a look that said he hated cops, and I gave him a look that said I hated his kind even more. While I tolerated prostitutes, I loathed pimps. Someone taking the money you earned just because they were bigger than you wasn't fair.

But I didn't come here to start trouble. I just wanted some food and caffeine.

I walked the room slowly, feeling the cold stares, and found counter space next to a portly man. I eased myself onto the stool.

"Coffee, officer?"

I nodded at the waitress. She overturned my mug and filled it up. I glanced at the menu, wondering if they had cheese curds—those little fried nuggets of cheddar exclusive to Wisconsin.

"The meatloaf is good."

I glanced at the man on my left. Big and tall, maybe fifteen years older than I was. He had a kind-looking face, but his smile appeared forced.

"Thanks," I replied.

I sipped some coffee. Nice and strong. If I got two cups and a burger in me, I'd be good to go. The waitress returned, I ordered a cheeseburger with bacon, and a side of cheese curds.

"Never seen you here before."

The voice, reeking of alpha male, came from behind me. I could guess who it belonged to.

"Passing through," I said, not bothering to turn around.

"Well, maybe you can hurry it along, little lady. Your kind isn't good for business."

I carefully set down my mug of coffee, then slowly swiveled around on my stool.

The pimp was sticking his chest out like he was being fitted for a bra, a few stray curly hairs peeking through his collar. One of his women, strung out on something, clung unenthusiastically to his side. Her concealer didn't quite cover up her black eye.

"I'm off duty, and just stopped in for coffee and some cheese curds, which I can't get in Illinois. I suggest you mind your own business. This isn't my jurisdiction, but I'm guessing the local authorities wouldn't mind if I fed you some of your teeth."

The older fat guy next to me snorted. The pimp wasn't so amused.

"The *local authorities*," he said it in a falsetto, obviously trying to

mimic me, "and I have an arrangement. That arrangement means no cops."
He gave me a rough shove in the shoulder. "And I'm sure they wouldn't
mind if I fed you—"

I drove the salt shaker into his upper jaw with my palm, breaking both
the glass and the teeth I'd promised. Besides being hard and having weight,
the shards and the salt did a number on the pimp's gums. Must have hurt like
crazy.

He dropped to his knees, clutching his face and howling, and three of
his women dragged him out of there. I did a slow pan across the room,
looking for other challengers, seeing none. Then I brushed my hand on my
pants, wiping off the excess salt, and went back to my coffee, trying to
control the adrenalin shakes. I hated violence of any kind, but once he
touched me, I didn't have any other recourse. I didn't want to play footsie
with the local cops he was paying off, trying to get an assault charge to stick.
Or worse, wind up in the hospital because some asshole pimp thought he
could treat me the same way he treated the women who worked for him.

Better to nip it in the bud and drop him fast. Though I didn't have to feel
good about it.

I took a deep, steadying breath, and managed to sip some coffee without
spilling it all over myself, all the while keeping one eye on the entrance. I'd
hurt the pimp bad enough to require an emergency room visit, but if he were
tougher and dumber than I'd guessed, he might return with a weapon. I set
my purse on the counter, my .38 within easy reach, just in case.

"You're Lieutenant Jack Daniels, aren't you?"

I glanced at the fat man again. Even though I'd been on the news many
times, I didn't get recognized very often in Chicago, and it never happened
away from home.

"And you are?" My voice came out higher than I would have liked.

"Just a fan. You got that serial killer Charles Kork, the one they called
the Gingerbread Man. How many women did he kill?"

"Too many." I turned back to my coffee.

"I saw the TV movie. The one that became the series. You're much better looking than the actress who played you."

I was in no mood to be idolized. Plus, there was something creepy about this guy.

"Look, buddy, I don't want to be rude, but I'm really not up for conversation right now."

The fat man didn't take the hint. "And you got Barry Fuller. He killed over a dozen, didn't he? He was both a serial killer and a mass murderer, due to all those Feds he took out at that rest stop."

I sighed. The waitress came by with my cheese curds. She set down the basket and winked at me. "These are on me."

"Thanks. I could use some salt."

I tried a curd. Too hot, so I spit it back out into my palm and played hot potato until it cooled off. My biggest fan refused to give up.

"There were others in the Kork family as well, weren't there? A whole group of psychos. I heard they killed over forty people, total."

I really didn't want to think about the Kork family, and I really didn't want to have a late-night gabfest with a cop groupie.

But, on the plus side, knocking out that pimp's teeth really woke me up.

When the waitress brought me the salt, I asked for my meal to go. The fat guy apparently didn't like that, because he gave me his back and had an intense whisper exchange with his buddy; a younger, attractive man in a flannel shirt. The young guy nodded, got up, and left.

"Just one last question, Lieutenant, and then I promise I'll leave you alone."

I sighed again, glancing at him. "Go ahead."

"Did you ever try to take on two serial killers at once?"

"I can't say that I have."

He smiled, lopsided. "Too bad. That would have been cool."

The fat guy threw down some money, then followed his buddy out.

No longer pestered, I decided to eat there, and settled in to eat my cheese curds.

Chapter Five

Taylor hadn't ever killed a cop. He came close once, a few years ago, when a state trooper pulled him over, and asked him to step out of his truck. Taylor had been ready to pull his knife and gut the pig, but the cop only wanted him to do a field sobriety test. Taylor wouldn't ever risk driving drunk, and he easily passed, getting let off with a warning and pulling away with a dead hooker in his sleeping compartment.

But he was itching to get at this cop. Taylor liked strong women. He liked when they fought him, refusing to give up. They were so much fun to break. Especially when they had such adorable feet.

As Donaldson suggested, Taylor had left the diner and gone back to his rig to grab the ether. Candi with an I was still out cold, but she held far less fascination for Taylor than this new prospect.

I'm going to have a little nip of Jack Daniels, he thought, smiling wildly. *Maybe more than one. And maybe not so little.*

For helping out, he'd let Donaldson have Candi. While Taylor wasn't into the whole *voyeur* scene, it might be interesting to watch another pro do his thing. Hopefully, it didn't involve any sort of sex, because he had zero desire to see Donaldson's flabby, naked ass.

Taylor grabbed the plastic bag—the ether-soaked paper towels still moist—and met Donaldson in the parking lot.

"The best spot is here, in the shadow of this truck," Donaldson said.

Taylor didn't like him calling the shots, but he heard the man out.

"She thinks I'm a fan," Donaldson continued, "so I'm going to call her over here, ask for an autograph. Then you come up behind her with the ether."

"She's armed. Her purse was too heavy to only be carrying a wallet and make-up."

"I saw that, too. I'll grab her wrists, you get her around the neck. We can pull her to the ground here, out of sight. How close is your truck?"

"The red Peterbilt, a few spaces back."

"When she's out, we throw her arms around our shoulders, walk her over there like she's drunk."

Taylor shook his head. "Only when we're sure no one is watching. I don't want a witness getting my plate number."

"Fine. We can walk her around until we're sure we're clear."

Taylor stared at Donaldson for a moment, then said, "She's mine."

Donaldson didn't respond.

"I'll give you the whore for helping me, Donaldson. But the cop is mine."

Donaldson eventually nodded. "Fair enough. Is the whore cute?"

"Too old, fat thighs, saggy gut from popping out kids."

Donaldson raised his eyebrow. "She's got kids?"

Taylor laughed. "You into kiddies, Donaldson?"

"Any port in the storm. But you can have fun with kids in other ways. Did the whore have a cell phone?"

"Yeah."

"Give it here."

Interested in where Donaldson was going with this, Taylor dug the phone out of his pocket and handed it over. Donaldson scrolled through the address book.

"Calling home," Donaldson told him.

"Can't calls be traced?"

"They can be traced to this cell phone, but not to our current location. To do that requires some highly sophisticated equipment—which I highly doubt the local constabulary possesses."

"Put it on speaker."

Donaldson hit a button, and Taylor heard ringing.

"Hello?" A child's voice, pre-teen.

"This is Detective Donaldson. I'm sorry to inform you that your mommy is dead."

"What?"

"Mommy is dead, kid. She was horribly murdered."

"Mommy's dead?" The child began to cry.

"It's an occupational hazard. Your mom was a whore, you know. She had sex with strange men for money. One of those men killed her."

"Mommy's dead!"

Donaldson hit the disconnect button.

Taylor shook his head, smiling. "Man, that is low."

"I'll call him back later, see how he's doing. This phone has a camera, too. Maybe I'll send him some pictures of Mommy when I'm done with her."

"What about the babysitter sending the cops here?"

"You think the babysitter knows what Mom's job is? And even if she calls the cops, Murray's pays them to stay away. Besides, we'll be in your truck by then."

Taylor thought it was reckless. But still, calling up a kid and saying his mother was dead was pretty funny. Taylor considered all of the cell phones he'd thrown away, and cursed himself for the fun he'd missed.

Donaldson dug into his pocket and produced a pair of small binoculars. He held them to his face and looked at the diner.

"The cop is still working on her burger. She is a sweet piece of pie, isn't she? *Jack fucking Daniels*. What a lucky day indeed. It's a small world, my friend."

"Not when you're driving from L.A. to Boston."

"Funny you should mention that. One of the reasons I'm a courier is to have a wide area to hunt in. I'm assuming you got into trucking for the same reason."

"The wider the better. You shouldn't shit where you eat."

"I agree. I don't think I'm even on the Fed's radar. And cops don't talk to each other from state to state. A man could keep on doing this for a very long time, if he plays it smart."

"So, what's your thing?" Taylor asked.

Donaldson lowered the binocs. "My thing?"

"What you do to them."

Donaldson did the eyebrow raise again, which was starting to get annoying. "Have we reached that point in our relationship where we can share our methods? You haven't even told me your name."

"It's Taylor. And I want to know, before I invite you into my truck, that you aren't into some sick shit."

"Define *sick*."

"Guts are okay, but don't puncture the intestines. That smell takes forever to go away."

"I'm not into internal organs."

"How about rape?"

Donaldson smiled. "I *am* into rape."

"I don't want to see it. No offense, but naked guys are not a turn-on for me."

"That's fair enough. We can take turns, give each other some privacy. My *thing*, as you put it, is to cut off their faces. One little piece at a time. A nostril. An ear. An eye. A lip. And then I feed their faces to them, bit by bit. You?"

"Biting. Toes and fingers, to start. Then all over."

"How long have you kept one alive for?"

"Maybe two days."

Donaldson nodded. "See, that's nice. I do all my work outdoors, different locations, so I never have time to make it last, enjoy it. You've got a little murder-mobile, you can take your time."

"That's the reason I'm a trucker, not a courier."

Donaldson got a wistful look. "I'm thinking of renting a shack out in the woods. Out in the middle of nowhere. Then I could bring someone there, really drag it out. You remember that old magic trick? The girl in the box, and the magician sticks swords in it?"

Taylor nodded. "Yeah."

"I'd love to build one of those. Except there's no trick. Wouldn't that be fun? Sticking the swords in one at a time?"

Taylor decided it would.

Donaldson peered through the binocs again. "Here she comes. Let's get in position."

Taylor nodded. He felt the excitement building up again, but a different kind of excitement. This time, he was sharing the experience with another person. It was oddly fulfilling, in a way his dozens of other murders hadn't been.

Maybe tag-team was the way to go.

He clenched the ether-soaked paper towels, crouched behind a bumper, and waited for the fun to start.

Chapter Six

The burger was good. The coffee was good. The cheese curds were heavenly. I had no idea why they weren't served in Chicago.

I paid, left a decent tip, then tried calling Latham to tell him I felt good enough to keep driving.

Still no signal. I needed to switch carriers, or get a new phone. It especially bugged me because I saw other people in the diner talking on their cell phones. If that *Can you hear me now?* guy walked into the restaurant, I would have bounced my cell off his head.

The parking lot had decent lighting, but all of the big trucks cast shadows, and I knew more than most the dangers of walking in shadows. I pulled my purse on over my head and tucked it under my arm, then headed for my car while staying in the light. The last thing I needed was the pimp to make a play for me. Or that—

"Lieutenant Daniels!"

—fat guy from the diner, who approached me at a quick pace, coming out from behind one of the rigs. I stopped, my hand slipping inside my purse and seeking my revolver. Something about this man rubbed me the wrong way, and at over two hundred and fifty pounds he was too big to play around with.

He slowed down when I reached into my handbag—a bad sign. People with good intentions don't expect you to have a gun. I felt my heart rate kick up and my legs tense.

"Don't come any closer," I commanded, using my cop voice.

He stopped about ten feet in front of me. His hands were empty. "I wanted to ask you for your autograph."

My fingers wrapped around the butt of my .38. Confrontation, even with over twenty years of experience, was always a scary thing. Ninety-nine percent of the time, de-escalation was the key to avoiding violence. Take control of the situation, be polite but firm, apologize if needed. It wouldn't have worked on the pimp, who was showing off for the crowd, but it might work here.

"I'm sorry, I don't give autographs. I'm not a celebrity."

"It would mean a lot to me." He held up his palms and took another step forward.

I was taught that you never pull out your weapon unless you intend to use it.

I pulled out my weapon.

"I told you not to come any closer."

"You're kidding, right?" Another step. He was six feet away from me.

I pointed my gun at his chest. "Does it look like I'm kidding?"

He put on a crooked grin. "Is this how you treat your fans, Lieutenant? I don't mean any harm. You want to shoot an innocent civilian?"

"I don't want to. But I will, if I feel threatened. And right now I feel threatened. Where's your buddy?"

"My buddy?"

He was lying, I could see it on his face, and I swirled around, sensing something behind me. I caught a flash of movement, someone ducking between two parked cars. I spun again, storming up to the fat guy, grabbing two of his outstretched fingers and twisting. My action was fast, forceful, and I gained enough leverage to bend his arm to the side and drive him onto his knees, my gun trained on his head.

"Get on the pavement, face down!"

He pitched forward, and I had to let him go or fall with him. Rather than face-first, he dropped onto his side and swung his leg at me.

I should have fired, but a small part of me knew I could be killing a guy whose only crime was wanting my autograph, and I had enough of an ego to think I could still handle the situation. I side-stepped his leg and rammed my heel into his kidney, hard enough to show him this wasn't a joke.

That's when his partner dove at me.

He hit me sideways, knocking me off my feet in a flying tackle that drove me to the asphalt, shoulder-first. His weight squeezed the air out of me, his hand pawing at my face, a cold, wet hand covering my mouth and nose, flooding my airway with harsh chemicals. I held my breath, bringing my weapon up, squeezing the trigger—

The trigger wouldn't squeeze. The gun didn't fire.

Now the paper towels were in my eyes, the sting a hundred times worse than chlorine, making me squeeze my eyelids shut in pain. I felt my gun being wrestled away, and the small part of my brain that wasn't panicking knew the perp had grabbed my .38 by the hammer, his grip preventing me from shooting.

I still refused to breathe, knowing that whatever was on my face would knock me out, knowing when that happened I was dead. That made me panic even more, thrashing and pushing against my unseen assailant. I tried to kick my feet, get them under me to gain some leverage, but then they were weighed down the same as my upper body—the fat guy had joined the party.

So I went for the fake-out, letting my body go limp.

The seconds ticked by, each one a slice of eternity since I was oxygen-deprived. I could hold my breath for over a minute under ideal conditions. But terrified and with two psychos on top of me, I wouldn't be able to last a fraction of that…

One second at a time, Jack. Just don't breathe.

I felt that vertigo sensation in my head, my mind seeming to stretch out and twist around.

"Is anyone coming?"

"It's clear."

Stay still. Don't breathe.

My eyes were stinging like crazy, and I wanted to put my hands to my face, rub the pain away.

Don't. Move. Don't. Breathe.

My chest began to spasm, my diaphragm convulsing and begging for air. In moments it wouldn't be under my control anymore. I would breathe in those toxic fumes whether I wanted to or not.

Hold it in don't breathe don't breathe DON'T BREATHE—

"Too much and you'll kill her." The fat guy talking.

The hand over my face eased up, the noxious rag being pulled away. I wanted to gasp, to suck in air like a marathon runner, but I managed to take a slow, silent breath through my nose.

The fumes still clinging to my face smelled like gasoline, and by sheer will I didn't sneeze or cough. I kept my breathing slow, like I was sleeping, even though my heart pounded so loud and fast I could hear it.

"She's out. Grab an arm."

I felt myself lifted into an upright position, my arms over their shoulders. Then I was dragged, my feet scraping against the asphalt, which tore at my bare toes like sandpaper. I bit my inner cheek. If I made a peep, they'd use the rag again.

"Her feet! Watch her feet! I don't want them messed up!"

"Shh! Lift higher."

Then I was completely off the ground. I tried to peek, to see where we were, but everything was blurry and opening my eyes made the pain worse. I could feel the weight of my purse still hanging at my side, and I had a dull throb in my shoulder where I'd hit the pavement, but it didn't seem dislocated or broken.

"It's this one."

My body was shifted, and I heard the jingle of keys and a vehicle door opening.

"I'll get in first, pull her up."

"Check around for witnesses."

"We're alone out here, brother."

Another shift, and then strong hands under my armpits, pulling me up, hands on my ankle, my right shoe coming off, and then...

Something warm and wet on my big toe.

Jesus... he's got my toe in his mouth.

His tongue circled it, once, twice, and then I felt the suction. Heard the slurping. Heard him moan.

This freak is sucking my toe.

Wet and sloppy, like a popsicle. I wanted to flinch. I wanted to scream.

Stay still, Jack. Don't kick him. Don't move.

His teeth locked on, scraping along the top and bottom, not enough to break the skin but enough to hurt, the pressure increasing...

I felt a surge of revulsion unlike any I've ever experienced, and my muscles involuntarily locked and my stomach churned, threatening to upload the burger and curds. I was half-hanging out of a truck, and I couldn't see, but I was going to take my chances and kick this bastard in the face, hopefully burying my shoe heel into his eye socket. It was two on one, and they had my gun, but I wasn't going to let him chew my toe off without a fight.

"Taylor, let's hold off until we get her inside."

My toe was abruptly released, and then I was violently shoved upward onto the fat guy's lap. I assumed he was sitting in the driver's seat of a semi. I felt his hot breath on my ear, and then the clammy touch of his lips. One hand pawed at my chest, tugging at my bra through my shirt. The other slid up my leg.

"Such a pretty lady," he said, nuzzling my neck. "I'm going to love feeding you your face."

When his lips touched my cheek it was like a taser shock, and my bile began to rise again.

"Take her in the back," Taylor said. "We'll bring her up to the sleeper."

The fat man gave my knee a final squeeze, then grunted as he hefted me up in his arms and shifted his bulk. Once again I was lifted, tugged, and pushed. I chanced a peek, everything dark and blurry, wanting so badly to rub my eyes, and all I could make out was a ladder of some sort.

"There's a handle on the trap door. Turn it."

"Where?"

"Right above your head."

I was shoved through an opening in the ceiling of the cab, then dropped unceremoniously onto a mat. It was hot. I smelled bleach, cheap perfume, and the copper-pennies stench of fresh blood. Also, underneath everything, was an odor that scared me to my core, an odor I recognized from hundreds of cases from more than twenty years or cases. A cross between meat gone bad and excrement that all the bleach on the planet couldn't ever fully erase.

The stink of dead bodies.

People have died in this room.

"Warm up here."

"When we get started, I'll put the air conditioning on. I've also got recessed stereo speakers, for mood music, and an AC outlet up by the fire alarm, if you want to plug in any power tools."

"I like power tools."

"Give yours a tap, see if she's awake yet."

I heard a slapping sound, skin on skin, and then a feminine whine.

"She's still groggy."

"She'll be up soon. I know she's not much to look at, but that really doesn't matter once you get started, does it?"

"Actually, Taylor, as grateful as I am to you for inviting me into your home, I've been reading about Jack Daniels for years. She's every killer's wet dream."

There was a long pause.

"What are you saying?" Taylor said.

"I'm saying I want the cop."

"We already agreed, she's mine."

"You can have her feet. I want her face."

"Maybe I want the whole thing."

Donaldson laughed. "You know, you remind me of my younger brother. I miss that kid, so much that I sometimes regret killing him. But I remember something my father used to say when we were fighting over a toy. He said, *If you can't share, then neither of you can have it.*"

Then I heard the unmistakable sound of my .38 being cocked.

Chapter Seven

Standing on the ladder, with his upper half through the trap door, Taylor stared at the gun in the kneeling fat man's hand. It was pointed at the cop's head, but Donaldson's eyes were focuses on him.

Goddammit, why did I let him grab the gun?

Taylor felt himself go dead inside, like his body turned to ice. He chose his words carefully, keeping his voice even. "You know what, Donaldson? Maybe you're right. Sharing seems like a fair thing to do, and it might even be fun. Besides, it would be a shame to deprive such a famous lady of either of our company. But I have to say that seeing you holding a gun makes me a bit nervous. We don't want to make enemies of each other, do we?"

Donaldson smiled, shrugged, and then uncocked the gun and shoved it into his front pocket. "I appreciate your generosity, Taylor. Really, I do. And normally I wouldn't be so ungracious to a fellow traveler. But this woman just *does* something to me. I haven't been this excited in years."

"I can see that." Taylor was eye-level with Donaldson's crotch. "Or maybe that's the gun."

"So let's have a meeting of the minds."

"Fine."

Taylor relaxed a notch now that the weapon was out of play, but he had no doubt Donaldson would use it again. His original fantasy of tag-team action had been replaced by the unpleasant image of Donaldson tying him up and feeding him his own face. When there are too many foxes in the henhouse, the foxes kill each other. A shame, because Taylor was starting to like the older man.

"Since you agree to sharing," Donaldson said, "would you be adverse to both of us going at her at the same time? You take the bottom half, I take the top?"

Taylor reached a hand behind his back and touched the folding knife clipped to his belt—Donaldson had given it back to him in the parking lot. Killing him right now would probably be the best bet, but the guy was big, and the knife blade was short. Unless he died quick, Donaldson would fight back and be able to grab his gun.

No, the knife wasn't the way to go.

But Taylor did have a sawed-off shotgun under his passenger seat. All he needed to do was jump down, lock the trap door, and grab it.

"Sharing would be okay." Taylor tried to look thoughtful. "But I want to look her in the eyes when I'm doing my thing. Be tough to do if her eyes were gone."

"They wouldn't be gone. They'd be in her mouth."

Taylor shook his head. "That wouldn't be good for me."

"I could leave her eyes alone. Maybe just take off her eyelids so she'd be forced to look. It could work. We could do a trial run on the whore, here."

Donaldson kicked Candi in her side. She moaned.

Taylor figured there were three steps beneath him. He would need to grab the door and tug it closed before Donaldson pulled his gun. He didn't know if the cop's bullet would go through the half inch steel the sleeper was made out of, but his shotgun slugs certainly would. Lots of damage, though, and it would make a lot of noise.

"I'm not exactly keen on a two on one. If you promise to leave her eyes alone, and that she'll stay conscious and not die on you, I could let you go first."

Donaldson's face remained blank for a moment, then he raised his eyebrow.

"I appreciate your offer. I sincerely do. But I can't help but think that while I'm doing my thing, you might make some sort of effort to do me harm. Or perhaps lock me in here."

Taylor began to wish he never parked at this truck stop.

"We seem to be at an impasse."

"No," Donaldson shook his head. "I believe we can work this out. I have no desire to harm you, Taylor. And I am grateful for this opportunity. I shouldn't have flashed the gun. That was a mistake. I've been playing this game solo for so long, I wasn't thinking clearly. I know you have a knife on you, and probably some other weapons in the truck, and I fear I just began a war of escalation."

"I don't want to kill you either." It was the truth. Not that he had any real affection for Donaldson, but trying to muscle the dead fat man out of his sleeper and drag him to a river didn't seem like a fun time.

"We don't know each other well yet. But we're kindred spirits. Maybe we could even become friends."

"It's possible."

"How long will the cop be out for?" Donaldson asked.

"A few minutes, probably more. Pinch her, see if she flinches. When they're really under, they don't flinch."

Donaldson leaned over Jack Daniels and squeezed her breast. She didn't move.

"She's out. You have some rope?"

"More bungee cords in the trunk."

Neither man moved to get them. Eventually, Donaldson raised an eyebrow. "Are you a gambling man, Taylor?"

"I've been known to play the odds."

"Let's flip a coin. Winner gets first crack at the cop."

Taylor considered it. "I'd be up for that, if it were a fair toss."

"We could go in the diner, have our waitress do the flipping. I'll even let you call it. Would be good to get out in the fresh air, clear our heads."

"Let's say I agree. You still have me at a disadvantage."

Donaldson nodded. "The gun. Firing it wouldn't be smart for either of us. Cops might already be on their way, after what Lieutenant Daniels did to that pimp."

"I've got a solution."

"I'm listening."

"An empty gun isn't a threat. Hand me the bullets. But do it slowly, or else I might get nervous and lock you up here for a few days with no air conditioning or water."

"Fair enough."

Donaldson gently reached back into his pants and removed the gun. He held it upside-down by the trigger guard, and swung out the cylinder. Then he dumped the rounds onto his palm and handed them to Taylor.

Taylor grinned.

Maybe this tag-team thing will work out after all.

"Are we good?" Donaldson asked.

"We're good. Let's hogtie this pig."

Taylor climbed into the sleeper, and after an uneasy moment of sizing each other up, the two of them began to bind the cop. Donaldson quickly got the hang of it, and they soon had Jack suitably trussed.

"You sure she's safe here?" Donaldson asked, admiring their handiwork.

"Never had an escape. Bungee cords are tighter than rope. The enclosure is steel, the lock on the door is solid. She's not going anywhere."

Taylor grabbed the cop's purse, wound it over his shoulder, and crawled down out of the sleeper after Donaldson. He made sure the trap door was locked, took what he wanted from the purse, and together they walked back to the diner.

Chapter Eight

The moment they were gone I rolled onto my belly and inch-wormed up to my knees. My hands were behind my back, the bungee cords so tight my fingers were tingling. I strained against the elastic, trying to twist my wrists apart, but couldn't free myself.

More cords wound around my chest and upper arms, and encircled my knees and ankles. I flopped onto my side, wincing at the pain. My shoulder still hurt, and there was a throb in my left breast where Donaldson had pinched me. If he'd done it for a few seconds longer, I would have screamed.

Pretending to be unconscious seemed like a better choice than really being unconscious, but when they tied me up I realized that maybe fighting back and yelling for help when I had the chance might have been the better move.

Panic threatened to overwhelm me, and I began to hyperventilate. Fear and I were old adversaries. There was no way to squelch it, but if I kept my focus I could work through the fear. The goal was to not think about any potential outcome to this situation other than escape.

Still unable to open my eyes because of the stinging, I rolled to my left, hoping to bump into anything that would help me free myself. I hit something soft. I brushed my cheek against it. Foam of some kind. I rolled right instead, eventually coming up against something more suitable. Something hard, stuck into the floor. After maneuvering around onto my knees, I rubbed my hands against the object.

It felt like a board, only two feet tall, and thin. Midway down the side was some sort of protrusion. Though my hands were quickly getting numb, I could tell by the sound when I jiggled it that it was a padlock.

I got my wrists under the lock, trying to wedge it in between my arms and the bungee cords. Then I took a deep breath and violently tugged my arms forward.

The elastic caught, stretched.

I pulled harder, feeling like my arms were pulling out of their sockets.

Then, abruptly, my hands were free, and I pitched forward onto my face, bumping my forehead against the padded floor.

I spent a few seconds wiggling my fingers, wincing as the blood came back, and made quick work of the other cords around my arms. Then I spit in my hands and rubbed them against my eyes. The stinging eased up enough for me to have a blurry look around the enclosure. There was moderate lighting, from an overhead fixture. I saw beige mats. A black slanted ceiling covered with sound baffles. A trunk. And a bound woman, her feet in some sort of wooden stock, my wrist bungee cord wound around a padlock on the side.

I unwound my legs, tugged off my remaining shoe, and crawled over to her, unhooking her bindings. "Can you hear me?"

The woman moaned softly, and her eyelids fluttered.

"You need to wake up." I gave her a shake. "We're in trouble."

"My... foot... hurts..."

"What's your name?"

"My... foot..."

I cupped her chin in my hand, made her look at me.

"Listen to me. I'm a cop. We're in a truck sleeper and some men are trying to kill us. What's your name?"

"Candi. I... I can't move my feet. It hurts."

I turned my attention to the stock. I crawled around to the other side, wincing when I saw the blood. I took a closer look because I had to assess the damage, then wished I could erase the image from my mind.

"What's wrong with my foot?"

"You're missing your little toe."

"My... *toe?*"

I studied the stock. Heavy, solid, the padlock and latch unbreakable. So I looked at the hinge on the other side. Six screws held it in place.

I scooted away from the stock, on my butt, and reared back my right heel.

"Stay still, Candi. I'm going to try to break the hinge."

I shot my leg out like a piston, striking the top of the stock once, twice, three times.

The stock stayed solid, the screws tight. And if I tried kicking any harder I'd break my heel.

"Don't you have a gun?"

I ignored her, turning my attention to the trunk in the corner of the enclosure. I crawled over to see if there was anything inside I could use.

"Don't leave me!"

"I won't leave you. I promise."

I found paper towels, paper masks, starter fluid, plastic bags, and a large Tupperware container. The lid had brown stains on it—dried blood—and I got an uneasy feeling looking at it. Fighting squeamishness, I pulled the top off.

It was filled with rock salt. But I could make out something brown peeking through. I shook the box, and it revealed a few of the brown things, small and wrinkled. They looked like prunes.

Then I realized what they were, and came very close to throwing up. I pulled away, covering my mouth. There had to be dozens, maybe over a hundred, of them in there.

That sick bastard...

"Did you find anything?"

"Nothing helpful," I said, closing the lid.

"What's in that box you were holding?"

Taylor was smart. He didn't leave any tools, weapons, or keys lying around. I eyed the starter fluid.

"Candi, do you smoke?"

"Yeah."

"Do you have matches on you? A lighter?"

"In my purse. He took it."

Dammit. But starting a fire in the enclosed space probably wasn't a good idea anyway. However, the chest itself had possibilities. It was made of wood, with metal reinforced corners. I picked it up, figuring it weighed at least fifteen pounds.

"What was in the box!"

I muscled the chest over to Candi and knelt next to her.

"Hold still," I said. "If I miss I could break your leg."

I reared back, clenched my teeth, and shoved the chest into the top of the stock. There was a loud *crack,* but both objects stayed intact.

I did it again.

And again.

And again.

And again.

My shoulder began to burn, and the corners of the chest were coming apart, but the hinge on the stock was bending.

Two more times and the chest burst open, spilling its contents onto the mat, the Tupperware container bouncing next to Candi.

I hit the stock one last time. The chest broke into several large pieces. I grabbed one of the slats used to make the chest, and wedged it in the opening I'd made between the top and bottom of the stock. I used it like a crowbar, levering at the hinge.

It was slowly giving... giving...

Then the stock popped open like a shotgun blast.

Candi sat up abruptly, grabbing her ankle to see her injury for herself. Then the tears hit, fast and hard.

"Ah shit... that fucker."

"We need to find a way out of here."

"My toe..." she sobbed.

"Candi! Focus!"

Her eyes locked on mine.

"We need to start rolling up the mats," I ordered, "find the way out of here before they come back."

She sniffled. "They? I only know one. Taylor."

"He's got a buddy now." I made a face. "And they're armed."

I watched Candi's face do an emotion montage. Anger, pain, despair, then raw fear.

"I have kids," Candi whispered. "A boy and a girl."

"Then we need to find the exit, fast. Start pulling up the mats."

"What time is it? My man, Julius, he'll come looking for me when I don't report back."

I thought about the pimp, running out of the diner with his teeth in his hand.

"Julius, uh, probably won't be coming to the rescue. Do the mats. Now."

She wiped her nose on her arm, and then reached for the Tupperware container.

"Candi…"

"I want to see."

She popped off the lid and squinted at the objects in the rock salt.

"What are these things?"

"We need to look for the exit, Candi."

"Are those… *aw, Jesus…*"

"Don't worry about that now."

"Don't worry? Do you know what these are?"

"Yes."

"These are… *nipples.*"

"I know, Candi. That's why we need to get the hell out of here."

That seemed to spur her to action. I joined Candi in pulling up mats, and we soon found the trap door. I pulled on the recessed handle.

Locked.

I tugged as hard as I could, until the cords on my neck bulged out and I saw stars.

It wouldn't budge.

"We're going to die up here." Candi was hugging her knees, rocking back and forth.

I blew out a breath. "No, we're not."

"He's going to bite off our toes. Then our tits, to add to his collection."

I reached up overhead, tugging at the baffling stuck to the ceiling. Under it was heavy aluminum. I did a 360, looking at all the walls.

There was no way out. We were trapped up here.

Then we both felt it. The truck cab jiggle.

Oh, shit. They're back.

Chapter Nine

Fran the waitress was happy to flip a coin for the two gentlemen who had tipped her so well.

"Tails," Taylor called.

Fran caught the quarter, slapped it against her wrist.

"Tails it is. Congrats, handsome."

Taylor gave her a polite nod, then turned to judge Donaldson's reaction. There wasn't one. The fat man's face was blank. Taylor left the diner, his cohort in tow. It was still hot and muggy outside, and the lot was still almost full, but there weren't any people around.

"Are we cool?" Taylor asked as they walked to his truck.

"Yeah. Fair is fair. You'll let me watch?"

Taylor shrugged like it didn't matter, but secretly he was thrilled at the idea of an audience.

"Sure."

"And you'll let me do her face?"

"Her face is all yours."

"You should try it once. The face. You peel enough of the flesh away, you can see the skull underneath. I bet Jack Daniels has a beautiful skull."

Taylor stopped and stared at him. "You've really got a hard-on for this cop, don't you?"

"I'd marry her if she'd have me. But I'll settle for a bloody blowjob after I knock her teeth out. Do you still have Jack's phone?"

Taylor had pocketed her phone and wallet. He tugged the cell out.

"Does Officer Donaldson want to inform the next of kin?" Taylor grinned as he handed it over.

"That's a possibility. Might also be fun to call up her loved ones while you're working on her, let them hear her screams."

"You've got a sick mind, my friend."

"Thank you, kindly. Let's see who our favorite cop talked to last. The winner is... *Latham.* And less than an hour ago. Shall we see if Latham is still up?"

"Put it on speaker."

The phone rang twice, and a man answered.

"Jack? I was worried."

"And you have good reason to be," Donaldson said. "Is this Latham?"

"Who is this?"

"I'm the man about to murder Jack Daniels. She's going to die in terrible pain. How do you feel about that?"

There was silence.

"What's wrong, Latham? Don't you care that..." Donaldson squinted at the phone. "Dammit, lost the signal."

Donaldson hit redial. The call didn't go through.

They stood there for a moment, neither of them saying anything.

"I hate dropped calls," Taylor finally offered. "Drives me nuts."

"Cops."

"I hate cops, too."

"Behind you."

Taylor spun around and froze. A Wisconsin squad car rolled up next to them. Its lights weren't on, but the driver's side window was open and a pig was leaning out. White male, fat, had something on his upper lip that an optimist might call a mustache.

"Did you men happen to witness a disturbance in the diner earlier?"

Taylor thought fast. But apparently so did Donaldson, because he spoke first.

"What disturbance?"

"Seems an Illinois cop got into a tussle with one of the locals."

"We're just passing through," Donaldson said. "Didn't see anything."

The pig nodded, then pulled up next to the diner. He let his fellow cop out, then began to circle the parking lot.

"I had to lie," Donaldson said, "or else we'd have to give statements. I don't want my name in any police report."

"I'm with you. But now we've got a big problem. One of them is going to talk to our waitress, and she'll mention us. The other is taking down plate numbers. He'll find Jack's car, realize she's still here, and start searching for her."

"We need to move our vehicles. Right now."

Taylor nodded. "There's an oasis thirty miles north on 39. I'll meet you there in half an hour. You've got the whore's phone, right?"

"Yeah."

"Give me the cop's," Taylor said. "We'll exchange numbers if we need to get in touch."

After programming their phones, Donaldson offered his hand. Taylor shook it.

"See you soon, fellow traveler."

Then they parted.

Taylor hustled into his cab, started the engine, and pulled out of

Murray's parking lot. He smiled. While he still didn't fully trust Donaldson, Taylor was really starting to enjoy their partnership. Maybe they could somehow extend it into something fulltime. Teamwork made this all so much more exciting.

Taylor was heading for the cloverleaf when he saw the light begin to flash on the dashboard.

It was the fire alarm. The smoke detector in the overhead sleeper was going off.

What the hell?

Taylor pulled onto the shoulder, set the brake, and tugged his sawed-off shotgun out from under the passenger seat. Then he headed for the trap door to see what was going on with those bitches.

Chapter Ten

The moment the cab jiggled, I began to gather up bungee cords and hook them to the handle on the trap door, pulling them taut and attaching them to the foot stock. When that door opened, I wanted it to stay open.

Then the truck went into gear, knocking me onto my ass. Moving wasn't going to help our situation. At least at Murray's we were surrounded by people. If Taylor took us someplace secluded, our chances would get even worse.

I looked around the sleeper again, and my eyes locked on the overhead light. Next to it, on the ceiling, was a smoke alarm. I doubted it would be heard through all the soundproofing, but there was a good chance it signaled the driver somehow.

"Candi! Press the test button on the alarm up there!"

She steadied herself, then reached up to press it. The high-pitched beeping was loud enough to hurt my ears. But would Taylor even be aware of it?

Apparently so, because a few seconds later, the truck stopped.

I reached for the Tupperware container and a broken slat from the chest, and crawled over to the side of the trap door. Then I waited.

I didn't have to wait long. The trap door opened up and the bungee cords worked as predicted, tearing it out of Taylor's grasp. The barrel of a shotgun jutted up through the doorway. I kicked that aside and threw a big handful of salt in Taylor's eyes. He screamed, and I followed up with the wooden slat, smacking him in the nose, forcing him to lose his footing on the stepladder.

As he fell, I dove, snaking face-first down the opening on top of him, landing on his chest and pinning the shotgun between us.

He pushed up against me, strong as hell, but I had gravity on my side and I was fighting for my life. My knee honed in on his balls like it lived there, and the first kick worked so well I did it three more times.

He moaned, trying to keep his legs together and twist away. I grabbed the shotgun stock and jerked. He suddenly let go of the weapon, and I tumbled backwards off of him, the gun in my hands, and my back slammed into the step ladder. The wind burst out of me, and my diaphragm spasmed. I tried to suck in a breath and couldn't.

Taylor got to his knees, snarling, and lunged. I raised the gun, my fingers seeking the trigger, but he easily knocked it away. Then he was straddling me, and I still couldn't breathe—a task that became even more difficult when his hands found my throat.

"You're gonna set a world fucking record on how long it takes to die."

Then Candi dropped onto his back.

Taylor immediately released his grip, trying to reach around and get her off. But Candi clung on like a monkey, one hand around his neck, the other pressing a wet paper towel to his face.

He fell on all fours and bucked rodeo bull-style. Candi held tight. I blinked away the stars and managed to suck in some air, my hands seeking out the dropped shotgun. It was too dangerous to shoot him with Candi so close, so I held it by the short barrel, took aim, and cracked him in the temple with the wooden stock.

Taylor crumpled.

I gasped for oxygen, my heart threatening to break through my ribs because it was beating so hard. Candi kept the rag on Taylor's face, and part of me wanted to let her keep it there, let her kill him. But my better judgment took over.

"Candi." I lightly touched her shoulder. "It's over."

"It'll be over when I bite one of his goddamn toes off."

I shook my head. "Give me the rag, Candi. He's going away for the rest of his life. Depending on the jurisdictions, he might even get the death penalty."

She looked at me. Then she handed over the rag and burst into tears.

That's when Donaldson stepped into the cab. He took a quick look around, then pointed my gun at me.

"Well what do we have here? How about you drop that shotgun, Lieutenant."

I looked at him, and then got a ridiculously big grin on my face.

"You gave him the bullets, asshole."

Donaldson's eyes got comically wide, and I brought up the shotgun and fired just as he was diving backward out the door. The dashboard exploded, and the sound was a force that punched me in my ears. Candi slapped her hands to the sides of her head. I ignored the ringing and pumped another slug into the chamber, already moving after him.

Something stopped me.

Taylor. Grabbing my leg.

Candi pounced on him, tangled her fingers in his hair, and bounced his head against the floor until he released his grip.

I stumbled out of the cab, stepping onto the pavement. My .38 was on the road, discarded. I looked left, then right, then under the truck.

Donaldson was gone.

A few seconds later, I saw a police car tearing up the highway, lights flashing, coming our way.

Chapter Eleven

"Thank you, honey."

I took the offered wine glass and Latham climbed into bed next to me. The fireplace was roaring, the chardonnay was cold, and when Latham slipped his hand around my waist I sighed. For a moment, at least, everything was right with the world. Candi had been reunited with her children. Taylor was eagerly confessing to a string of murders going back fifteen years, and ten states were fighting to have first crack at prosecuting him. No charges were filed against me for my attack on the pimp, because Fran the waitress had sworn he shoved me first. My various aches and pains were all healing nicely, and I even got all of my things back, including my missing shoe. It was five days into my vacation, and I was feeling positively glorious.

The only loose end was Donaldson. But he'd get his, eventually. It was only a matter of time until someone picked him up.

"You know, technically, you never thanked me for saving your life," Latham said.

"Is that what you did?" I asked, giving him a playful poke in the chest. "I thought I was the one who did all the saving."

"After that man called me, I called the police, told them you were at Murray's and someone had you."

"The police arrived after I'd already taken control of the situation."

"Still, I deserve some sort of reward for my cool-headedness and grace under pressure, don't you think?"

"What have you got in mind?"

He whispered something filthy in my ear.

"You pervert," I said, smiling then kissing him.

Then I took another sip of wine and followed his suggestion.

Epilogue

Donaldson kept one hand on the wheel. The other caressed the cell phone.

The cell phone with Jack Daniels's number on it.

It had been over a week since that fateful meeting. He'd headed southwest, knowing there was a nationwide manhunt going on, knowing they really didn't have anything on him. A description and a name, nothing more.

He'd been aching to call the Lieutenant. But it wasn't the right time yet. First he had to let things cool down.

Maybe in another week or so, he'd give her a ring. Just to chit-chat, no threats at all.

The threats would come later, when he went to visit her.

In the meantime, he'd been so busy running from the authorities, covering his tracks, Donaldson hadn't had any time to indulge in his particular appetites. He kept an eye open for likely prospects, but they were few and far between.

The hardest thing about killing a hitchhiker was finding one to pick up.

Donaldson could remember just ten years ago, when interstates boasted a hitcher every ten miles, and a discriminating killer could pick and choose who looked the easiest, the most fun, the juiciest. These days, cops kept the expressways clear of easy marks, and Donaldson was forced to cruise off-ramps, underpasses, and rest areas, prowl back roads, take one hour coffee breaks at oases. Recreational murder was becoming more trouble than it was worth.

He'd finally found one standing in a Cracker Barrel parking lot. The kid had been obvious, leaning against the cement ashtray near the entrance, an oversize hiking pack strapped to his back. He was approaching every patron leaving the restaurant, practicing his grin between rejections.

A ripe plum, ready to pluck.

Donaldson tucked the cell phone into his pocket and got out of the car...

For a continuation of Donaldson's adventures, read SERIAL UNCUT by Jack Kilborn & Blake Crouch.

For a continuation of Jack's adventures, read FUZZY NAVEL by J.A. Konrath.

For a continuation of Taylor's adventures, read AFRAID by Jack Kilborn.

J.A. Konrath Interviews Jack Kilborn

Jack Kilborn is as secretive as he is enigmatic, and was tough to get a hold of. This interview was conducted by J.A. Konrath via email.

JA: Thanks for taking time to answer some questions, Jack.

Jack: I remember you. You write those chick novels, right?

JA: I write about a female cop who chases serial killers. Some folks think they're pretty scary. Both men and women enjoy the series, but it's a bit harder-edged than the average suspense novel. Jack Daniels was the lead in the story we just wrote together, TRUCK STOP. Weren't you paying attention?

Jack: She sort of sounds familiar. Aren't you the guy that visited 600 bookstores in one summer? Signed thousands of books?

JA: That's me.

Jack: I haven't seen your name on any bestseller lists.

JA: So, how would you describe your first novel, AFRAID?

Jack: I tried to write a thriller that included every kind of fear possible. Fear of the dark, or being chased, of drowning, of authority, of burning, of losing a loved one, of pain, of disfigurement... and, of course, fear of being horribly murdered.

JA: What's the plot?

Jack: A helicopter crashes near the small town of Safe Haven, Wisconsin. It's so tiny it has a population of 904. But not for long.

JA: So the helicopter lets something loose in town?

Jack: Something horrible. The town can't defend itself either—no police force. Soon it's quarantined, and everyone is fighting for their lives.

JA: I was lucky enough to read an advanced reader copy of AFRAID. It scared the hell out of me.

Jack: Thanks. I predict that at least 25% of people who start the book won't be able to finish it because it's too frightening. It gave me nightmares when I was writing it.

JA: There certainly are some memorable scares.

Jack: I didn't use any chapters in the book. My goal was to go from one high point to another without any breaks. I hope it worked.

JA: It worked for me. You call it "technohorror." What is that?

Jack: The technothriller genre is about fusing modern day science and technology with big thrills. Michael Crichton perfected the form, which has been used to great success by Dan Brown, James Rollins, Steve Berry, and many others. Technohorror views technology in a more sinister way.

JA: Do you think the scenario in AFRAID could happen?

Jack: I wouldn't be surprised if it already has.

JA: You've sort of come out of nowhere. Care to share your writing background?

Jack: It's probably similar to yours. Bitten by the writing bug at a young age, getting a lot of rejections, finally landing a two-book deal with a big publishing house.

JA: I like the Afraid Game on your website.

Jack: Thanks. It's a fun little Flash thing I did. People seem to enjoy it.

JA: There's also an excerpt from AFRAID on www.jackkilborn.com.

Jack: Almost forty pages worth. A healthy dose of horror. I've already gotten some hate email, people saying it's too graphic. But it's not really graphic. It's violent, sure, but I leave most of the details up to the reader. Do you have excerpts on your website?

JA: Yes, at www.jakonrath.com. But I'm not doing an excerpt from my new book, CHERRY BOMB. That's because at the end of my last Jack Daniels novel, FUZZY NAIL, there was a cliffhanger, so I don't want it to spoil what the big secret is.

Jack: Can't people just search on the Internet and find the answer?

JA: So what's the next Jack Kilborn book?

Jack: I just finished TRAPPED, my follow-up to AFRAID. It's sort of a sequel, and explores many of the same themes. The people who have read it believe it's scarier than AFRAID is.

JA: I don't see how that's possible.

Jack: I'll send you a copy.

JA: Thanks. I'd be happy to blurb it.

Jack: I'm sort of holding out for blurbs from bestselling authors, if you don't mind. No offense.

JA: No offense taken. Maybe you'd like to blurb one of my books, if you have time.

Jack: One of those chick books? Sure. But I can't promise I'll like it.

JA: CHERRY BOMB has a four page sex scene, several torture-murders, and an extended woman-on-woman fist fight.

Jack: I'll give you my address so you can send me a copy. The cover makes it look harmless.

JA: None of my books are harmless. If you want proof, there's an excerpt following this interview.

Jack: I thought you didn't want any excerpts.

JA: This one doesn't contain any spoilers.

Jack: What's CHERRY BOMB about, by the way?

JA: Jack Daniels chases the most brilliant and sinister serial killer she's ever faced. One who killed someone dear to her, and plans to kill more.

Jack: How come the serial killers always have to be brilliant? How about having a serial killer with average intelligence?

JA: They'd get caught too quickly. Make for a pretty short book.

Jack: True. So can anyone just pick up CHERRY BOMB and start reading, or do they have to start at the beginning of the series?

JA: You can begin anywhere in the series. But for those who want to read them in order, it goes WHISKEY SOUR, BLOODY MARY, RUSTY NAIL, DIRTY MARTINI, FUZZY NAVEL, CHERRY BOMB.

Jack: Maybe we should talk about this e-book thing. We're both doing well with e-books on Kindle.

JA: I noticed you had the #1 Kindle bestseller for over three weeks. The novella SERIAL, that you wrote with Blake Crouch.

Jack: Yeah. I think I remember Crouch. Good writer. It's got Donaldson from TRUCK STOP in it.

JA: And Taylor from TRUCK STOP is a character from AFRAID.

Jack: I know. I wrote it, remember?

JA: I've noticed SERIAL has gotten a lot of one-star Amazon reviews.

Jack: People think SERIAL is too sick. It probably is. No worse than TRUCK STOP though. Or AFRAID. Or your books, from what you say.

JA: Do the negative reviews bother you?

Jack: They amuse me. I love the ones from people who give it one star and stopped reading on page 3.

JA: It's a nasty little story, but fun. And it's free, right?

Jack: SERIAL is 100% free. So I see from searching Amazon.com that you've got a bunch of books you put up on Kindle yourself. You've priced them all under $2.00. Why so cheap?

JA: I don't feel ebooks should be expensive. There's no cost to print or ship. Why should I charge the same price as a print book?

Jack: I agree. Cheap and free are what readers want. What's ORIGIN about?

JA: It's technohorror. The US government is studying Satan in a secret research lab. He's the Dante version: horns, hoofs, wings, eats live sheep. The book is sort of JURASSIC PARK meets THE EXORCIST.

Jack: What's THE LIST?

JA: I don't want to spoil it. Let's just say it's a technothriller about some very famous good guys and bad guys. Jack Daniels also has a cameo.

Jack: Jack Daniels is in another one of your exclusive Kindle books, SHOT OF TEQUILA.

JA: She's the co-star in that. It's sort of an Elmore Leonard-type crime novel, with a lot of action.

Jack: How about DISTURB?

JA: Another technothriller, with a medical slant. A pharmaceutical company invents a pill that replaces a full night of sleep. But it has some pretty horrible side-effects.

Jack: Violent and gruesome?

JA: Of course.

Jack: What is 55 PROOF?

JA: A collection of fifty-five short stories. It has some previously published Jack Daniels shorts, and also some horror stuff. Some of the horror is pretty hardcore. Tread lightly.

Jack: FLOATERS?

JA: Another Jack Daniels novella, that I wrote with Henry Perez.

Jack: PLANTER'S PUNCH?

JA: Jack Daniels again, a novella I wrote with Tom Schreck.

Jack: You're really milking this Jack Daniels thing. Is she in SUCKERS too?

JA: I wrote SUCKERS with Jeff Strand. Jack isn't in it, but one of her series regulars, Harry McGlade, is the hero. It's funny, and pretty sick.

Jack: Finally, you got this poetry collection called DIRTY JOKES & VULGAR POEMS for only eighty cents. Does it suck?

JA: I'd have to say that's the greatest thing I've ever written. Some of the jokes and poems are so disgusting, so bad, so totally wrong, that I expect it will someday become a TV series.

Jack: Poetry is stupid.

JA: This isn't like the crap you had to read in school. This is funny stuff.

Jack: For eighty cents, maybe I'll try it. So are you working on another Jack Daniels novel?

JA: It's called SHAKEN. There's an excerpt in PLANTER'S PUNCH. What are you working on now?

Jack: Another in-your-face technohorror novel.

JA: Go figure. Should we discuss what it was like working together on writing TRUCK STOP?

Jack: Why? You think anyone is actually still reading this?

JA: It's possible.

Jack: Working with you was fine. No problems. Except for that dumb pun you wanted to keep in the story.

JA: At the end, I wanted Latham to say to Jack, "First you hit that pimp with the salt shaker, then you threw salt in Taylor's face. So, technically, you *asalted* two men."

Jack: Yeah. That pun. There's something wrong with you.

JA: I like it. Maybe I'll stick it back in the story.

Jack: So, we done here?

JA: I think so.

Jack: Good. This was getting kind of long. Besides, I've got plans later that involve sleeping with your wife. I think she likes me more than you.

JA: I think you're right...

Jack Kilborn is the author of the technohorror novel AFRAID, already released by Headline Books in the UK, and Grand Central in the US. Visit him at www.jackkilborn.com.

JA Konrath is the author of the Lt. Jack Daniels thrillers. His sixth, CHERRY BOMB, was just released in hardcover by Hyperion. Visit him at www.jakonrath.com.

All of Jack's and JA's books are available as ebooks, and as audiobooks from Brilliance Audio.

Read the Jack Daniels series by JA Konrath:
Whiskey Sour
Bloody Mary
Rusty Nail
Dirty Martini
Fuzzy Navel
Cherry Bomb
Shaken

Exclusive ebooks by JA Konrath:
55 Proof – Short Story Omnibus
Origin
The List
Disturb
Shot of Tequila
Crime Stories – Collected Short Stories
Horror Stories – Collected Short Stories
Jack Daniels Stories – Collected Short Stories
Suckers by JA Konrath and Jeff Strand
Planter's Punch by JA Konrath and Tom Schreck
Floaters by JA Konrath and Henry Perez
SERIAL by Blake Crouch and Jack Kilborn
Truck Stop by Jack Kilborn and JA Konrath

Writing as Jack Kilborn:
Afraid
Trapped
Endurance

Non Fiction
The Newbie's Guide to Publishing

Visit Joe at www.JAKonrath.com

Made in the USA
Lexington, KY
13 December 2010